The Alchemy of Forever

The Alchemy of Forever

Avery Williams

SIMON & SCHUSTER BFYR

New York London Toronto Sydney New Delhi

An imprint of Simon & Schuster Children's Publishing Division
1230 Avenue of the Americas, New York, New York 10020

Also available in a SIMON & SCHUSTER BFYR hardcover edition

Produced by Alloy Entertainment
151 West 26th Street, New York, NY 10001
Book design by Liz Drezner
The text for this book is set in Janson.
Manufactured in the United States of America
2 4 6 8 10 9 7 5 3 1
Library of Congress Control Number: 2012936766
ISBN 978-1-4424-4316-7 (hc)
ISBN 978-1-4424-4317-4 (pbk)
ISBN 978-1-4424-4318-1 (eBook)

FOR CONOR

He ne'er is crown'd
With immortality, who fears to follow
Where airy voices lead.
—John Keats

prologue

london, 1349

I feel as though I've been waiting for the masquerade ball for my entire life. At fourteen, I am eligible for marriage and finally old enough to attend. The torchlight flickers on the sandstone facade of Lord Suffit's palace on the Thames, and the roses woven into my hair are heady and sweet. I remember to push my mask up over my face before I walk through the great arched doorway.

I catch sight of myself in a mirror.

I wear a high-waisted white gown—punctuated with golden threads on the seams—that flows over my body like water. The sleeves are fitted at the tops of my arms and flare out at my elbows like wings. The mask is golden and shaped like a butterfly, dotted with crystals and glass beads. It points back from my face toward the silver net that holds my hair in a thick bun at the crown of my head.

I am momentarily disoriented by my mask, not sure if the reflection I see is really me. I tentatively touch my hand to my cheek, and the mirror-girl follows.

Satisfied, I turn around and follow my parents and the sound of the music—lyres and lutes, tambourines and drums—until we arrive in the ballroom. I stand there for a moment, watching the masked dancers: women in silk and velvet gowns that brush the floor as they twirl in a circle, men forming a larger circle around them, the sinuous glow of the candelabras glinting off their headpieces. Although I have spent my entire life in London, I don't recognize anyone.

I feel a presence at my side and turn to look. A young man, all in black, with a red mask and white-blond hair, is standing next to me. He offers me a goblet of pomegranate wine, and I take a sip, feeling the burning sweetness in my throat. "You should dance," he tells me.

"But I don't recognize anyone," I answer, wondering if I know him.

"That's the point," he replies, his blue eyes vivid beneath the scarlet mask. "The disguises are meant to offer freedom, to let us do things we wouldn't normally do, to let us be someone entirely different for one night."

I study him for a moment. "Do we know each other?"

He tilts his head back and laughs. "I don't think so. I would remember you, I'm certain. But then again, maybe we do. We'll never know." He offers me his arm and leads me toward the dancers.

We are partners only briefly, soon separated as we move down the line in formation. But I glance up at him more than once, and each time he is looking at me, following me around the room with those vivid blue eyes. I am grateful that my face is covered, as I feel my usual blush heating up my cheeks. But when the song is over, he is gone.

I wander alone through the crowd, feeling hot and dizzy. The wine, the dancing, the press of people—it is too much. I follow torches down a stone-walled hallway through a courtyard, then outside to the garden, where a magician is entertaining a group of people. I watch, amazed, as he produces a dove from the empty air, then releases the bird above his head.

"He's a charlatan," says a voice behind me. I whirl around to see the man with the scarlet mask.

"It's amazing!" I exclaim. "He conjured a bird."

"He did no such thing. He merely tricked you. But"—he holds out his hand—"if you will join me, I will show you something truly amazing."

I am intrigued. I take his hand and let him lead me away from the crowd. When we reach the palace gates, I hesitate.

"I should not leave. My parents will worry."

"It is just here, on the street," he promises, and I reluctantly follow him around a corner toward a garden of rosebushes just opposite from the Thames. I can smell their sweet blooms mingling with the torch smoke. We stop next to a stone bench, and he lets go of my hand.

"May I?" he asks.

I am not sure what he is going to do, but I nod my assent. He reaches for my hair, gently pulling out one of the roses and cradling it in his palm. It is still deep red, but wilted, the edges of the petals already drying out.

"People are always looking for magic, when the natural world holds true miracles," he says, pulling a small glass vial from his pocket. "This flower is dead. No offense meant, my lady." He smiles. "But the roses here in the garden are still very much alive."

He opens the vial and lets a few drops of liquid fall onto the base of the dead rose's stem, then holds it up to a thorny branch of the living rosebush. After a few seconds he takes his hand away, and I gasp.

The red rose I had once worn in my hair is in full bloom, the velvety surface of its petals no longer dried or wilted.

"Magic?" I whisper.

"Science," he replies.

I am astounded, and delighted. "I don't care what you call it," I say. "It's still magic to me."

"Will you take off your mask?" he asks, looking deep into my eyes. "I must know who you are."

"Only if you remove yours as well."

He nods, and I untie the ribbons that hold the butterfly mask to my face, and pull it aside. He does the same with his scarlet mask, the same color as my rose.

We look at each other and let out small gasps of surprise.

"Seraphina," he says breathlessly.

"Cyrus," I say wonderingly. Cyrus is the apothecary's son, and I've stolen more than a few glances at him when he and his father come to the house to visit. He is handsome with his white-blond hair, solid cheekbones, and vivid eyes. When I dream of my marriage, I often imagine Cyrus as my husband.

"You are even more beautiful than I remember," he says, and it is clear that he has thought of me, too. "And so I give you a promise. I will come to your home to speak with your father. And next time I will bring you something more than flowers."

There is no holding it back; I blush a deep crimson. I am

overwhelmed, dazed, dazzled. The roses' heady scent fills my senses and I close my eyes. Is this my destiny?

We hardly notice when the two figures appear from the shadows and approach us: a man and a woman wearing filthy clothes, their faces half covered with cloths to conceal their mouths. The swords strapped around their waists, however, look well made and sharp.

"Sir!" spits the man, addressing Cyrus. "Pass me your purse."

I stiffen with fright, and Cyrus shields me with his body. "Be gone," he commands. "I have nothing for you."

The man draws his sword. "Your lady, then."

I am not carrying any money either. But I do have a jeweled crucifix that I always wear around my neck, and I hurriedly unfasten it to hand it to the man.

He grabs it roughly, nearly breaking the chain. "Is that it?" He grunts, turns his head, and spits on the ground.

"It is all I have," I tell him in a tremulous voice.

Before I can move he has me pinned under his arm. His teeth are rotten, and I can smell alcohol on his breath.

"Get away from her!" Cyrus screams, springing to action. In one swift movement he grabs the woman's sword, kicks the man with his boot, and sinks the sword into his belly. His blood, sickeningly warm, splashes onto the front of my gown. We watch his body slump to the stone.

Cyrus locks his eyes with mine, and I see his expression change, his eyes grow round, terrified. And then, for the second time in an evening, my world changes forever.

To say that the woman's small dagger pierces my back sounds too delicate, as if she is preparing my earlobes for jewelry. It is an eruption of pain. I feel the knife go in, feel it scrape against bone, feel a hot gush as blood starts pouring down my back, pumping in unison with my alarmed heartbeat.

Cyrus knocks the woman over. She falls hard, her head cracking against the stone. She does not get up.

I sink to my knees, looking up at the moon shining brightly, as if nothing horrible has just happened.

I feel Cyrus's arms encircle me, feel his breath as he leans close, putting pressure on the wound, see my blood running over his white fingers, turning them completely scarlet.

In a haze, I see him rip open his tunic and pull out a small vial. The world grows dim as I close my eyes.

"I will save you, Sera. Don't leave me!" He pours a drop of liquid from the vial onto his finger and holds it to my lips.

As it touches my tongue, I cry out in pain. "What is this poison?" I gasp.

"It is an elixir," he explains hurriedly. "My father and I

created it during the Black Death. He fell ill, and we used this to save him. The body you know—he was not born into it."

I feel a tug as something in my throat burns. "I am on fire!"

"It's the silver cord that binds your soul to your body," he says urgently, "and this potion is unraveling it. You'll soon be free."

I begin to feel weightless, like I could drift toward the sky, like I could join the planets in their joyful arcs.

"Sera. Don't go." I hear Cyrus's voice, but it sounds so unimportant. I want to explain to him where I am going: to the stars. He could join me.

When he holds the filthy woman up to me, I rouse myself from my thoughts. He wants me to kiss her. What a ridiculous, revolting idea. Isn't she dead? Aren't I dead?

No, I realize slowly, coming back to Earth. She is alive; she merely lost consciousness when she fell. I don't know why, but I obey Cyrus. I kiss her until I taste something sweet. Then suddenly it feels as though the world has exploded. Thunder cracks, and it sounds as though an entire fleet of ships is firing its cannons. I shift, careening through space and time, and then all is still. Miraculously, the pain in my back is gone.

"Sera. Open your eyes," Cyrus commands.

I obey, with great effort. The view is all wrong. I can see my body, lying on the stones, so pale and cold, blood soaking my gown.

I am a ghost, I think wildly. It is the only explanation. Except that when I reach out, my hand makes contact with my own cheek. But it is not *my* hand that I reach out with—it is dirty, with ragged nails. Somehow *I* am now the filthy female thief.

I jump to my feet, suddenly strong. "I don't understand."

Cyrus stands in front of me. "Sera, you're alive. And if I am correct, you'll never have to die."

"But my body . . ."

Cyrus hesitates a moment, thinking. Then he scoops it up and drops it in the Thames. It lands with a loud splash. "It's the only one you'll ever leave behind. Your new body is different, no longer human or attached to your soul. When you are done with it, it will break into dust."

Cyrus's words wash over me, but I cannot comprehend what he is saying.

Just then I hear my mother's panicked voice cut through the silence of the street.

"Seraphina Ames! Sera, where are you?"

Cyrus turns panicked. He grabs my hand, pulling me

away from the sound. "Seraphina, we must go."

Not knowing what else to do, I run after him.

"Good-bye," I whisper to my mother, but she doesn't hear. She will never see her daughter again.

one

san francisco, present day

The late autumn day is oddly hot for San Francisco. The morning fog has lifted and the sun's rays reach my pale skin, but do not warm me. For the past year I've stayed bone white, no matter how much time I spend in the sun, and I'm freezing, all the time. It is always this way when death is near. I've put this body through hell, and it's finally catching up with me.

I wince as I lean back on one of the steel chaise longues scattered around the pool on the roof of my apartment building, a brash glass tower, all angles and blue tints, jutting upward over the SOMA neighborhood. The sunlight glints off the surface of the pool; it's almost too bright for me, even behind my large sunglasses. I blink, watching a hummingbird make his way to the roof deck, zigzagging madly between the ruby-colored morning glory blossoms spilling out from galvanized planter boxes I had bought at the local flea market. I am always amazed when birds appear here, twenty stories up in the middle of the city. How did he know there were flowers? Was it instinct that drove him upward, or blind luck?

When I try to fly away, will I be as lucky and find what I am looking for?

Living like this—the persistent cold, the pain radiating through my joints at a constant interval, the shortness of breath accompanying my every movement—has made my choice for me. For once my body is as weary as my soul. I've dragged it all over the globe for six hundred years—it's time to let go of this life and figure out what comes next. I would be lying if I said I wasn't terrified, but a thrill of excitement runs up my spine every time I think about it. It's been so long since I've ventured into the unknown.

"I know that look. What are you thinking about?" Charlotte, my best friend, asks as she comes through the glass door to the deck. She carries a tray of iced tea, moisture already beading like wobbly diamonds on the outside of the glasses. When I take one, the little droplets fall to the ground and immediately turn to steam.

I push my sunglasses up into my dark hair and smile at Charlotte. "Nothing," I lie. "Just enjoying the sun."

I can tell no one of my plan to die, not even Charlotte. Cyrus would never let me leave. Not without a fight, and one that I would surely lose. More than anything I want to be free of the man who controls me with his fists, his words, and his iron will—the man who made me what I am.

Charlotte narrows her hazel eyes at me, but says nothing. After two centuries of friendship, I can't get anything by her, but I also know she won't pry. I cherish her understanding and acceptance; it is what I'll miss most when I leave. That and the sunshine, but I can't afford to think about what I'm leaving behind if my plan is going to work.

Moving around the deck, Charlotte offers drinks to our other friends. Jared pulls out a flask to spice up his, looking every bit the pirate he was when I first met him in 1660, a row of studs and hoops trailing up his earlobe like a rocky coastline. Amelia declines, her white-blond hair gleaming in the sunlight and her deep tan a stark contrast to my milky skin.

When Charlotte approaches Sébastien, his long dreadlocks pulled back in a low ponytail, a shy smile flickers across her face. He leans on the orange metal railing that encircles the deck. I notice his fingers grazing hers as he takes his tea, making her shake her head, slightly embarrassed, her copper curls falling forward in her face.

I have always loved her red hair, which is not so different from the hair she was born with. All of us have had a similar experience: When Cyrus made us Incarnates, we went through periods of trying out different kinds of bodies. Old, young, male, female. But we all found the experience too disorienting, and eventually settled in forms that reminded us of our former selves. I've been a different incarnation of myself—brown eyes, long brown hair—for centuries.

The glass doors open once more, and Cyrus, our leader, joins us on the deck. He's wearing a well-tailored black shirt that sets off his platinum hair and tall, lean frame. Around his neck is the vial of elixir he used to make us Incarnates. I can't say he's not beautiful, though the magic I once felt when looking at him has long since dissipated.

He sits next to me, regarding me with his icy blue eyes and running his hands through my hair possessively. I shiver but don't pull away. "I want to discuss Sera's party," he tells us. Yes, the party in my honor. Although it would be more apt to call it an execution.

I sit up, my muscles straining from the effort, and

am momentarily dizzy. When my vision clears, I see the hummingbird fluttering around a cluster of lilies, his wings a red blur.

"It's going to be at Emerald City," he announces, and Amelia's eyes brighten. Emerald City is the most exclusive nightclub in San Francisco. People more important and more beautiful than Cyrus have been turned away at the door.

Jared lets out a low whistle and pulls his chair closer to Cyrus, the metal screeching against the concrete deck. "Pulling out all the stops, eh?"

Amelia chuckles, arching her back toward the sun. "It's not that often that Saint Sera deigns to take a new body."

I detect an undercurrent of nastiness, but I don't let it get to me. She's right. I've been putting off this moment for as long as I could. We get about ten years in a body, even if the body we take is already sick, broken, run down by years of abuse. When we transfer our spirits, the body regenerates. But the energy expended in healing the body is also its doom, leading to organ failure five or ten years down the road. Unlike my friends, I try to stay in a body for as long as possible rather than switching into a new one as casually as I might try on a dress. Even Charlotte has no qualms about killing. *It's the only way for us to stay alive*, she says. *Why waste this gift?*

"My little darling," Cyrus murmurs affectionately, pulling

me into his lap. I try not to cringe at his touch. "I'm going to miss this body when it's gone. Only one more week. But don't worry, we'll find you another just as beautiful." Amelia looks away, scowling.

He does love me, I've never doubted that. I'm his touchstone, his only link to his real past, to the body into which he was born. He's told me as much, crushing me in embraces that leave bruises the following day. *Seraphina, I would die without you.*

What will he do when I'm gone?

Jared and Sébastien will be fine, as long as they continue to follow orders. Amelia will be happier without me—she's always had a crush on Cyrus. I worry about Charlotte, though. Cyrus has never liked her.

I met Charlotte in New York in the early 1800s. I bought flowers from her at the market in Five Points and, much to Cyrus's dismay, struck up a friendship with her. I took her shopping for dresses she could never afford on her own, and she regaled me with stories about her seven brothers. When she did not show up at her stand one morning, I sought her out at her home and found her and her younger brother Jack in the throes of scarlet fever.

I begged Cyrus to let me save her, and he finally said yes to shut me up. I don't think he really considered the consequences—that I would finally have an ally, someone who knew my true self. I turned her into a killer so I could have a friend, and I will regret that for eternity.

The hummingbird approaches the railing, then dips under it, taking off into the sky. I catch Amelia watching it from her perch two seats down. She was an aerialist when Cyrus turned her and used to "fly" for a living.

Cyrus turns his attention to the group. "Amelia, you're in charge of the guest list. Under my *close* supervision, of course." She beams. "I want plenty of options for Seraphina."

Plenty of options for himself, he means. He would pick for me—he always did. He has a type: willowy build, long dark hair, Mediterranean skin. She would be a failed model who had turned to drugs or an aspiring poet with a streak of madness who would never live to see age thirty. I stopped caring long ago what my body looks like; I only care that my new host either doesn't want to be alive or doesn't deserve to be.

I do have one request. "Amelia," I say, "please don't invite anyone too young."

She smirks at me, but it doesn't feel cruel. Just matter of fact. "Don't worry, you can go straight to confession afterward."

"Jared," Cyrus continues, "you're in charge of security. I

don't want the club staff on this—we need a crew who will be discreet."

"Of course, Cy." Jared nods, pushing his black hair off his tattooed neck.

The mention of security sends a jolt of nervous adrenaline through my veins. Jared won't mess around. He knows this is more than a dance party. Someone is going to die.

I'm trying to control my breathing, which is coming in quick, shallow gasps. I glance down, willing myself to stop fidgeting with the heavy ring on my left hand. Its antique garnet catches the sunlight like a glass of red wine—or blood.

I asked Cyrus to buy it for me a couple of weeks ago, on a fog-swathed day in Hayes Valley. "It's a Victorian antique," the saleswoman had remarked. I silently thanked the other customer who drew her attention just then, keeping her from saying more. Because it was more than just a Victorian bauble. It was a poison ring, with a hidden compartment under the bloodred stone. Not much room, just enough for the tiniest pinch of powder or a single pill. It would be enough.

Sébastien, who has been silent until now, shoots me a concerned glance. "You okay? You seem tired." Next to me, I feel Cyrus stiffen.

"She's fine," he says coldly. "Aren't you?" I can feel the

rage burning under his skin. He hates it when anyone else thinks they know how I feel, as though he's the only one allowed that ability.

I smile weakly. "I'm just . . . excited."

Cyrus sighs heavily and stands up, the sun shining around his platinum hair like a halo. "I think I'm done for the day. We'll continue this later. Sébastien, I'll need you to work on the DJ lineup."

Sébastien flashes one of his rare smiles, white teeth brilliant against his brown skin. Music is one of the only things he cares about. Music and Charlotte. When I'm gone, I hope he will comfort her—and protect her. Because if Cyrus suspects she had any involvement in my escape . . . well, he's killed for much less.

two

"I think I want coffee. Or maybe pistachio. Or . . . I don't know, green tea."

Charlotte ties her curls in a loose bun on the top of her head. "You can get all of them. An added bonus of switching bodies tomorrow—no need to eat healthy."

"True," I say. "In that case, I guess I should get hot fudge, too."

The night before my party is moonlit and clear, warm enough to wear only a light jacket. I link my arm through Charlotte's and skip as much as my aching muscles allow, pulling her toward Michael's, my favorite ice-cream parlor in all of San Francisco—perhaps in all the world.

Although ice cream wasn't around when I was little, my mother and I used to flavor our cream with fruit and herbs from the garden. We'd make it when my father was away, staying up late and eating it right in the kitchen in our nightclothes. A century later, after I'd complained of missing my mother, Cyrus had fed me my first bite of real ice cream and smirked triumphantly at my delight in it. "See? Why ever long for something from the past when the future brings things that are so much better?" he'd asked.

"I still can't believe Cyrus let you out of his sight the night before your switch," Charlotte says as we turn the corner and walk toward Michael's. I strain my eyes to see the daily specials written in neon on the window—hazelnut, raspberry swirl, and mint gelato.

"Yes, well, he has to learn to live without me sometime," I say lightly. *Starting tomorrow*, I add silently.

He didn't want me to go out tonight—"There's still so much planning for the party, Sera," he'd said—but he relented after much begging on my part. He's never quite been able to resist when I stick out my lower lip. Juvenile, I know, but it does the trick and I needed one last girl's night with my best friend.

We walk through the doors of Michael's, and a cold, sweet smell instantly envelops me. Michael's looks like it was scooped up in a tornado in the Midwest and plopped down in the middle of San Francisco. Painted wooden cutouts of chickens, cows, and corn line the wall, and a row of rusty tin milk pails hang from the ceiling. We are the only people in the shop other than the girl behind the counter, who has hair the same color as the Blue Moon sorbet, and two little piercings that stick out of her bottom lip like fangs. She takes a break from whispering into her cell phone to serve us our cones, then instantly goes back to gossiping.

Charlotte and I sit in our usual spot, two stools facing the front window, so we can watch people walk by.

"Gerald, 1913," she says without preamble, pointing to a man in his midforties with a wobbly chin and a healthy outcropping of ear hair. This is the game we always play. Although as far we know we are the only Incarnates in the world, we always wonder if others have found a different route to immortal life, perhaps by a philosopher's stone that allows them to stay in their original bodies. We watch people on the streets and on TV, deciding who they could be from our past.

I frown. "No, Gerald had nose hair, not ear hair."

"Oh, right," Charlotte says with a snort, then takes a bite of her mocha-chip ice cream.

As it's a Friday night, we watch a steady stream of beanie-wearing teenagers and singles rushing to dates, but no one else looks familiar. These bodies are all new.

After a few minutes I voice the question that's been haunting me ever since I made my decision to die. "Do you believe in true reincarnation?"

Charlotte turns her hazel eyes toward me. "What do you mean?"

"What do you think happens to people's souls when they die? Do they just evaporate, or are they reborn into new bodies with no memories of their past lives? And what about our souls? We've been around so long, would ours even know how to move on?"

Charlotte takes a bite of her cone and crunches thoughtfully. "Well, you know what Cyrus says."

I do know what Cyrus says. He told me his theory in 1666 while we sat together on a boat on the Thames during the Great Fire of London. As we watched the world burn around us, I confessed that I sometimes considered dying, so I could join my parents in heaven. The flash of anger that came over him was sudden and intense. The flames flickered red in his eyes, and for the first time in my life, I truly feared him.

"The soul is nothing but a concentration of energy, held

together by will, or, in our case, years of practice," he said fiercely. "Our Incarnate souls are different from human ones. Ours are stronger."

"But—" I began.

He grabbed my arm so tightly that his fingernails drew blood. "There is nothing after this life for humans, but your soul is strong, too strong. If you are killed, Seraphina, your soul will want to leave, yet after years of being intact, it will not know how. You will become a hungry ghost, unable to affect the physical world." The idea that I could stay on Earth in purely spiritual form terrified me, and I huddled against Cyrus for protection while the city where I'd grown up disintegrated before my eyes.

But now, as I truly face my own mortality, I have to wonder: How can he possibly know what comes next? Did he say those things just to scare me into staying with him, so he wouldn't have to wander the world alone?

"I don't care what Cyrus says," I reply, watching as a young couple kisses briefly under a streetlamp outside. "I want to know what you think."

Reflected in the window, I see the corners of Char's mouth turn down. It is rare that we flout Cyrus, even in his absence, and it troubles her to do it now. Still, she answers. "I suppose anything's possible." She lowers her eyes and whispers, "Sometimes I hope Jack is still out there somewhere."

I touch her arm. "I look for my mom, too."

We finish our cones in silence, listening to the electric hum of the freezers and the girl behind the counter laughing happily into her phone, unaware that she's in the presence of two seasoned killers. Then Charlotte gestures suddenly at something scurrying outside. "Seamus from Ireland, 1878!"

I furrow my brow. "What, that squirrel?"

"Yes! He was always hoarding food. And his front teeth were abnormally long," she says mischievously.

"You are terrible," I chide with a laugh.

"You love me," she says. Her expression turns serious. "Sera, I know you're nervous about tomorrow. But it'll be okay, I promise."

A lump forms in my throat, and I don't look at her for fear that I will accidentally give something away.

"You've done this a million times," she continues. "Cyrus will make sure your new body is perfect."

"But don't you think it's wrong?" I press. "Who are we to decide who lives or dies?"

"It's what we are, Sera. It's a choice we all made. I wish everyone could be like us." What she doesn't say is, "I wish Jack could have been like us." It had been hard enough to get Cyrus to make Charlotte an Incarnate. He would never have accepted her brother as well.

"Mmm" is all I say, not wanting to argue with Charlotte on our last night together. It took me six hundred years to come to terms with death. It is not my place to rush Charlotte. "Let's go home. I'm in the mood to watch *While You Were Sleeping.*"

"Ugh, again?" Charlotte groans.

"Yes! It's my favorite." I push myself onto my shaky legs and wave good-bye to the blue-haired girl. She's so absorbed in her phone call that she doesn't even notice we're leaving until the cowbell over the door rattles loudly.

"Come back soon!" she shouts as she does every time a customer leaves.

The wind has picked up outside, bringing with it the vaguest hint of fall, a smell I've always associated with possibility.

"Okay, fine," Charlotte relents, crunching through a pile of fallen leaves on the sidewalk. "We can watch *While You Were Sleeping.* But then can we watch *Casablanca*?"

"Ugh, again?" I mimic. She elbows me and we both laugh. I hook my arm through hers again and pull her close. "You never know, Char. Maybe Jack is with us right now."

Charlotte raises a red eyebrow and smiles wistfully. "Maybe."

We walk back to the house. I lean on Charlotte for balance, and I wish this night, and our friendship, could last forever. But I settle for living in this moment. Because even though it took me six hundred years, I finally know better. Time can't be cheated, not really. Everything—even me, and one day even Charlotte—must come to end.

three

The next morning, the day of my party, I wake to an empty house. I didn't sleep well. No matter how much I fuss, I can't get comfortable. The bed's cool gray sheets match too closely to the sickly pallor of my skin, and my bones jut out through my skin at odd angles now.

I throw on my white terry-cloth robe and pad through the condo. Its design is modern, all neutral shades, and I fit in too well. In the kitchen I find a pot of hot coffee. Next to it is my mug, laid out by a bud vase holding a single velvety purple morning glory blossom. It is the most colorful thing in the entire place. A note is tucked under the lip of a shiny silver teaspoon. With stiff fingers, I unfold it and see Charlotte's fine script:

> *Good morning, S, I'm out with Amelia. Boys are at the club. Let's get ready together later?*
>
> *—Char*

I pour myself a cup of coffee and take a sip, grateful for the warmth it brings on its path through my body. In the bathroom Cyrus and I share, I stand in front of the mirror and let my robe fall away from my body, regarding myself without emotion. I am too thin, ribs prominent on my sides and collarbones creating dark hollows on my chest. I look sick. Weak. Still, my chapped lips curve into a smile. Dying is the bravest, most human thing I will have done in six centuries.

After a hot shower, I dress in my favorite pair of faded green pants and a fuzzy hoodie and make my way to Cyrus's library. It's locked—none of us have ever dared enter here without his permission—but I know where he hides the key.

The library is the one room in our home that is not sleek and modern. Floor to ceiling bookshelves line all the walls, holding a jumble of handmade bindings, sewn Coptic spines, and ancient leather-bound volumes. An Oriental carpet in red and turquoise stretches across the floor, a souvenir from the year we spent in Iran. The room smells like old paper, with a faint trace of Cyrus's soap, notes of vetiver and cedar.

This is his collection, a record of his hundreds of years of knowledge. As much as Cyrus appreciates human progress and technology, nothing can replace these weathered volumes. They have an almost talismanic power over him, which is why no one else is allowed in this room. We've taken the library with us every time we've moved to a new city. I cringe, remembering the trouble it caused on the voyage from Barbados to New Amsterdam. At least one person has died for these books.

I run my fingers over the spines till I find what I'm looking for, and pull a slim book from the shelf. It has a lock closed over its front edge, like a diary. But I don't need to read it to know what's inside: the formula for making the elixir. Cyrus, the son of an alchemist, had learned how to make the elixir that unbinds the silver cord that anchors the soul to the body. He wears a vial of it around his neck at all times. It only takes a few drops to turn a mortal being into one of us: an Incarnate, a soul untethered from a specific body, who can live forever by stealing others' lives. We only need the elixir once—then we can switch at will.

Cyrus may have the formula memorized by now, but

there's a chance he doesn't—after all, he hasn't changed anyone into an Incarnate in almost a hundred years. That chance is enough for me.

I sit at his desk and pull out a creamy sheet of stationery.

Dear Cyrus,

I loved you once, with all my heart, and I stayed alive, in one form or another, for centuries because I could not bear to be apart from you. But the years have changed us, and not for the better. Every death we've caused has killed our love, bit by bit. I cannot kill another human in order to live. When my current body is lost, I will be too.

Until the next life,

Seraphina

Back in my room I fold the note and put it in the pocket of the dress I'll wear tonight. Everything is in place. Doors open and doors close; I just have to walk through.

By nightfall the fog is so thick that I can't see more than twenty feet in front of me. The streetlights glow amber in the haze, reminding me of minerals in a fire. Cyrus once charmed me with colored fire instead of a bouquet of flowers, the pale powders in his palm giving little clue to the hue they brought to the flame. It seemed like magic, those little flames glowing red, glowing violet, the color of cat's-eyes lapping at the dark. But it was only science—borax, copper chloride, potassium sulfate. I know that now.

It's just before ten PM when Charlotte and I arrive at Emerald City; the others have been at the club all day preparing. A large crowd of people is gathered outside the doors, bouncers holding them at bay while they check the guest list. Jared gives me an appreciative glance and parts the crowd for us to go inside.

I shiver in my oyster-colored silk shift dress, a modern version of the one my real body died in so many years ago. I've always valued symmetry, and this feels like a fitting tribute to my original incarnation. A small car key is pinned to the underside of my bra strap, laying flat against my heart. I wear no jewelry except for my poison ring, the hidden compartment of which contains my parting gift for Cyrus.

The second I step inside I'm overwhelmed by the thumping bass and loud voices. I walk slowly up the stairs, my heart pumping weakly. Charlotte places a steadying hand on my lower back.

"Sera, you really shouldn't wait this long to take a new body," she whispers in a worried tone. "You're pushing it."

"You know me," I say with a forced laugh. "Always living on the edge."

Cyrus is waiting for us just inside the door. His eyes flicker with purpose under the low tracking lighting. "Seraphina, you look so beautiful," he murmurs, pulling me close. I am enveloped in his herbal scent, his strong arms. A memory of the masquerade ball rises in my mind, but I push it down. Nostalgia is my enemy tonight. I can't look backward.

"This is amazing," Charlotte says, smoothing down her green sequined dress. "I've never been inside Emerald City before."

The interior of the club is all shades of green—velvet couches the color of damp pine needles, intricate stained-glass chandeliers in chartreuse, wallpaper in turquoise. Waitresses cross the crowd with trays of absinthe and Midori in small crystal glasses.

Not long ago I would have loved a party like this—dancing till dawn, slipping through the crowd with purpose, making eye contact with Cyrus as we decided, together, who my victim would be. There is something undeniably thrilling about this part. The promise that, no matter what, I can change my body. That I can walk out a new person, presenting a brand-new face to the world. If only my memories were as easy to shed.

"You fit right in with that dress," I tell Charlotte. "But in the first Oz book, the Emerald City isn't really green. The Wizard makes everyone wear green-tinted glasses, so that's what they see."

Cyrus frowns, as though I've insulted his choice of venue. I put my hand on his arm. "I think I'll get myself a glass of champagne."

He brightens. "Yes, go get a drink, and don't forget to . . . look around." He finishes this statement with a sly grin and a knowing look. My stomach turns, but I make myself return his smile.

Charlotte and I cross the dance floor, which pulses with bodies dancing to electronic beats. The DJ is playing a remix of the old Neil Young song "Heart of Gold." It makes me unaccountably sad.

I crossed the ocean for a heart of gold. And I'm getting old.

Charlotte looks behind her to make sure I've followed. "Let's dance after this?" She has to shout to be heard. I grab her hand and give it a squeeze. Yes.

She asks the bartender for two Midori sours with wedges of watermelon, and we toast. "To new beginnings, and old friends," she says.

"Cheers." I smile, and we clink glasses. "Friends forever."

The cold melon-flavored sweetness of the Midori trickles down my throat, and I am reminded of the summer we lived in Alabama. Cyrus found us a broken-down farmhouse with a brilliant red barn out back and a massive watermelon patch. Charlotte and I spent hours in the cool shade of the barn, the smell of hay and horses all around us, eating watermelon after watermelon and making wishes on the sticky black seeds.

I wish to fall in love.

I wish to live forever.

I wish to be friends until the end of time.

I have only one wish for Charlotte now. I take her wrist, suddenly urgent. "Charlotte, you need to tell Sébastien how you feel. Promise me this."

Charlotte's smile falters. "Sera, you know what Cyrus would say."

"Screw Cyrus." When I see the stricken look on her face, I soften my tone. "What is eternal life without love?"

Cyrus appears behind us at the bar and encircles my waist with his arm. I twist to the side so he won't notice the folded note in my pocket. "There's someone I want you to meet," he murmurs. He must have already made his choice. It didn't take long.

I take a deep breath and pluck the empty wineglass from his hand. "Let me refill that for you, then I'll be right there." He kisses the side of my neck, then nods toward a girl standing alone under a chandelier, light falling in lacy patterns on her gleaming chestnut hair. She looks almost exactly like me, a minor variation on a theme.

When he's gone, I pull Charlotte toward me in a tight hug. "Thanks for being my best friend, Char. I mean it." When I pull back, my eyes are filled with tears. I blink them back.

"My sensitive Seraphina." She pushes my hair back and holds her palm to my icy cheek for a moment. "I will see the new you soon enough."

I swallow hard as the bartender places a full glass of red wine in front of me. I pick it up and make my way through the crowd toward Cyrus and the girl. When I'm confident no one is looking, I flick open my poison ring and, in one practiced movement, dump its contents into the glass. Then I stride forward, catching Cyrus's eye. He looks pleased.

I feel a flash of sadness for him. Cyrus, my alchemist love, the one who made magic real, the one who lives for illusion, who says, *Yes, the fire only burns violet for you, Seraphina.* Cyrus, who grips me so tightly I feel like I'm choking, who made me a killer, who would rather kill me himself than lose me. He's told me so, many times. But after tonight, I'll be gone—and for the first time in hundreds of years, we'll both be alone.

four

I walk toward Cyrus, my strides matching the incessant thump of the music. My heart hammers in my chest, and I am careful not to let the wine slosh over the edge of the glass. I don't look at it, knowing from long experience that I am more graceful when I don't try to be. *Trust yourself, Sera. Don't think, just act.*

"Hi, I'm Sera," I say to the girl, handing Cyrus his wine and taking her hand in mine. She's stunningly beautiful, with rich, espresso-colored hair and warm brown eyes framed by inky lashes. A rosy flush on her prominent cheekbones sets off the light olive hue of her skin. Apart from our coloring, we could be sisters.

"I'm Claudia," she responds, with a hint of a German accent. "Cyrus tells me you're a photographer?"

Cyrus catches my eye, urging me to follow his lead. "I was telling Claudia about the photo shoot you're working on—you're still casting models, right?"

"Right—yes, we're still looking." The girl is watching me with hopeful, innocent eyes, and I picture how this night could progress in some alternate reality. We'd go upstairs and talk. I'd draw her in, build her trust in me, tell her about the months I spent in Munich and about Café Frischut, my favorite coffee shop there, until she came willingly to my arms. My cold mouth would close over hers and in a flash of violet light, I would feel a surge of power and claim her body for my own.

Suddenly my resolve slips. My soul may be ready to die, but there is a part of me that only knows how to keep living, no matter the cost. *I can still change my mind*, I think. I can take her body, find Charlotte and dance with her, lose myself in the unrelenting music. I can go home with Cyrus. I can stay his.

But then I look at Claudia, at the way she nervously twirls the marcasite ring on her index finger, and remember exactly why I must hold firm.

Cyrus takes a sip of wine and furrows his brow. "Is this the Pinot Noir?" he asks. My heart starts to slam in my chest—I can't decide if I'm more terrified that he'll taste the sedative, or that he won't.

"No," I reply as innocently as possible, "the Cabernet."

He takes another sip. "It's good," he says, flashing me a dazzling smile.

"It's so loud down here." I turn to Claudia. "Why don't we go somewhere more private, where we can talk about the shoot?" Cyrus tips the wineglass to his lips again, and I silently will him to slow down. I've got to get him out of here before the powder takes effect.

"Yes, that would be fantastic," she agrees. I lead them to the back of the club, where a heavy green-velvet drape obscures a stairway.

"There's a private lounge up here." I glance behind me. The girl is sure-footed, confident, while Cyrus misses a step and nearly drops his glass. But hundreds of years of existing in human bodies have granted us an effortless, feline grace, and he recovers easily.

The walls of the stairwell are lined with jade-and-gold-striped wallpaper, and dim rose-colored bulbs flicker in copper sconces. At the top a long hallway leads us to our destination. Jared and Amelia stand guard outside but move aside to let us pass. I float by them on a nervous cloud.

Amelia gives me a strange look, as though she can see deep inside me, her avian eyes wary and her head cocked to the side. I want to say I'll miss her, but it is actually a relief to know that I will soon be free of her.

Claudia and Cyrus enter the lounge, and I close the heavy walnut door behind us, locking it. Cyrus is surprised—I know he wants it open for Jared and Amelia in case anything goes wrong—but he doesn't say anything.

"It's beautiful," Claudia says breathlessly, taking in the walls made of milky green glass, backlit by twinkling lights. The ceiling is covered with gossamer fabric, billowing softly in the breeze wafting in from the open balcony doors. This private room with its balcony is exactly why I asked Cyrus to hold my party here.

"Glad you like." Cyrus's voice is slightly slurred as he steers her toward a cluster of couches and sits down. He rubs his eyes as if to clear his vision. I take a nervous gulp of air and hand Claudia a glass of absinthe, trying to find a comfortable position on the pillows piled on the floor. I try not to look at the balcony doors. Even in his impaired state, I'm terrified that Cyrus can read my intentions. My good-bye note feels heavy in my pocket.

"So, Claudia, tell me about yourself. You're not from San Francisco, are you?" I lace my fingers together to keep from tapping them impatiently. Cyrus's wine is half gone.

"No," she replies. "I am from Munich."

"Traveling with friends?" I ask.

"Oh no, traveling alone. I adore it. I've been all over, but San Francisco is an amazing city. That's why I want to get a job here, so I can stay."

Even though Claudia will ultimately survive the night, rage courses through me. Cyrus knows my one criterion—that I only take bodies ready for death, either physically or spiritually. But Claudia is clearly healthy and happy and looking forward to her future. She is alone and beautiful—all that Cyrus needs to know to decide she deserves death.

Cyrus, pale and with dilated pupils, shoots me a smile devoid of any trace of remorse. I close my eyes for a moment, willing myself not to give in to the anger that's sparking in my heart.

Claudia smiles shyly. "So tell me about the photo shoot." She crosses her legs and touches her hair. "I have done some modeling."

I stand up, needing to dispel my anger somehow, and the effort causes the room to swim briefly in misty gray. I walk slowly over to the bar, feeling their eyes on my back. I pull a bottle of water out of the minifridge. "The shoot, right." My voice sounds thick. "It's an editorial piece. It should feel like a fairy tale."

"Like Snow White?" she asks. "That is my favorite story."

I glance at Cyrus. "You remember that story. Is it like that?" I ask him.

His expression is dreamy. "The wicked queen demands Snow White's heart," he whispers, and something snaps inside of me. I walk over to the leaf-green sofa where he sits.

"But she doesn't get it!" I say. "Snow White tricks her and sends her the heart of a deer instead."

He sees my rage, but just smiles and drains his glass in one swallow. Suddenly I realize just how much I'm going to enjoy what's about to happen.

One, I count silently.

His eyes, which had begun to close, fly open, and his hand snakes out and grabs my wrist.

"What's going on?" asks Claudia.

Two.

I lean close to Cyrus, ignoring the pain in my wrist. "She doesn't deserve to die. None of them did."

"Sera?" His voice is weak and his grip on my wrist loosens.

"Good-bye," I answer.

Three.

His eyelids flutter, then close, as he slumps forward. I plunge my hand into my dress and pull out the note, slipping it into his pants pocket. I feel his hand fall away from my arm as he crumples onto the low table, his head making a loud thump as it hits the glass.

Claudia lets out a scared gasp. "Run!" I whisper. Then I dash toward the balcony doors, and like a bird taking flight, I am free, out into the night.

five

The balcony swirls with fog. I swing my legs over the railing, slippery with marine air. I lose my grip and force myself to focus. One misplaced hand and I will tumble to the concrete below. I do intend to die tonight, but not here. Not like this.

I can hear Claudia yelling inside and grit my teeth. I should have spiked her drink too. One of my shoes slips off. As it disappears into the fog, I picture it bouncing on the sidewalk. I struggle to find a foothold. Amelia had trained me as an acrobat, but that was a long time ago, and my body is very weak.

Breathing hard, I kick off the other shoe and ignore a

pounding sound above—Jared and Amelia kicking in the door. I can't afford to dwell on it, so I keep moving. Bit by bit, I make my way down.

Once on the sidewalk, I can't hear anything else from above; all other sound is swallowed by the dance music pouring from the club. I shove through the crowd still waiting to get in to Emerald City, then start running up Spear Street.

Each time my foot lands on the pavement, hot pain shoots up through my body. My breath comes in rasps and my lungs feel as though they're collapsing. But I know what I'm running toward and push myself forward. It's 11:17 PM; I have ten minutes before the next train leaves the BART station.

I hear a shout behind me and whip my head around, nearly losing my balance. It's only an old homeless man having an argument with a street sign. After that I keep my gaze focused straight ahead, too terrified to glance backward.

"Sera! Stop!" Jared yells. I run even faster, my dress swishing against my thighs and my hair lifting high behind me in the damp wind. It feels like my skin is falling off my bones, and I know my bare feet are probably bleeding. My failing heart beats erratically in my chest, fluttering like a trapped bird. I pray I have the strength to reach my getaway car. *That's all I need*, I plead with my body. *Please.*

Finally daring to look behind me, I see Jared gaining on

me, Amelia only a few steps behind. He would love nothing more than to drag me back to Cyrus like a puppy who'd gone off leash. Amelia, on the other hand, would probably be happier if I disappeared forever, though loyalty to Cyrus is all the impetus she needs to join the pursuit.

The BART station sign looms in the distance, its black-and-blue logo illuminated but out of focus in the fog. There's more foot traffic as I get closer to the Embarcadero stop, and I shove people out of my way. "Watch it!" I hear as I blaze by.

It's a game night, and every other person is wearing the Giants' colors. A woman decked out in an orange-and-black jersey pushes an empty stroller. I misjudge her direction and trip over the stroller, falling to my knees on the sidewalk.

"Sera! Stay there!" Jared's voice has an undercurrent of panic. If he goes back empty-handed, Cyrus will surely "have words" with him. I know all about the very real scars those words can leave.

Scrambling to my feet, I take off again, Jared and Amelia only a block behind me now. I look back once more and make sure they're watching as I finally reach the BART station entrance, shoving through drunken baseball fans down the escalator. I hop the turnstile without paying, hurrying toward the rising wind and industrial screech of the trains rumbling into the station.

The platform is packed with Giants fans, all orange and disorganized and jubilant. The arriving train is headed for the East Bay, and the crowd struggles to board. I catch sight of my reflection in a window: wild-eyed, hair a tangled mess, dress torn, blood dribbling down my knees.

"Seraphina! You need. To. Stop!" Jared's voice is urgent and close. I turn around and catch his eye, then push my way onto the East Bay–bound train. People give me a wide berth, and I feel someone touching my hand. I gasp and look down—but it's only an older woman sitting near the doors. "You okay, honey?" I nod wordlessly, eyes trained on the platform. Amelia and Jared dash into a car two down from mine.

"The doors are closing. Please stand clear," says the conductor.

That's my cue. I spring into action.

The rumble and horn of an approaching train—heading in the opposite direction—are the only sounds I hear. I dart out of the car just before the doors close and dodge across the platform, sidestepping people and slipping toward the front of the crowd as the San Francisco–bound airport train opens its doors with a sigh. Pinned by the window, I turn and look behind me, where the East Bay train has yet to depart. Jared and Amelia are still on the other train, scanning the crowd.

Amelia's eyes lock with mine. I've been seen. It doesn't

matter. Their train is already chugging to life and sliding out of the station. They'll be stuck on it for the long ride under the bay, between the Embarcadero and West Oakland stations, giving me a good twenty-minute head start if they decide to come back after me.

I ride for only two stops and exit with the crush of people at Powell Street. No doubt Jared and Amelia will think I'm headed deeper into the city, toward the airport. But when Cyrus wakes up, he'll find my note and realize I haven't boarded any planes.

The rush of adrenaline has worn off, and I'm exhausted. But still, I am free to follow this night's course of action to its dark finish. The wind has stopped, allowing the fog to settle thickly over the neighborhood. It turns city blocks into something more private, like small, silent rooms. Through the haze the fractured beam of a streetlight glints off a metal surface. I squint—it's the car. I had kept it hidden near our apartment and driven it over earlier today. Two soggy parking tickets are plastered to the windshield, but I say a prayer of thanks that it hasn't been towed.

I bought the dusty old Ford off Craigslist a few weeks earlier. I gave the seller a fake name and paid his price without complaint, though I knew it was high, handing over an envelope filled with cash. I'd been saving money bit by bit for years—ten dollars here, twenty there—small enough amounts that Cyrus would never notice. I didn't even start saving it consciously—it was more instinctual. One day after buying a coffee I slipped the change into the book I was reading, then told Cyrus the cashier must have shorted me. It gave me a small thrill to disobey him, to finally have something that was mine.

I reach into the bodice of my dress and unpin the key I'd affixed to my bra strap. In the trunk I find my getaway bag—it holds a change of clothes, Cyrus's book, and the rest of my emergency money. I'm going to drive down to Big Sur tonight. I want to be among the redwoods and waterfalls when I die.

I tug on my jeans and sweater, dropping my soiled dress in the trunk and slipping my bruised feet into a pair of sneakers. My hands shake as I slide into the driver's seat and press the key into the ignition. The throbbing in my temples and the blue hue of my fingers tell me I may not make it to Big Sur. But I have to try.

The engine starts and I pull out into traffic, heading toward the bridge. I shake my head with disbelief—after six hundred years with Cyrus, I am finally free. I will never again, I promise myself, kill an innocent. I press harder on the accelerator as the car rumbles onto the bridge, leaving San Francisco—and my past—far behind.

six

I drive with the windows wide open, drinking in the world and fresh air while I still have time. The pavement thrums under the wheels, carrying me forward, and I feel a flush of excitement. I know it's morbid, but death is unexplored territory. Not even Cyrus knows what happens after we die.

With every mile I put between me and Cyrus, I feel a weight lifting. Even in the rain, California has never looked so beautiful and alive. I glance up at the stars, pinpricks pushing through the clouds, like they might fall into the bay.

I hope you're out there, *Mother*, I think, *because I'm coming.*

But my euphoria comes at a high price, quickly sapping

my remaining energy. My hands shake on the steering wheel and my vision blurs, turning the oncoming headlights into long yellow ribbons. I barely have enough energy to push the gas pedal. A car honks and swerves around me, and I fear that I'm no longer in charge of my body.

I let out a little sigh and tighten my grip on the wheel. I had wanted to go all the way to Big Sur, to be deep in the pines, listening to nothing but the cold wind and the hooting of owls on gnarled branches, but I'm fading—fast. I won't make it to Big Sur. Even if I tried, I would probably get into a car accident and end up killing someone else in the process.

Oakland, I decide, is as good a place as any to die. The road turns sharply as I begin the descent from Treasure Island toward Oakland, passing a tattered and faded billboard advertising a judgment day that never came. Beyond that, an eerie cluster of shipping-container cranes look out over the Oakland port like ancient guardians of the city.

I guide the car down Franklin Street, toward Jack London Square. A lone light shines on the loading docks of Second Street, illuminating the small droplets of mist that hang in the night air. I pull over on a side street, holding my head in my hands. The wave of weakness crests, then recedes. Trembling, I pull the key from the ignition, hoist my bag on my shoulder, and set off silently through the gloom. Sidestepping slicks of oil and crumbling potholes, I make my way toward a neon sign that reads SALOON, tucked under a termite-gnawed eave.

I know my time is short, but still, I'm not going to die sitting in my car. Though our original bodies die a human death, our stolen bodies collapse into dust when we leave them, exhausted from the energy it takes to host a foreign soul. I want my dusty remains to return to nature, not add to the layer of grime in this old Ford.

I decide to go in and get something to drink. I have to admit I'm scared, and wine will take the edge off my nerves, make me brave, before I chase my destiny into the great beyond.

Once inside I set my getaway bag on the ground and slide onto a heavy oak bar stool, smiling briefly at the two older men who sit next to each other not talking. After a moment I feel their eyes fall away, and they return to their beers. Catching sight of my high cheekbones and espresso-colored hair in the mirror behind the bar, I understand why they were looking. Even this close to death, I am beautiful.

The bartender mops the area in front of me and tosses down a napkin. He is skinny, with tattoos snaking up his arms, and eyes that suggest too few hours of sleep. He reminds me vaguely of Jared. "What can I get you?" he asks in a flat tone.

"Glass of red wine, please."

"I'm going to have to see some ID."

I look up and meet his eyes. "Is that really necessary?" I hold his gaze for several long seconds. When he holds firm, I sigh and dig out the ID that matches my face: Jennifer Combs, age twenty-two. The bartender studies the ID and for one giddy second I imagine telling him my real age, just to see his reaction. But I hold myself in check. The last thing I need is to draw attention to myself.

The bartender passes the laminated card back to me before pouring my drink. I stick Jennifer Combs—a name Cyrus made up when I took this body—back into my purse. I won't be needing her anymore.

"Thanks." I take a long sip of what will be my last drink ever, then sit back and survey the room. The bar is old, with an intricately detailed tin ceiling covered in multiple coats of chipping paint. Booths upholstered with cracked blue vinyl line the walls, and several wooden chairs are strewn haphazardly across the linoleum floor.

In the corner a thin girl with shaggy black hair and feather earrings is locked in a heated conversation with a dark-haired boy. She wears a bright red T-shirt; on her arms are telltale track marks. My stomach sinks.

The girl pushes the boy's shoulder. "Let me out!" she demands.

"Taryn, please," he pleads in a low voice, grabbing her arm. "Just calm down."

Taryn sets her jaw, an angry vein throbbing in her temple. "I mean it, Dan. Let me out."

The boy sighs heavily, but after a moment he slides over and lets her out. Taryn ducks her head, hiding her face behind her lank hair as she stalks across the bar.

"That girl has a death wish," the bartender observes, worry lines creasing his forehead.

I watch as Taryn shoves open the door and disappears into the night. "Looks like it," I say.

The bartender turns to refill someone's drink, and instantly I am gone, out into the foggy night, my bag in my hand. Standing so quickly makes me dizzy, but my head is clear, and I am suddenly so glad I came inside the bar.

I've known a thousand Taryns—the girls who have nothing left to live for, no will to stay alive. I can spot them anywhere, can smell their desperation. I used to prey on them; without the Taryns, I would not have survived all these years. But only one person will die tonight, I vow. And it won't be her. Saving Taryn will be a small penance for all the lives I've taken.

seven

Taryn is just ahead of me, slipping in and out of view in the thick fog. Lights, flashing red and orange, illuminate her thin frame from behind. She is stumbling, off-balance—drunk, at the very least.

Keeping to the shadows, I silently follow her as the streets grow closer to the Oakland estuary. There are no other people around, despite the brand-new condos that loom, unsold, over rotting produce warehouses.

The girl unsteadily approaches one of the steel shipping-container cranes. They look more animal than machine, with four legs and an extension over the water that resembles a head, looking out to sea.

Taryn begins climbing the ladder, slipping as she grabs the rungs before finally making it to the top. She approaches the edge of the crane, high over the murky water. After a beat I follow, the effort nearly unbearable.

The wind is strong at the top. It whips my dark hair around my face and muffles my footsteps. I feel unsteady on my feet, but I am determined to get her down.

"Taryn?" I say softly when I reach the girl. In the past I would have stalked this girl, but now I hope to save her.

She jerks around, her face registering slight surprise. Her cheeks are sunken, but her eyes are wide-set. She was probably pretty at some point.

"What do you want?" Taryn asks, hugging her arms around her torso.

I wait a moment before replying. "Are you going to jump?"

Taryn exhales, her shoulders slumping. "Why do you care?" Tears shine in her green eyes.

I search my heart, wanting to say the right thing. But all that springs to mind are six hundred years of platitudes, so I settle on the same question I asked myself when I decided to let myself die: "Do you have a good reason?"

She turns away from me, and I follow her gaze across the water. The twinkling lights of downtown San Francisco are barely visible through the fog, swirled and smudged like the Milky Way. When I was little, my mother and I used to lie out in the grass behind our house in London and spell my name in the stars, like a celestial connect-the-dots. "*Seraphina*" *means* "*angel,*" she would tell me. *Can't you see it written in the heavens?*

"Do you have any family?" I ask, stepping close enough to touch her.

"I don't have anyone," she says, the wind lifting her hair behind her.

I reach out for her thin shoulder. I look deep into her green eyes. "Not even the boy at the bar?"

"Especially not him," Taryn says fiercely.

I nod, understanding. "You won't find any comfort in death," I promise her. "It's a void. It's nothing. You only want to die if you desire that nothingness. If you don't want to be alone, that means you're still alive. There's hope."

"Who are you?" she asks. I can barely hear her voice over the wind.

I think back over my unnaturally long life—my childhood in London, swimming in the sea in the south of France, arriving in San Francisco in the 1960s—and scroll through all the names I've gone by, starting with Seraphina and ending with Jennifer. I look her in the eye. "I am no one."

She takes a step away from me, closer to the edge. I look

down at the hard, glittery pavement, some forty feet below. The surface glistens with moisture.

"Taryn," I say urgently. "You can't fly. The stars aren't your friends. Climb down. Go back to the bar. Find some people."

She hesitates, chewing her lip. I see her resolve softening. "I can't promise I won't be back here later, though."

"That's fine. You decide to live one moment at a time. When it's time to die, really time, you will know."

Taryn walks back toward me and I again put my hand on her shoulder. For the first time I see fear in her eyes. Good. Fear indicates a desire to live. "Get down," I tell her with a little push. And she does, her small hands gripping the ladder, moving slowly, trying not to fall.

I hold my hand to my brow, watching Taryn fade into the foggy night, her red T-shirt slipping away like a heart. When she's gone, I let out the breath I've been holding. I saved a life tonight. Two, if I count Claudia. It doesn't erase all the lives I've taken, all the borrowed time I've lived on. But it's something.

I take a step closer to the edge, retracing Taryn's footsteps. If I run and jump, I should be able to hit the water. But first, I fish in my bag and pull out Cyrus's book and a lighter. This knowledge dies with me. The cover is leather, dyed a brilliant shade of blue. It reminds me of Cyrus's eyes—I have seen them in every shade of blue. Currently, they're an icy blue, like the snow-covered part of a glacier. But when I first met him, they were this exact shade. The rich color of the morning sky before the sun rises. In one smooth motion, I bang the book against the metal platform beneath my feet, and the lock breaks away.

The pages are thick, smooth vellum. The smell transports me back in time, when I used to sit with my father in his study as he scratched away at his balance sheets. But I realize, my heart sinking, that they won't burn quickly. My father told me that vellum is made from animal skin—not plant fibers, like modern paper. It's why the book, at least as old as Cyrus, has lasted.

I run my hand over the surface of the pages. They are a jumble of Latin, Greek, and Old English, plus other languages I don't recognize, mixed in with astrological and scientific symbols: the output of Cyrus's alchemy studies. One page has a rough sketch of two people facing each other, a braided cord joining them at the navel. It's been painstakingly shaded with metallic ink. I know instantly what it is: the silver cord that binds the soul to the body.

I don't have time to burn it, but I can take it with me into the sea. The water will do its job, eventually, washing all the ink away. Hugging the book to my chest, I squeeze my eyes shut, a few tears escaping their corners as I say my final farewells—to my coven, the Incarnates; to Charlotte; to my mother, whom I never got to say good-bye to the first time. I savor the moment as the wind whistles through the crane like a hymn.

I am ready.

But before I can send myself into the air, I hear the squeal of tires shredding across asphalt and the sound of shattering glass pierces the night like a gunshot. A girl's terrified voice screams out. I whip around. Only one thing makes these sounds: a car accident—a deadly one.

Taryn.

eight

The ensuing silence yawns around me, a dark formless presence that pushes me toward the ladder. I have to see if it's Taryn, to see if my penance, my last act on Earth, has failed.

Time is of the essence and my strength is waning by the second, so I throw the book in my bag and leave it on the crane, then begin to climb down. My sneakers slip on the rungs and my breath comes in ragged waves. I stagger toward the deserted streets.

The smell of smoke and acrid burnt rubber assaults my nose, mingling with spilled gasoline. My pulse is rapid, my legs are shaky, and my vision is blurring again. I turn a corner and stumble over a pothole in the slick asphalt. My ankle buckles beneath me.

"Damn," I mutter. Ahead of me, I see the car. Flames lick through a gap in its hood, casting strange orange shadows on the rusty, rippled loading dock doors. The car is upright, but a spiderweb of cracks on its windshield tells me it flipped at least once before landing here. I smell a coppery wash of blood. Dizzying, overwhelming—it is everywhere.

I grab the door handle, gather what little strength I have left, and yank. It won't budge, and for a split second I have the sensation that I am not here, that I am dead, a ghost girl trying, laughably, to move objects in the physical world. I close my eyes, picturing the windswept crane, and steel myself for one final tug. Metal scrapes metal and sends a jarring reverberation up my arm the door finally opens.

My breath catches in my throat, relief mingled with horror. It is not Taryn, but a young girl, maybe sixteen, with tangled blond curls and a silver bracelet around her tanned wrist. Blood runs down the side of her face, soaking the embroidered neckline of her white peasant blouse like a bloom of red flowers.

She isn't dead—a vein still pulses weakly in her neck—but she is close to it. Her right arm and leg appear to be broken, as does her neck, and blood seeps from a wound in her head. Up and down, up and down, her chest rises and falls, her breaths small and pitiful. She coughs, and a ruby drop of blood escapes from the corner of her lips. She takes another breath. And then, with chilling finality, she goes still.

In a fog I hold two fingers to her neck. There is no pulse. A little voice in the back of my head tells me she is beyond help, but I wrap my arms around her waist and pull. I hear a metallic snap as I manage to get her out of the car and lay her down on the street, and I can only hope I haven't broken something else in her. She's small, but I am so weak that I nearly black out from the effort. Kneeling, I tilt her head back. I lay my hands over her heart, her blood sticky on my skin, and push down hard, pumping rapidly. Moving to her face, I pinch her nose closed, put my mouth over hers, and blow.

I have every intention of saving her, however unlikely her recovery is, but the second my cold, dying lips touch her warm ones, the sudden urge to take her body overwhelms me, as strong as a riptide.

No! I tell myself, jerking myself away from her lips and beginning to pump her chest again. But the smell of her jasmine perfume is so heady and I am so light-headed that when I lock my mouth back on hers, instinct takes over. Instead of blowing into her lungs, I hungrily breathe in again and again. Power surges through my veins, a feeling of simultaneous falling and rising up, like a playground swing. After a few minutes I taste something sweet: her life essence.

I try to stop, but it is beyond my control. Tears stream down my face as I draw out her soul, her life force flowing through my mouth, its sweetness expanding, then finally beginning to wane as it makes its way into the ether. A sensation like thousands of static shocks pierces my body, small blue sparks dancing between her forehead and mine. I think of heat lightning, those far-off strikes in the night sky. They are so common in summer, flashes unaccompanied by thunder. I see waves crashing on the beach of a lonely planet, deep in space. Small silvery chimes, the voices of stars singing a hymn. My mother's face appears in my mind, but she looks different from what I remember. Her skin is smooth, glassy and glittery, celestial dots of light making up her irises. Her dark hair, a mirror image of my own, is made up of the void of space, comets trailing through its ebony tresses. Her mouth opens, but there is no sound when she speaks. It doesn't matter; I can read her starry lips. *Not yet, Seraphina*, she's saying. *Not yet.*

Purple, then white, the little lights move at ever more dizzying speeds, and I realize with a jolt that I have badly miscalculated. I have never inhabited a body this broken and close to death, and fiery agony shoots up and down my broken limbs, even as I feel them being slowly repaired by my immortal essence. I roll over on the asphalt and see my old body has already turned to dust and is quickly dissipating in the breeze.

The far-off wail of sirens penetrates my consciousness. I need to get out of here before the police show up. And I need to get my bag—it's got my ID inside, the one with the name Cyrus gave me, as well as the book that can never fall into human hands.

Knees buckling, I push myself to standing and take a wobbly step forward. *Just a few more feet.* But the smell of blood and gasoline makes me sick, and I fall to my knees, and that's when I realize that Taryn is there, watching.

I'm dizzy and frantic—just how much has she seen?—and try to call out to her. But the flickering lights from a police car round the corner and she takes off down the alley. I will myself to move, to get to the crane and retrieve my bag, but again the pain takes over, pulling me down. My eyes flutter closed and I sink into blackness.

nine

Through the faint pink of my eyelids, I see fluorescent lights overhead. The air is sharp with antiseptics. The feeling of terror, of something being off, seeps in from the edges of my mind, but I can't remember why I'm scared. Tentatively, I open my eyes. The windows reveal a hazy afternoon, the sun pushing its way through the approaching fog and shining on the palm trees. Muffled voices blend with a clattering of wheeled carts and heels clacking down a tiled hallway.

Reaching up to my temples, I feel a bandage and circular sensors connected to wires. I touch my hair, which falls just above my shoulders in loose curls. *What the—?* I shake my head, trying to clear it of the dizzying panic that is beginning to take hold. A white plastic bracelet stands out on my tanned arm: *Kailey Morgan, F, age 16.*

In an instant, the events of the previous night come flooding back: the crash, the blood, the moment when I ceased being Jennifer Combs or Seraphina Ames or whoever I truly was and instead became Kailey Morgan. Bile rises in my throat as I sit up in the hospital bed and scan the room. The monitor to my right beeps rapidly, echoing my thudding heart.

A nurse enters through the propped-open door. "You're awake!" I regard her with wide eyes, too alarmed to speak. "I'll go get your parents." The woman exits as quickly as she came, leaving me in stunned, frantic silence.

An experimental wiggle reveals that my broken arm and leg have already healed. I only hope that happened *before* the ambulance came for me. I wonder how close the doctors came to figuring out that I'm not quite like any other human patient—that I'm something more: a body snatcher, an immortal, a killer.

With horror I remember my bag with Cyrus's book in it. Is it still on the crane? What had I been thinking, leaving it behind? I have to get back to the docks and find the book.

I swing my legs over the side of the hospital bed and stand. I will have to run— What choice do I have? Kailey's parents will realize immediately that there is something horribly different about their daughter. As I rip the sensors off my temples and wrists, I hear voices coming closer.

". . . concussion . . . needs rest . . . might be a little confused . . ."

I look down at the hospital gown—white with a pale-blue daisy print—and realize how ridiculous I will look running past the nurses' station, out the door, and down the street. Grimacing, I slip back into bed and rearrange the sensors on my skin.

Moments later a woman rushes through the door. She is pretty, though the dark circles under her eyes call attention to the shallow lines at their corners. Following her is a rugged-looking man, blond hair mixing well with the gray threads in his sideburns. He looks as sleep deprived as the woman.

"Kailey! Oh, thank God!" The woman pulls me into a tight hug, then leans back to look at me. I recoil slightly. "What happened?" The couple, along with the nurse, waits for my answer.

"Um . . . there was . . . a dog. I didn't want to hit it." My new voice is high-pitched, a far cry from my last body's throaty cadence.

Kailey's father winces. "Oh, Kailes."

The woman tucks a stray curl behind my ear. "Your

brother's down in the cafeteria. I don't know *how* he can think of food right now—" Her voice breaks off as a boy enters the room. He is lanky and looks slightly older than Kailey, with the same dark blond hair and bronzed skin.

"Thanks for trashing my car, sis," he says. His tone is casual, but I can tell from his bloodshot eyes that he's been crying.

"I'm sorry," I say distractedly, my mind fixed on the untenable situation I've woken up to and on my bag, vulnerable and exposed, with its dangerous secrets.

"Bryan," Kailey's mom says warningly.

He holds up his hands and grins. "Kidding!" Then his expression turns serious. "What were you doing in Jack London anyway? It's dangerous down there. I thought you had that art gallery thing in Berkeley."

My eyes dart between Bryan and Kailey's parents, who lean in expectantly. What can I say? *I was trying to end my unnaturally long life, then when I tried to save your daughter, I accidentally took her body?* "I . . . yes. I did. And . . . I—" The heart-rate monitor beeps at a faster pace.

Just in time, a young doctor in a white coat knocks on the doorframe, then comes in without waiting for a response. I lean back on the bed and force myself to take deep, calming breaths. "I'm sorry. I feel really dizzy right now."

The doctor elbows past Kailey's mother and waves a pen

flashlight quickly in front of both of my eyes. He returns it to his pocket with a blank expression and consults my chart.

"When can we take her home?" Mrs. Morgan asks.

My heart sinks. *Home?* The only place I want to go is back to the cranes to get my bag. After that . . . I shake my head. Then what? Waking up as a teenager with a loving family is so far out of my plan, I can't even begin to contemplate my next move. Hot tears sting the back of my eyes, and I look up at the ceiling, forcing them back.

I'd been so ready to let go, but here I am, in the body of girl whose family doesn't even know she's dead. The rational part of me knows that there was no way Kailey could have survived that crash, but the guilt that I have taken yet another life is overwhelming. The heart-rate monitor picks up once more with my swell of emotion, and I focus on taking deep, calming breaths.

"Normally I'd want to keep any patient who'd been in a serious crash overnight," the doctor says with a frown, "but all her tests have come back normal. There's nothing physically wrong with your daughter." He checks my pulse. "To be in an accident like that and come away without a scratch, it's . . . unbelievable. Do you know what a miracle it is that you are alive?"

I blink my new eyes. "Trust me, I know."

ten

I stare through the station wagon window as the Morgans' car pulls up to a single-story Craftsman house in North Berkeley. It looks like a fairy-tale cottage, set back from the street and surrounded by redwood trees, a colorful herb garden poking up in front of its old, leaded-glass windows. As Bryan and his parents walk through the heavy oak front door, I pause on the porch, listening to the low tones of junk-sculpture wind chimes jingling in the breeze. The chimes are beautiful, made of antique silver spoons, pieces of jewelry, skeleton keys, and dried bones.

Entering Kailey's house feels horribly wrong. I've taken

more lives than I can count in the years since I left my original body, but never have I stayed around to see the life the person left behind.

Bryan turns and looks at me. "What's up? You waiting for a hand-delivered invitation?"

I force a weak smile. "Give a concussed girl a minute to smell the roses," I say lightly as I step through the threshold onto a vintage hardwood floor inlaid with a dark walnut border. In front of me is the living room, where well-worn velvet couches sit on an artfully clashing selection of Persian rugs. Beyond that is a kitchen that is welcoming in its messiness. Kailey's mother sets her purse on the counter. "You should go lie down, honey. Doctor's orders."

I pause. To my right and left are two hallways, each leading, I guess, to bedrooms. But which way is Kailey's? I take a chance and head to the right, taking a few cautious steps before Bryan clears his throat.

"You think just because you're a medical marvel, you get the master bedroom?" His tone is still lighthearted, but the look in his eyes is not. I can tell that he's worried about me. Well, not *me*—he's worried for his sister. I am gripped by the sudden urge to tell him the truth, but I am fully aware that the Morgans won't believe me. At best they would think my concussion was worse than the doctor said. At worst they'd suspect I needed to be in a mental institution.

"Just checking to see if you were paying attention," I say, smoothly exiting down the other hallway. My voice sounds hollow, the veneer of playfulness utterly false.

The first open door reveals an unmade bed strewn with jeans and hoodies. A multicolored jumble of Chuck Taylors spills out of the closet.

I continue down the hallway to the next room. The scent of jasmine perfume hangs heavy in the air and I know it's Kailey's room even before I look inside. I shut the door behind me and exhale deeply. *You're almost there. Just wait for them to fall asleep tonight, then you can go to the cranes, get the book, and figure out Plan B—whatever that is.*

The room is painted a vivid shade of dark turquoise, and the bedspread is a silk quilt in a lighter green, closer to lime. Purple throw pillows with black beaded fringe are piled at its head. The effect is that of being surrounded by giant peacock feathers.

I'm drawn to a violin case that leans against the desk. The violin is one of my favorite instruments. Was Kailey a musician? Looking more closely I see that it's covered in a thick layer of dust. But in the corner is an easel with a half-completed painting of a girl standing on a beach, staring out to sea.

The scene is all gray: cloudy sky, fog bank rolling in over choppy whitecaps. The girl looks like Kailey, her sparkling eyes the most colorful spot on the canvas. Despite the bleakness of the scene, she looks happy, as though she can see something, just out of view, that gives her hope. Looking closely I see that she's outlined the shapes of mermaids just visible beneath the surface of the choppy sea. She never had a chance to fill in their details, but they are undeniably there.

It reminds me of our voyage from Barbados to New Amsterdam. I had been furious with Cyrus for killing our servant in a fit of rage and had spent as much time as possible alone on the upper decks, the ocean breeze whipping my hair across my face. The opaque surface of the Atlantic frustrated me. I wanted to see beneath. I wanted to believe there was another world below us, where mermaids combed their hair under a permanent drift of golden silt and played music on a sunken harpsichord.

Turning away from the painting, which fills me with inexplicable sadness, I regard a mirrored vanity that hugs one wall, postcards and ink sketches tucked between the glass and the frame. I pick up a stack of photos of Kailey and her friends: on a camping trip, at a school dance, lounging next to a gleaming pool. One girl appears in several of them; the magenta streaks in her dark hair make her easy to spot. Kailey's eyes stare out at me in photo after photo, shining with life.

I regard my new body in the mirror and furrow my brow.

This is the first time I've been a teenager since my original body died, and the feeling is jarring. My eyes are a grayish green, with long, thick lashes, and my hair meanders from light brown to a shimmery gold where the sun has bleached it. It hangs past my jaw in loose curls, with a swoop of wavy bangs. My nose is a bit too pert for my liking, and my lips are a dark shade of coral, striking against Kailey's tanned skin.

There is no tangible difference between the face that I see in the mirror and the face in the photos, nothing I could point to with certainty to prove that everything has changed. And yet I don't think I look like her, that smiling girl that Kailey was.

"What do I do now?" I ask the stranger in the mirror. "Do I keep being you? Or do I go back to the cranes and jump?" Kailey doesn't answer me.

The choice to die had been easy when my body was falling apart around me. If I follow the same course now, I will be actively killing a human body. But if I don't follow through on my plan, where will I go? I have no ties to the world, no real skills. Cyrus always made sure I was dependent on him for everything.

I tear my gaze away from the mirror. The most important thing now, other than the bag, is Cyrus. By now he knows I'm gone. But will he accept my letter at face value or will he wonder if I am still out there, on my own, away from him? He knows me so well—he used to even be able to predict my dreams. Will he somehow instinctively know what happened? Will he feel my presence and come searching for me? Will he read a news report about an accident and wonder if, in a misguided attempt to save a teenage girl, I switched into her body? With Cyrus, anything is possible, and being dragged back to the coven is the worst thing that can possibly happen. I'd be under constant surveillance. And Cyrus would make me very, very sorry for tricking him.

On the desk is a laptop computer. I swipe my finger over the track pad and the blank screen is replaced with an Internet browser window. I pull up the *San Francisco Chronicle* website. There were plenty of murders and car accidents reported in Oakland over the weekend, but thankfully, nothing about Kailey's incident.

I click back to Google and type "jack london car accident," which brings a slew of results. Narrowing by date, all but one disappears.

It's a hit on the police blotter page on the *Oakland Tribune*'s site. "October 16th, 12:38 AM, Alice and Second Streets, Oakland: Police were called after a Berkeley minor was involved in an injury accident. No fatalities and no arrests were made." I let out the breath I had been holding—the report wasn't too bad and didn't stand out among all the other incidents in the area.

Google Maps tells me it's only two miles from the Morgans' house to the downtown Berkeley BART station, and then a straight shot to downtown Oakland. Studying the map, I realize that Berkeley High School is right next to the BART station.

Kailey's backpack is slouched on her desk, next to her purse. I take a rapid inventory of their contents, keeping her wallet and cell phone, but disabling the GPS. I add a change of clothes and, on impulse, a slouchy hat and oversize sunglasses.

A knock at the door startles me—I barely have time to dart to the bed before Kailey's father comes in, carrying a tray. He still looks tired, but he doesn't have the same anxious expression that he did in the hospital. He doesn't know his daughter is dead; he thinks everything will be okay.

"Your mom wanted me to bring you dinner. Tortilla soup, your favorite."

"Oh . . . thank you," I say cautiously, wondering what the real Kailey's response would have been.

"Listen, kiddo." He sits down next to me on the bed. "Don't worry about explaining where you were last night. I told your mom to leave it alone. If you've got a boyfriend or something . . . well . . . you can tell us later." He gives me a hug, his voice cracking with emotion. "We're just glad you're okay."

My heart twists painfully in my chest. Of everything I've done over the years, this is the worst. Kailey's death would have destroyed this family, but at least they would have the finality of knowing she was dead. And when I disappear tonight, will they think their daughter ran away? That Kailey killed herself? Either of those options feels so much worse than a tragic car accident.

I ask myself, for what feels like the millionth time since I woke up in the hospital, what was I thinking? I knew CPR would be fruitless. Why did I try, when the risk was so great? I should have let nature take its course. Did I interfere because, as an Incarnate, I have learned that nature's course can be altered? Or was there some small, unconscious part of myself that still wanted to live?

I turn away from Mr. Morgan to hide the tears in my eyes. "I am so, so sorry for making you guys worry. I feel terrible."

"Hey, I'm a dad. Worrying is my job. See you in the morning, kiddo." Mr. Morgan gives me a small smile before closing the door with a soft click, leaving me alone with my guilt and sadness.

eleven

I wait several hours until the house is swathed in silence and the darkness outside is thick. Slinging Kailey's backpack over my shoulder, I open the window and hop out onto the brick path below in one smooth motion. I can't deny that it feels invigorating to be in a new body after months of painfully inhabiting a dying one. But that realization is followed by a wave of crushing remorse that hurts more than my old body ever did.

I creep softly by the side of the house and head to the street. At the edge of the driveway, I turn back and look at the house once more. *I'm sorry. I really am.*

A deep growl startles me out of my silent farewell. I whip my head around and peer through the darkness, eyes flashing, prepared to run. Or fight.

"You look pretty active for a girl who just got out of the hospital."

I freeze. The voice belongs to a tall, dark-haired boy standing in the shadow of one of the redwood trees. He holds the leash of an enormous dog. The dog growls, straining against its chain.

"I mean," the boy continues, "did you really need to go out the window? Or was that for added drama?"

"You were watching me?" Fear makes my voice tremble slightly. "Who are you?"

"Very funny, Kailey." Then a worried look crosses his face. "Wait, do you really not remember?"

I exhale. So this is one of Kailey's friends. For a moment I had been certain that it was Jared in a new body. Or, even worse, Cyrus.

"Just a little concussion humor," I reply, forcing myself to smile. "Who told you about the accident?" I ask, keeping my tone light even as panic rises in my gut. Had I missed something in the news after all?

"Bryan. I ran into him earlier."

I nod with relief, regarding the boy again. His hair is

dark and long enough to fall into his face. He rakes it off his forehead with strong-looking, well-shaped hands. His eyes are a surprising color of turquoise, staring at me from under thick brows. A camera dangles from his neck. There's something about him that feels familiar, but I can't quite put my finger on it.

"It was no big deal. I'm actually pretty embarrassed about it, so if you can keep it on the down low, that would be great." If word of my accident isn't out there yet, I have to do my part to keep it quiet. Cyrus has unraveled mysteries with far less information.

The boy's dog snarls again, baring its teeth at me. Animals are tougher to fool than people. I've always wondered how they know something isn't quite right about me. He jerks on the leash. "Harker! Stop it!" Harker whimpers and stops growling, though he continues to regard me with a baleful glare. The boy's eyes lock on mine, and I see him noticing my backpack. "That's cool. I can keep a secret."

I exhale and take a step back. There's an awkward pause. "So what are you doing out?"

An anxious look flashes across his face, but quickly disappears. He's hiding something. We have that in common. "I love being out at night," he says, tipping his face to the sky.

"It's quiet. You can see the stars, if the fog will let you. You know. Obvious reasons. What about you? Going AWOL?" He nods toward my bag.

"I just . . . needed some air. I guess I should go back inside." There is no way I can escape now. I'll have to wait another hour, until the boy is home and asleep.

"Sleep is probably a good idea." He bends to scratch Harker's ear as the dog lets out another low growl. "Hey, if you need a ride to school tomorrow, I can give you one. I hear your 'no big deal' totaled Bryan's car."

School. Of course Kailey would have to go to school. How would her friends handle her disappearance? "Um, sure. Thanks. G'night . . . *Harker* . . . and . . . g'night . . ." I finish weakly.

"Take care, Kailey," the boy says, briefly putting his hand on my shoulder in a friendly gesture. I can feel the heat from his palm through my sweatshirt. I turn and make my way back through Kailey's window.

Back in Kailey's room, I lie on the green silk coverlet and stare at the ceiling. It's covered in tiny glow-in-the-dark stars. If I squint my eyes, I can imagine they're real, except they aren't arranged in actual constellations. This is a sky of Kailey's own creation, the pretend universe she slept in, the safety and stillness she sought in her small world.

My eyes are heavy, and I close them—just for a second,

I promise myself—hoping that wherever Kailey is now, she's at peace. In my mind I still see the stars, rearranging themselves in brand-new patterns, their gentle light flickering down to Earth, shining on the neighbor boy's crow-black hair.

twelve

I'm awoken by the clatter of dishes and the scent of coffee and food. Ruby-tinged light floods through the lace curtains. I jolt upright, my heart racing, sure that Cyrus has found me. Then I see the green bedspread and realize where I am. I groan, berating myself for having missed my opportunity to sneak out. It's far past dawn and the Morgan family is most definitely up.

I hear the sound of approaching footsteps, and moments later Mrs. Morgan's face appears in the open door. "Morning, sweetie. How do you feel today?"

"Um, okay," I stammer. Truthfully, I feel like hell. I

tossed and turned all night, my mind churning with nightmares. In them I was chasing my mother through a dense forest, her dark hair streaming out behind her. I couldn't see Cyrus, but I knew he was near. Little piles of powder kept erupting into colorful flames around me, dizzying violet and red, pale starlit yellow and lime green, and Cyrus's voice rang out through the trees: *Sera, I told you death was only an illusion.* Just as I finally caught up to my mother, her hair turned a shocking blond and Cyrus's voice boomed from her mouth. *I'm coming for you,* he said with a snarl.

Mrs. Morgan sits on the bed and looks at me with concern. I realize I'd fallen asleep in jeans and a sweatshirt. "I think," she says firmly, "that you need to stay home from school today. I'll stay with you."

I'm not sure how to respond. I imagine Kailey would be psyched to stay home from school, but the thought of spending the day with the mother of the girl I killed makes me feel physically ill. I need to get to the docks, and it will probably be easier able to slip away between classes than to escape from Mrs. Morgan's watchful eye.

I manage a weak smile. "I think I should go to school. Honestly, I feel fine."

Bryan sticks his head in the door, a piece of toast in his hand. "Are you *seriously* asking to go to school? Kiss ass."

"I'd really rather go," I tell him.

"I know." He grins. "Just giving you a hard time."

Mrs. Morgan looks between the two of us, hesitating. "Okay. You can go. But you need to eat first. I'll go make you something." She heads back to the kitchen, and Bryan turns to follow her.

"Hey, Bryan?" I push myself into a sitting position.

"Yes, O spoiled one?"

"Could you . . . not say anything to anyone at school about the car accident? I don't want this getting around."

Bryan looks shocked. "I thought your life goal was being in the limelight."

I feel my cheeks growing hot. "I just don't want to make a big deal about it."

He stares at me. "You're blushing."

I turn away from him. I've always been a blusher, no matter what body I'm in.

"Bryan, please."

"Okay. Whatever you want, weirdo." He pops the rest of his toast in his mouth.

After he's gone I look through Kailey's vintage armoire for something to wear. It smells of oiled cherry wood and laundry detergent, and the neatly hung clothes are organized by color, like an artist's palette.

I wonder what she would pick to wear, running my hand along a purple cashmere sweater and a deep fuchsia dress covered with a blue geometric pattern. I ultimately settle on a pair of cropped, rust-colored jeans and a burgundy, lace-trimmed tunic. The scent of jasmine has entwined itself in the fabric, reminding me with each inhale just whose clothes I am wearing.

I race through breakfast—eggs over easy with chicken sausage—as Bryan enters the kitchen.

"We've gotta go. I think I hear Noah's car out front."

Noah. I wonder if that's the neighbor boy's name. I grab Kailey's backpack and stare at Mrs. Morgan. Her hair is combed neatly back into a ponytail and the dark circles that had been so prominent under eyes yesterday have vanished. After a moment's hesitation I pull her into a hug. "I love you," I say softly, wishing I could ease the pain she'll feel when her daughter doesn't return home tonight.

"Love you, too, Kailes," Mrs. Morgan says in a slightly surprised voice. She kisses my cheek, then shoos me out the door.

Bryan is waiting next to Noah's ancient VW Bug, tapping his foot. "Finally," he says, pointing toward the backseat. "Invalids have to ride in the back," he explains with a grin.

I feel Noah's eyes on me as I climb into the car. In the sunlight they are a warm turquoise, the same color as Cyrus's had been two bodies ago. I pull the seat belt across my lap. The boys thankfully fill the silence and ignore me, though I catch Noah glancing back at me in the rearview mirror now and then. I place my forehead against the cool window, letting Noah and Bryan's conversation wash over me as I pray over and over again that my bag is still on the crane.

We pass a line of small houses—Craftsman, A-frame, and a squat shingled one that would have been more at home in Cape Cod. Wildflowers grow chaotically all around it, Queen Anne's lace mixing with bright yellow goldenrod and purple sage. My mother would have loved it. My father allowed her a small patch of garden that the servants weren't allowed to touch. She spent hours out there, teaching me the Latin names of each seed: *lilium*, *rosa*, *cosmos*, and *orchis*. She would weave me halos of daisies and belladonna, always warning me how dangerous flowers could be. "Never put these in your mouth, my little angel. But atop your pretty hair they do no harm."

Soon we pull into the parking lot, joining a stream of beat-up cars jockeying for spots close to the front entrance. The school looms large, all glass and curved walls. I wonder if Kailey liked it here, if she looked forward to gossiping with her friends between classes or if she spent her time staring out of windows, counting the hours until she was free again. I have never been to school. My parents had hired tutors for me when I was young; everything else I know I'd learned from Cyrus.

Noah comes to a stop next to a green Volvo with a

BERKELEY HIGH WOMEN'S SWIM TEAM bumper sticker and turns off the sputtering engine. Bryan pushes his seat down to let me out, and I stand up in the dim sunlight.

"See you in bio," Noah says, and departs, holding a book over his head as he dashes toward the school.

Bryan looks at me expectantly, and I follow him across the parking lot. "See ya," he says when we reach a covered walkway.

I watch as he walks away, nodding and high-fiving friends as he passes. He has the same easy smile as Kailey, the same buoyancy and happiness I saw in her pictures. No doubt his sister's death will change that.

This is it. I swear my hammering heart must be audible to those milling around me.

"Good-bye, Bryan," I whisper, then, making sure no one's looking at me, I dart back across the parking lot against the wave of arriving students. I try to appear casual yet purposeful, and avoid eye contact with everyone I pass. When I turn the corner and am out of sight of the school, I break into a flat-out sprint for the BART train that will take me close to Jack London Square, where I will have to decide what—if anything—comes next.

thirteen

I get off the train in downtown Oakland, and the scent of fetid water and rotting produce surrounds me as I walk toward Jack London Square. The area is much busier during the day—trucks parked in front of loading docks, men hoisting boxes of melons, tourists gingerly making their way down to the waterfront. The sun has broken through the clouds and warms the top of my head, and I'm surprised to find myself smiling—it has been so long since I've felt anything other than cold.

My pace quickens as I near the docks. In the distance I

see the bar where I'd met Taryn; it looks even more dilapidated during the day. Paint is peeling off the storefront in long strips and the sunlight catches on windows covered in a film of dust. Just beyond that is the side street where I parked my car and the crane where I so stupidly left my bag.

Just as I reach the intersection, I realize with a start that a police car is parked at the curb about fifty feet in front of me. I freeze, blood draining from my face. Rationally, there's no reason for the police to be looking for me—for Kailey—but still. In my mind there is a giant sign over my head proclaiming MURDERER.

You were trying to save her! I remind myself, pleading with my feet to take casual strides. I feel a prickling sensation as the hairs on the back of my neck stand up. I don't turn around, even though I'm certain the officer is following me. Instead, I walk faster, just short of a run. A glance in the side mirror of a parked car confirms my fear: The police car is trailing behind me.

I duck into an alleyway and hide in the doorway of an industrial garage. I hold my breath and cross my fingers, hoping the cop will drive past. After a beat he does, and I exhale with relief.

A hand falls on my shoulder. "Do you need something?"

My heart in my throat, I whirl around and find myself

staring at a thin-lipped construction worker. "N-No," I stammer, and take off once more. But when I reach the side street where I had parked my car, I stop short. There are dark brown drips on the asphalt, drips that might look like oil stains to anyone else. But I know they're blood. Kailey's blood. And the black tire tracks are still there, like scars, on the surface of the road.

The car is gone.

Panic courses through my veins, but I force myself to take a deep breath. *It was probably just towed*, I remind myself. *There was nothing in it that tied it to you, except fingerprints from a body that is now dust.*

These thoughts aren't reassuring, and dropping all pretenses, I sprint to the crane and start climbing the ladder. My foot slips on the second rung from the top, and I let out a loud gasp as I nearly lose my grip. Clinging to the bars, I regain my footing and hoist myself onto the top of the structure.

The wind up here is forceful, bringing with it a far-off giggle and a loud, catcalling whistle. But I hear nothing, feel nothing, because just like my car, the bag is gone.

At that moment a gray cloud blots out the sun and it begins to rain. As the steady stream soaks through Kailey's hair, dampening her loose curls, panic fills my body. This cannot be happening. That bag had everything in it—my old ID, my money, Cyrus's book.

Taryn.

I sink to my knees. She was an addict and after six hundred years of observing human behavior, I can picture the scene too well. After seeing my body disintegrate into dust—something she would not be sure was a drug-induced hallucination—she climbed back up the crane, looking for the angel who tried to save her. Instead she found the bag, which contained car keys, money, a brand-new identity, and a strange old book.

The horn of a boat in the harbor emits a mournful cry, a crane nearby groans to life, and the smell of rotting lettuce assaults my nostrils. What will Taryn do with the book? My mind catalogs a million possibilities. She could try to sell it to a rare-books dealer when she runs out of money and needs her next score. It could end up in police custody if she's arrested—or dies from an overdose.

Or worse, maybe she already tweeted a picture of it, along with a post about how someone in Jack London Square gave a teenage girl CPR, then turned to dust, giving Cyrus a roadmap to find me in 140 characters or less. No doubt Cyrus would be prowling the Internet for any mention of me, for any hint that I could still be alive. And Jared, as penance for losing me in the crowd, would go to the ends of the Earth to bring me back.

I don't know what it means that I am still alive right now and whether I should keep this new, healthy body or dive into the harbor to finish what I started last night. But I do know one thing: I am never, ever going back to Cyrus. And if I can help it, Cyrus will never find his book.

I scale back down the ladder, jumping onto the pavement when I'm still four rungs from the ground. Ignoring the burning pain this ignites in my shins, I push my legs fast, making a sharp right onto Second Street and dashing toward the bar. Maybe the bartender there knows Taryn, and if I could get her last name, I could track her down.

I am thirty feet from the saloon when the wail of police sirens pierces the air. My forehead is covered in a fine mist of sweat, my stomach clenches, and I feel the precursor to an anguished cry choke my throat. I consider making a break for it, but I'll never be able to outrun a police car. So I stop in my tracks, panting as I watch the officer who had been following me earlier get out of his vehicle and walk toward me.

"Excuse me, miss," he says, "but shouldn't you be in school?"

Bending at the waist to catch my breath, I swallow a stream of curse words. I had forgotten how young I look in this sixteen-year-old body. The backpack isn't helping, either.

"N-No, sir," I stammer. My mouth feels stuffed with cotton. "I'm on my way to work. I don't have class at the university until tomorrow." It's a plausible lie—UC Berkeley isn't far and being a college student would certainly explain the backpack.

"Sure you do," he says, with a withering smile. "Let me see your ID."

"Oh. Um, I don't have it with me," I try.

"I mean it, miss. Hand it over."

I feel my face go hot and have no words as I open the bag and hand over Kailey's driver's license. He looks at it for a long time, then shakes his head.

"Get in." He nods toward the police car.

"Why?" I ask.

"I won't make you ride in the back, but we need to go to the station where we'll call your parents."

Oh my God, the Morgans. The last thing they need is to think their daughter, who they almost lost yesterday, has turned into a delinquent overnight.

"Please, sir," I beg. "Please don't call them. I promise I'll never skip school again."

The officer smiles ruefully. "Do you know what your problem is, Kailey?"

My problems would fill his citations notebook and make

him question everything he thinks he knows about the world, but I keep my mouth shut.

"Your problem," he continues when I don't respond, "is that you're a terrible liar."

fourteen

The station smells like old coffee and men's cologne, and the fluorescent lights overhead turn my hands a sickly shade of yellow green. I am sitting on one of the hard plastic chairs behind the reception desk when the entire Morgan family walks in. Mr. and Mrs. Morgan won't look at me, but Bryan raises his eyebrows with grudging respect.

The officer pulls Kailey's parents into a private room to talk to them, and Bryan takes a seat next to me. "I had no idea you were such a badass," he whispers.

I don't say anything—I just shake my head slowly. He elbows me in the side, and I allow a small smile.

Mr. and Mrs. Morgan exit the conference room, both of them tight-lipped and still refusing to make eye contact. Mr. Morgan's face stands in flushed contrast to Mrs. Morgan's ashen pallor, but I can tell they're both furious.

As soon as we pull out of the parking lot, the floodgates open.

"First we have to come pick you up at the hospital, and then at the police station. What's next? The morgue?" Mr. Morgan explodes, banging his hands on the steering wheel for emphasis.

I flinch at the word "morgue," where this body should be right now. Before I can answer, Mrs. Morgan sighs. "Honestly, I blame myself. We've been entirely too permissive."

"No!" Mr. Morgan snaps. "This is not our fault. Kailey, the officer told me you *lied* to him. Sneaking off is one thing, but I thought we raised you to always tell the truth." He frowns. "I'm very disappointed in you."

"Where were you even going?" Mrs. Morgan demands. "Does this have something to do with why you were there on Saturday night?"

"I, um," I hesitate. Why *would* Kailey have been down there that night?

I glance at Bryan, who's enjoying this way too much. I shoot him a poisonous look, but he just smiles wider.

"I'm painting the cranes," I finally finish. "It's my new project."

"At night?" Mr. Morgan says skeptically.

"You're grounded, of course," says Mrs. Morgan, watching us in the rearview mirror. Bryan smirks. "For two whole weeks, if not longer."

Mr. Morgan nods vigorously. "No going *anywhere* but school. And no TV."

They continue to berate me the entire way home, but I tune them out, instead focusing on the whisper of an idea that's taken root ever since the police officer slammed the door of his car on me.

Every push I've made to end my life has been thwarted. Every single one. It could be simple incompetence—after all, I've been with Cyrus for six hundred years, and I should expect some hiccups making my way through the world alone. But then I think of the night I switched into Kailey's body, of the vision of my mother whispering, *Not yet*, and it feels like something, or someone, doesn't want me to die.

I think of the disgusted expression Cyrus would wear if I said such a thing to him. Cyrus doesn't believe in fate or anything at all beyond the physical world that he moves through so certainly. *Modern science is the child of alchemy*, he'd say. *All magic has a rational explanation.*

The hairs on my arm stand up as I consider that the universe might be trying to tell me something. As much as I think Cyrus is close minded in his staunch rejection of anything resembling spirituality, I have to admit that I've never actually witnessed anything to convince me otherwise. I've never seen a ghost, never heard a prophecy, never really believed in anything beyond this life. But now, as I've tried to leave it, I feel as if I'm brushing up against an invisible hand that is steering my course.

And though the body I'm in now is completely different from any other I've ever occupied, its heart beats as surely as any other's, reminding me with each thud that I am very much alive. *Maybe*, the voice whispers, *you should stay that way.*

I shift in my seat, the seat belt scraping my neck, and train my eyes out the window. I pull Kailey's hat down over my ears and close my eyes, letting the sun wash over my eyelids. I don't know the specifics of my plan, but I've come to a decision.

I'm not going to end my life. Not right away. I am not this family's daughter, but I owe them a debt. I will stay here, pretend to be Kailey, and figure how I can bring the Morgans peace. I will try to track down Taryn so I can find and destroy the book. And I will work on my plan of escape. Today's events tell me it won't be easy— My car is missing,

I have no money, and I have no idea if Cyrus is on my trail, but thanks to Kailey's healthy body, I have some time to figure it all out.

After a stone-silent family dinner, I return to Kailey's room, close the door behind me, and immediately boot up her laptop. I try every possible search for Taryn—Facebook, MySpace. I Google "Taryn + Berkeley," "Taryn + Saloon," "Taryn + black hair," but my attempts yield nothing. I next turn my attention to the saloon, finding a phone number listed on Yelp.

It rings twice. "Hi, is Taryn there tonight?"

"Who?" the man on the other end barks.

"Taryn. She's a patron—she was there two nights ago," I say, wondering if I'm speaking to the man who had studied my ID before begrudgingly serving me.

"Taryn?"

"Yes! She has black hair—"

"I have no idea who you're talking about," the man interrupts, then the line goes dead. I stare at the phone for a few seconds, disappointment mingling with frustration. Now that I'm grounded, it will be difficult to get back to the bar to ask more questions in person.

But Taryn's not the only person I have to find. I need to learn every detail of Kailey's life if I'm going to pull off living as her. I look around the room, pondering the best way to prepare myself.

Considering her artistic skill, I am betting there is a diary around here somewhere. I approach the bed and reach between the mattress and the box spring, but come up empty.

My eyes are drawn to a framed print to the right of the vanity. It's of a young girl wearing a wreath of flowers, a silvery crescent moon rising behind her. She holds one hand to her mouth as though she's afraid to speak.

I gently lift the frame off the wall, feeling its uneven heft. Turning it around, I see that a sketchbook has been tucked into the gap between the frame and the wall. Bingo.

Sitting at her desk, I thumb through the pages. I feel guilty, like I'm spying, but looking at her artwork, I can almost sense her presence. It comes through so strongly. I feel like she'd want me to look at these, that she'd want me to recognize what she lost.

They are mostly portraits: a drawing of her mother in their garden, of Bryan tying his shoes, a wry expression on his face. She had a remarkable ability to capture the essence of their personalities with the smallest of details. This was her language, I realize. This was her way of interacting with, and chronicling, the world.

Several of the portraits look like Kailey herself, but they're fantastical. In one she is kneeling next to a fire hydrant, a pile of broken glass in front of her, wings erupting from her shoulders. In another she has her hand outstretched, one finger pointing down a deserted street to a dragon who stands next to a parked car. They are gritty, realistic, but always with one detail that tells me this is a girl who believed in magic.

It reminds of Cyrus's book, the carefully painted manuscript where he recorded his research. My stomach twists at the thought of Taryn poring through it just as I'm scouring Kailey's journal now.

Flipping to the inside back cover of the sketchbook, I find a cryptic message: "FB—fairy510, EM—same." I immediately grasp what it is: her Facebook and e-mail passwords. *Score*, I think, and settle in for some research.

Her e-mail doesn't provide much personal information, though I do find an attachment with her class schedule. I pull up the website for Berkeley High School, which has a map. The campus is made up of many different buildings arranged in a square, with common areas mostly outside. I compare the layout to the locations of Kailey's classes and commit everything to memory.

I click over to Facebook and log in. Kailey has more than seven hundred friends. My mind reels— Despite my long life, I can't even think of seven hundred people that would know my name, let alone those that I would call friends.

I begin to sort through her list of friends and am quickly overwhelmed. There's no way I can memorize them all. My heart sinks. I start scrolling faster, and the faces blend together and become meaningless. But one face jumps out at me. It's the neighbor boy, and his name is indeed Noah. Noah Vander.

Scanning the posts on her wall, I see that there are only four girls who write with any regularity. These must be her close friends. There's Leyla Clark, the girl with the magenta-streaked hair who I recognize from the photos. It seems that she is Kailey's best friend, and therefore will be the hardest to fool. The easy camaraderie of her posts makes me sad; I miss Charlotte deeply. I wish I could contact her somehow, let her know I'm okay and ask for her help, but I know it's impossible. She could never keep the secret from Cyrus. He would punish her for her involvement, then come straight for me.

I copy down the names of Kailey's other close friends—Chantal Nixon, Madison Cortez, and Piper Lindstrom—and study their photos. There's one girl who appears in many of the group shots, though oddly she's not on Kailey's friend list. I note her name as well: Nicole Harrison. She's pretty, with shiny brown hair and a light dusting of freckles. She appears to be friends with the rest of Kailey's crew. I wonder what happened between her and Kailey.

Kailey's profile says she's single, and though there are a couple messages from boys in her in-box, they're not overly familiar or flirty. No boyfriend, as far as I can tell, which will make things easier. Although it does deepen the mystery of where Kailey was going the night she died. Like her parents, I realize I had assumed she was going to meet a boy.

A *thwack* from the direction of the window sets my heart thudding, and I leap up and back away toward the door. *Oh God*, I think, suddenly sure I will see Cyrus's face at the window. The thought arrives with a sheen of sweat and a shot of adrenaline coursing through my veins.

I grab the nearest heavy object—a metal jewelry box from Kailey's dresser—and flick off the light switch next to the door. The room is plunged into darkness, and I kneel on the floor. I hear sounds from outside, scratches and scuffles on the exterior walls. I squeeze my eyes shut and then open them, my breaths coming in alarmed gasps.

"Kailey! It's okay," a voice whispers. I open my eyes and reluctantly look at the window, where a face slowly comes into focus. It's Noah.

"You scared me!" I say sharply, standing up. I am furious, but relieved.

He rather unceremoniously climbs the rest of the way through the window, a canvas grocery bag banging into the wall. I hold my finger to my lips and murmur a low "Shh."

"I hear you're grounded," he whispers with a smile. "Bryan told me." He climbs over the bed and stands next to me. He's quite tall and is wearing gray corduroy pants and the same black sweatshirt he had on the first time I met him. I can smell the night air from the folds of his clothes.

"You really shouldn't sneak up on people. You almost gave me a heart attack," I hiss, gesturing for him to sit on the bed. I flick on the light, but it feels overly bright. I'm hit with the fear that it will bring the Morgans in to check on me and quickly turn it off.

Noah unzips his hoodie. "You know, light doesn't actually make any noise," he informs me. I can't suppress a small laugh.

"I'm sorry if being on lockdown's made me paranoid!" I whisper, sitting in Kailey's desk chair, but pushing it back a few feet. There's an awkward silence.

"Yeah, I heard you did some hard time today."

"The hardest," I joke feebly. "Two whole hours."

He rakes back his black hair. It's hard to tell in the dark, but I think I detect a blush on his tanned face. For some reason I'm reminded of the first time I met Cyrus, and I wonder why Noah has come here tonight. Is this a usual occurrence?

As if reading my thoughts, he clears his throat. "*Any*way, I knew you were trapped in here, so I come bearing gifts." He reaches into the bag and pulls out treats: a cupcake, a brownie, and a bottle of sparkling pomegranate soda.

"Thank you," I say, sincerely touched that Kailey had someone in her life who would sneak her cupcakes.

"Sure." He looks away and fiddles with the shoelaces on his worn sneakers. "It's no big deal."

There's another long silence, but I make no move to fill it. Experience has taught me that people will always start talking if the gap is long enough, and right now I need as much information as possible.

"So where did you sneak off to today?" He looks me in the eye.

"I didn't sneak off anywhere. I just wasn't in the mood for school," I say curtly. "Did anyone ask about me at school? You didn't say anything about my accident, did you?"

He tugs at the collar of his button-down shirt, looking stung. "Of course not, Kailey. I promised."

I realize I've hurt his feelings. "I'm sorry." I heave a sigh. "I've just had a long day."

He smiles again, brightening. "Yeah, I suppose a run-in with the law could take it out of you."

"You have no idea," I admit. "Thanks for the cupcake, though. Chocolate is my favorite."

"Anytime. I guess I should leave you to your beauty sleep." He flashes me another smile as he climbs onto the ledge, and I'm struck again by his deep blue eyes and strong jaw. "Oh! I almost forgot." He jumps back down and picks up Kailey's iPhone. "I assume you're not allowed TV. What about phone?"

"They didn't mention the phone," I reply.

"Fair game, then," says Noah, tapping on the touch screen. He hands it back to me. "Good night," he says softly, slipping back out the window. I close and latch it behind him, shutting out the autumn night air, then look to see what he typed into Kailey's phone.

He's opened Words With Friends, the free Scrabble-like application. I tap the icon and see he's already started a game with me. His first word is "sneak," the *K* landing on a double-word square.

I look at my own letters: *ZPJNMNY.* No vowels at all. I build off his *S*, writing "spy," then sit back down on the bed where he had been sitting. It's still warm.

I wonder what Noah and Kailey's relationship was like—Were they actually friends? I pick up the jewelry box from the floor and return it to the dresser, turning on a lamp. A small framed photo catches my eye—it's a picture of her and Noah when they were kids, maybe five or six years old. She looks impatient, hands on her little hips, her eyes looking straight at the camera with a challenging glare. I guess she didn't feel like smiling.

fifteen

Tuesday morning dawns gray and rainy, water coursing down the old wooden windows of the Morgan house. The morning plays out as the previous one did, except Mrs. Morgan is icy toward me and now Bryan makes me sit in the back, not because I'm an invalid, but a "criminal." Little does he know.

We drive in silence, listening to Noah's new Broken Bells album, and arrive in the school parking lot much too soon. I check Kailey's schedule for the umpteenth time, then get out of the car. Once again Noah jets away, but now that I know they share the same first-period biology class, I wonder why he runs off without his friend. Bryan motions me forward, and we hurry across the parking lot, dodging puddles, their filmy surfaces covered by rainbows from the oil slicks on the asphalt. This time—no doubt on his parents' instruction—he waits to make sure I'm actually inside the building before he takes off with a quick "See ya."

Then I'm on my own. Taking a deep breath, I enter the fray. I've seen depictions of modern teen life on TV, but I've never actually set foot in a school. My first impression is that it's noisy, students laughing and jostling, their shouts echoing off the bright white stucco walls of the various buildings. The architecture is an eclectic mix of 1930s to recent styles, and the student body is just as diverse.

Which way to go? I try to reconcile the physical place with the map I'd studied and take a few hesitant steps to my right. Fat drops of water fall in my eyes from a leak overhead, and I quickly dodge out of the way, swiping at my eyes.

A couple kids say hello to me, and I wave uneasily in return. I try to walk faster and with confidence, but I soon realize I'm completely turned around, and turn on my heel in the opposite direction. A bell rings, and I jump, panicking. Unless I can figure out where to go, I'm going to be late. Everyone will stare at me.

I pass the girls' bathroom and gratefully duck inside, locking myself in a stall and closing my eyes till my breath has returned to normal. Digging in my pocket, I find the map I had sketched out the night before. Suddenly, I realize where I am.

More composed, I leave the bathroom and find my way to the biology classroom. I don't think the classes will be difficult. Cyrus, for all his faults, was an excellent teacher, giving me a solid education in mathematics, sciences, and literature. I could easily solve chemical equations, debate the finer points of Socratic discourse, or expound on the entire history of Greece.

I reach the door of the classroom and freeze—where should I sit? I spot Noah near the front and wonder why he would drive me around, bring me cupcakes, and then ignore me at school. My many years of living have not made the actions of teenage boys any less enigmatic. Still, I start to make my way toward him—he is, after all, the only person I know—but the teacher stops me. "Ms. Morgan," he says in a gravely voice. "Please take your *assigned* seat so class can begin." I stop in my tracks and look where the teacher gestured.

There are two empty seats near each other, and I move toward them hesitantly. "Any day now, Ms. Morgan," the teacher prods. I take a breath and flip an imaginary coin, choosing the seat in front of a pretty girl with long, shiny brown hair. She gives me a smile, but her eyes are cold. I glance once more at Noah before sitting down, the girl following my gaze. With a start, I realize this is Nicole Harrison, the girl Kailey wasn't friends with for whatever reason.

The other students already have notebooks and textbooks open on their lab tables, and I follow their lead. Kailey's notebook is filled with doodles in the margins: flowers, portraits of other students, abstract patterns. Art was clearly where she excelled.

I turn to a fresh page and write the date, October 18, in my old-fashioned script. I stare at it for a moment and realize I've got to try to copy Kailey's handwriting, which is, to my discerning eye, atrocious. I turn to a new page and start again, letting my hand relax and relying on muscle memory to approximate her stylized printing.

"Cellular respiration," the teacher writes on the whiteboard behind him, then begins the lecture. I dutifully copy down the phrase, but my mind starts to drift almost immediately.

How am I going to make my escape? I realize now that I can't just disappear. The Morgans would no doubt issue an AMBER Alert, and my face would end up plastered all over every major news outlet in the state. An AMBER Alert for a teen girl in the Bay Area would likely catch Cyrus's notice. I silently thank the officer who picked me up yesterday.

No matter which train of thought I follow, I keep coming back to the same conclusion: The Morgans will need to think Kailey is dead. It's the only way to stop anyone from looking for Kailey ever again. Should I fake another car crash? A fire? Plant a suicide note saying I've leaped from the Golden Gate Bridge?

Bile rises in my throat at my callous planning, although in an odd way, I know that staging an accident is the kindest thing I can do for the Morgans and the truest way to respect Kailey's memory. Beyond that, all I can do is promise myself that Kailey's is the last body I'll ever inhabit. I will stay in it for as long as possible, till the last damned breath it's able to breathe. It feels paltry, and it is, but it's all I've got.

A buzz from Kailey's iPhone, wedged in the back pocket of my jeans, brings me back to the present. The clock on the classroom wall tells me class will be over in a few minutes. The teacher is droning on, and I wonder how any of the students are able to stay awake. Glancing around, I see a sea of sleepy, bored eyes.

Surreptitiously, I pull the phone from my pocket and glance at it underneath the desk. It's a text from Leyla.

i miss you! are you actually here today?

Not really, I think as the bell rings.

* * *

By lunchtime I'm exhausted and on edge. The classes are easy, but the social dynamics are not. I never know where to sit or who to talk to, and my teachers seem baffled every time I know an answer. Kailey, it seems, wasn't the most diligent student, but I have no idea if she wasn't smart or was simply disinterested.

I exit Kailey's English class—Shakespeare I—and let myself be pulled along with the river of students toward the cafeteria. It's a large, circular room flooded with natural light, its walls almost entirely made of glass.

Searching the faces of the crowd, I suddenly panic. Some people look vaguely familiar, but I don't see any of the girls whose faces I memorized last night. I don't even see Noah or Bryan—in my entire long life, I have never felt more out of place.

"What do you think you're doing?" I hear the voice in my ear at the same time I feel a hand grab hold of my elbow.

Whirling around, I recognize the elbow tugger: It's Leyla Clark, Kailey's best friend. I plaster a smile on my face to cover my surprise. "Hi, Leyla."

"Why, hello, *Kailey*," she mocks, turning me around and marching me away from the cafeteria. I'm mesmerized by her skirt, a colorful, patchwork affair that looks handmade. I don't question where we're going—I'm so relieved that I don't need to enter the cafeteria by myself that I'd gladly go anywhere.

"I'm *so* glad you're back. You feeling okay? Bryan said you were sick. Actually, I should thank you for giving me an excuse to talk to him!" She keeps chattering all the way through the empty drama wing, till we reach a narrow staircase. For a flash, I'm reminded of the staircase at Emerald City. I'm gripped by the sensation that, like that night, I'm about to cross a threshold.

"What's wrong with you? Everyone's waiting!" Leyla gives an impatient smile and leads me up the creaky stairs. She ducks behind a curtain, and I follow her into a small, secret room.

The smell of Chinese food and the sound of laughter hit me as I walk in. "Hey, Kailey! Welcome back!" says one girl, her ivory cashmere sweater complementing her coffee-colored skin. I recognize her as Chantal Nixon. She's decidedly preppy, unlike the rest of Kailey's friends.

"Thanks," I say, joining their circle on the cushy carpet. The room is covered in graffiti and a swirling collage. I think I recognize Kailey's style in several of the paintings: a girl lying under a tree, a purple bicycle, a deer with flowers and ribbons in its antlers.

Piper Lindstrom and Madison Cortez are here, too, and I congratulate myself on my successful Facebook research.

They both look vaguely rock-and-roll, with ripped skinny jeans and T-shirts for bands I've never heard of.

I immediately recognize Nicole as well, the girl who'd given me a dirty look that morning in biology. She's not, I notice, eating Chinese food out of the takeout containers like the other girls. Instead she's got a wooden bowl full of salad. Her style is upscale hippie, with comfortable, expensive-looking leather shoes and a soft, green top.

In the coven we all had defined roles: Cyrus was the tyrannical leader; I was his subservient love; Jared was Cyrus's yes-man and enforcer; Amelia, his doting sidekick. Sèbastien moved behind the scenes, and Charlotte served as my best friend. I wonder what role Kailey played in her group.

Piper hands me a takeout container full of fried rice, and I take a few bites before passing it along. Nicole shoots me a smile laced with ice. "Feeling better? You seemed pretty out of it in bio this morning."

Madison, holding the fried rice, pauses and looks up with worry shining in her blue eyes. "You're still sick?" She looks back at the food container and sets it down gingerly.

"No, but thanks for your concern, Nicole." My tone is neutral, but in my mind I've already classified her as someone to watch out for.

A silver charm bracelet on Nicole's wrist catches my

attention. Glancing around subtly, I realize that Piper and Madison are wearing the same bracelets, though Leyla just wears a strand of thin red leather. “What are you looking at?” Nicole demands.

“Nothing,” I mumble, taking a bite of broccoli from the next container that Piper passes me. Leyla gives me a strange look.

“I thought you hated broccoli,” she says.

“It’s . . . um . . . healthy,” I stammer.

Leyla points at my chest. “Who are you and what have you done with Kailey?” I feel the blood draining from my face and the muscles tensing in my legs. I glance at the door, calculating how quickly I could be down the stairs and outside.

But Leyla just chuckles, tossing her magenta-streaked hair. “*Anyway*,” she continues, “can we get back to discussing the party?”

“You’re coming, right, Kailey?” Madison waits for an answer.

“To what?” I ask. I figure that since I missed school yesterday I don’t have to pretend to know about it.

“Dawson’s party Thursday night,” she huffs incredulously. “It’s up in the hills, in Montclair. Dawson’s parents are gone. We’ve only been talking about it for the past two weeks.”

"Oh, right. Um . . . I can't go," I say, hoping I sound sincerely disappointed. "I'm grounded."

"You are?" Chantal is incredulous. "What for?"

For being a very bad body snatcher, I think. "I got in a fight with my mom. It was stupid."

"Does this mean Bryan's not going?" Leyla asks, an urgent tone to her voice.

"I have no idea," I reply. "Why don't you ask him?"

Her brown eyes sparkle. "If you insist."

Nicole clears her throat. "I thought we were forbidden to talk to your brother?" A rosy flush appears under her freckles and a defiant glint flashes in her eyes. She tucks a loose lock of hair behind an ear.

A look passes between Leyla and Nicole that I don't understand, and Madison seamlessly changes the subject.

While the girls prattle on about what to wear to the party, I look around at Kailey's friends, bonded by years of history and inside jokes. I think of how well I knew Charlotte—that she snorted when she was embarrassed, that she could only memorize things if she made up a song for it—and how well she knew me. My decision to leave the coven was the only secret I had ever kept from her.

I have been so distracted by waking up as Kailey and by looking for Cyrus's book that I am only realizing just now how utterly alone I am. No one knows my real name or what I really am. And the thought makes me want to burst into tears.

But then my phone buzzes and I look down. It's from Noah; he's played another word: "friend." And I wonder if I am not quite as alone as I think.

sixteen

My second day at school is a little easier. I know where I'm going and where to sit. I speak up in my English class, offering my thoughts on *Hamlet* and impressing the teacher. I eat lunch with Kailey's friends, still feeling slightly shy, but not like a cannon about to go off. It helps that Nicole has a doctor's appointment—"Isn't that, like, her fifth appointment this month?" Chantal asks suspiciously—and isn't there. *Fake it till you make it*, Charlotte and I would joke every time we were disoriented after a switch or had to move to a new house we didn't like, and I repeat the mantra to myself on a continuous loop.

I have to stay late to make up a French test Kailey had missed when I ditched, but I breeze through it, finishing in a half hour, and dash out the front door with other detention-goers. Bryan's at practice and Noah's long gone, so I have to walk. I've only gone a few steps when I stop, noticing a pay phone just outside the school.

All day I've been mulling over how to find Taryn. I keep circling back to one idea: calling my car in as stolen. It's risky, I know—it could raise a lot of questions—but I decide it's worth it if it means I get Cyrus's book back. I won't be able to give them Kailey's cell, so I quickly download Google Voice and create a second line on her phone with a different number. Then I drop a few quarters in the pay phone and dial the police.

It rings three times before a perky woman picks up.

I cross my fingers behind my back, hoping I am doing the right thing, and lower Kailey's voice to make it sound older. "Hi, I'd like to report a stolen car."

I give her the details—the license plate, the fake name I bought the car under, the location where it was stolen, and the new number I just programmed into Kailey's phone. I hear the woman typing loudly as I speak.

"I wouldn't get your hopes up," she warns. "Stolen cars rarely turn up. The thieves usually change the plates or get it to a chop shop within hours. But we'll call you if we find anything."

I thank her and hang up, then set off toward Kailey's home, my mind working overtime. I don't need the car back, I just need to smoke out Taryn. I feel badly possibly getting her arrested, but she really shouldn't have taken my bag and my car.

I'm a few blocks away from the Morgans' house when I hear someone shout Kailey's name. I turn around and spot a familiar silhouette behind me: Noah is out walking his dog. As they approach, Harker growls at me again, but this time I kneel in front of him and rub his ears.

"It's okay, Harker," I murmur, feeling the silky fur. After a minute the dog calms down. It appears we have a temporary truce.

"I don't know why he keeps doing that," says Noah. I catch his gaze, his eyes as blue as the Caribbean Sea.

"He's just protecting you." I stand, and we fall in step, meandering down the street. I take a breath. There is something I want to know. "Why do you run off to bio without me every morning?" I don't look at him, instead watching the trees, the way the last long-limbed reaches of sun are lighting them up against the sky.

I am surprised when he laughs. The sound is warm.

"Kailey, you've made it pretty clear that our friendship only exists outside of school. I'm not the one ignoring you."

I look down awkwardly. I'm getting a fuller picture of who Kailey was. And she was . . . complicated. Imaginative and artistic, with plenty of friends who cared for her. But also somewhat manipulative, if she really did forbid her friends from talking to her brother. And now this.

"Sorry," I mumble.

Noah pulls a small digital camera from his pocket and points it at me. "What are you doing?" I ask.

"Recording this moment for posterity." He grins and takes a photo. "I can't remember the last time Kailey Morgan issued an apology."

We pass a house with open casement windows, taking in the cool breeze. Inside, someone is playing the piano. Noah stops, his head cocked. "I love this song."

"It's the second movement of the *Pathetique* sonata," I answer reflexively. Beethoven is one of my favorite composers.

He looks at me wonderingly. "There's definitely something different about you. Don't get me wrong—I like it."

I stiffen as the song continues, the notes uneven on the soft wind—the kind that only comes after a storm. Noah's still looking at me. For some reason I think of Cyrus's icy blue eyes. Noah's are nothing like that.

"Let's walk," I say, keeping a space between us as we continue down the street. Our shadows stretch out in front of us in the orange light, an optical trick making the distance between us appear very small.

We pass an antiques shop, and Noah stops to peer in the window. It's absolutely packed with objects—old books, teacups, musical instruments. A small handwritten sign in the corner of the window captures my eye: HELP WANTED. I pause, thinking.

"Do you think they'd hire me?" I ask Noah.

He looks at me curiously. "What happened to 'I'd rather be poor and have time to paint'? Besides, what do you know about antiques?"

This makes me laugh. "I know a *lot* about antiques, for your information."

"What's so funny about that?" he asks.

I shrug. "Inside joke."

Harker whimpers and pulls on his chain. "He wants to run," Noah explains, with an apologetic tone.

"We should run, then. Running is fun. You should use your body to its full potential while you're young." I know it isn't the kind of thing Kailey would say, but I don't care.

Noah's long hair falls into his eyes, and he pushes it back behind an ear. "You keep saying the weirdest things." He smiles. "But I like weird. Let's go."

The three of us race down the street, and I easily take the lead. It does feel good to run, to feel alive, to crunch through fallen leaves on the wet sidewalk, to splash through puddles and soak the legs of my jeans.

When we reach our houses we stop, gasping for breath and laughing.

"Kailey?" Mrs. Morgan appears at the door. "Where have you been?"

I look apologetically at Noah. "Uh, I should head inside."

"See you," he says, waving to Mrs. Morgan.

As I head up the front walk, I glance back at Noah, bending down to pet Harker, and am struck suddenly by how alive, perfectly alive, and human he is. He is both his spirit and his body, bound by the silver cord. Cyrus says it's a physical phenomenon, that modern chemistry just hasn't figured out how to quantify it yet, but I don't believe him. I may be immortal, but Noah is the magical one.

seventeen

Having spent a few days with the Morgans, I know what it's okay to talk about: Bryan's upcoming football game, my homework, Mr. Morgan's job as a librarian. I smile and nod at all the right places, even though I'm distracted. I can't stop thinking about the help wanted sign in the antiques shop window.

Finally, I clear my throat. "I know I'm grounded, but—"

"Here we go," says Mr. Morgan. Bryan leans in eagerly, sure I'm about to get into even more trouble.

". . . but I was wondering if I could get a job?" I finish.

Mrs. Morgan raises her eyebrows, and Mr. Morgan

nods slowly. Bryan's jaw drops slightly. "That is not what I expected you to ask," he says.

Kailey's parents look at each other, communicating silently, the way longtime couples learn to do. Mr. Morgan glances back at me. "I don't see why not," he says thoughtfully.

"We'd have to approve the job, of course," adds Mrs. Morgan.

I tell them about the antiques store. "Who knows if they would actually hire me, though," I demur.

"I think it's a great idea, Kailes. Just as long as you have time for your schoolwork," says Mrs. Morgan.

"Of course," I assure her. "School comes first." Bryan rolls his eyes and mimes gagging, but I ignore him, happy with my little victory.

Just as we're starting in on apple pie, the house phone rings, and Bryan jumps up to answer it, his chair scraping across the black-and-white checkered linoleum floor. I hear him talking softly in the hallway, but I can't make out what he's saying. "Must be a solicitor," Mr. Morgan observes.

"Kailey, it's Leyla. She wants to know if you'll study with her tonight," announces Bryan, returning to the kitchen. He has a funny half smile on his face.

"You should," says Mrs. Morgan. I look up, surprised.

"You're still grounded," she adds, trying to look stern. "But studying is allowed."

"We haven't seen Leyla around much lately," Mr. Morgan says.

"Kailey? Phone?" Bryan reminds me, sitting back in his chair and taking an enormous swig of milk, emptying half the glass.

"Oh, right." I go to the phone in the hallway and pick it up. "Hello?"

"Why have you been ignoring my texts?" Leyla demands, but continues before I can respond. "I'll come get you and we can get coffee, okay? I'll be there in ten minutes."

"Oh, okay," I answer hesitantly.

"Good. Ciao."

"Leyla's coming to pick me up," I inform the family. I'm not imagining the disappointed look that flickers across Bryan's face.

"Oh, I thought she was coming here," he says.

"That's fine, honey." Mrs. Morgan takes a sip of wine. "Have fun."

I run outside when Leyla pulls up in her Honda. I expected her to drive a car that matches her personality a little bit more—a pink Cadillac, a vintage Volvo, or a painted school bus. She's wearing glasses and concentrates on the road as we drive, whipping them off as soon as we find a parking spot near Telegraph Avenue.

"I'm so glad they let you out tonight," she says, tossing the glasses onto the dashboard.

"I have to admit I'm surprised. But I asked them if I could get a job, so maybe they're rewarding me for showing initiative or something."

Leyla stares at me. "You're getting a job? Will you still have time to paint?"

I think of the unfinished portrait on Kailey's easel. It will have to remain undone because art is something I never managed to master. "Yeah, I'll still have time to paint," I lie. "And I'll have more money for art supplies."

"Fair enough." She smiles. We climb out of the car, and I follow her lead as we walk down Telegraph, inhaling the Nag Champa incense that wafts out from nearby head shops. I try not to stare at the punk kids that sit on the sidewalk, begging for change. I know their type all too well: runaways, probably from wealthy families, but angry at the world. The type that no one would miss. A girl with oily white-blond hair wearing patch-covered camouflage pants pets a mangy-looking dog, looking at me hopefully. I turn away. These are the kinds of kids I've preyed on in the past.

Leyla takes me to a café across the street from UC Berkeley. It's packed with students, laptops open and books piled on tables, but a low chatter tells me that they're not all here to study. I grab a table inside while Leyla gets us drinks.

"So, what's going on with you?" asks Leyla as soon as we're seated, steaming mugs of chai in front of us. She squints slightly.

"Not one to beat around the bush, are you?" I ask, with a wry smile.

"No, sorry, I just mean that you seem . . . different. Distracted. And I can usually tell what you're thinking, but right now I can't." She leans back in her chair, looking at me expectantly.

I take a sip of the chai, but it's too hot. "I've just been . . . tired," I finish lamely, because what else can I say? As much as I wish I could take her hand and tell her that her best friend is gone, I simply can't.

"Oh, okay." Leyla looks disappointed, but just like Charlotte, she doesn't pry. "So can you believe Nicole?" she says, changing the topic at lightning speed.

I think of Nicole's pointed glares and conspicuous absence from Kailey's friend list and shrug. "She hates me. Not much I can do about that."

"She doesn't hate you. You guys will make up eventually. You always do. I don't think she was *that* serious about Bryan, anyway. She'll get over it." I hear a trace of wistfulness in her voice.

"Maybe. But she's been really mean this week," I point out.

Leyla shakes her head, her hair swinging back to reveal earrings made of feathers and miniature skeleton keys. I'm reminded of the wind chimes on the Morgan porch, and I wonder if they are another one of Kailey's creations. "Look, if you feel that badly, you can always refriend her on Facebook. I've always respected your wishes. I understand why you don't want your friends dating your brother. I wouldn't either. Too complicated." I don't miss the undercurrent of anxiety when she talks about Bryan.

Once more, Charlotte pops into my head—how she was always sneaking looks at Sébastien, how they would smile at each other when they thought no one was looking. "You know, maybe I was wrong about that."

"No, no. It's okay, Kailey. Don't back down now." She smiles, but won't look me in the eye.

"I don't—I don't want to control anyone. And I'm sorry if you feel that way." I'll never be like Cyrus, trying to control people, telling them how to feel and act and punishing them when they disobey.

Leyla cocks her head. "Seriously, are you okay? Something seems . . . off."

I force a laugh. "Everything's great. Same old me!"

She drains her drink, looking unconvinced. She has a foamy mustache from the chai, and I tell her so. She pulls a mirror from her purse to inspect the damage and lets out a long laugh. "Can't take me anywhere! I'll be right back," she says, leaving for the bathroom.

I'm staring out the window, lost in thought, when a boy approaches our table. He's older, probably late twenties, and has jet-black hair and a nose ring. "Hey, Kailey," he says. I narrow my eyes. He's clearly too old to be in high school and smells like leather, cigarettes, and beer. I wonder how she knows him.

"Hey," I say hesitantly.

"Haven't seen you around much lately. Thought you were coming out on Saturday." He's looking at me intently, and not in an entirely friendly way. There's something about him that I don't like.

"I've been really busy," I say stiffly. I want him to leave.

Out of the corner of my eye, I see Leyla coming out of the bathroom. "So I should really get back to my studying," I say.

He follows my gaze and nods. "I get it. Well, hopefully you make it back down to the club one of these days. I miss dancing with you." He winks at me and walks away. My skin crawls.

"Who was that?" Leyla asks curiously, settling back into her seat.

"I have no idea," I answer honestly. "Hey, let's get out of here."

As we make our way back down Telegraph, she links her arm with mine. "I'm so glad we got to hang out tonight." I'm surprised by the sudden physical closeness, but relax into it. I know this isn't my life, but I've been so lonely and I genuinely like Leyla. She's kind, and she loved her friend.

"Me too," I say.

eighteen

The next day Bryan has an early morning football practice, so it's just Noah and me in the car. I sit in the front seat and feel suddenly shy, staring straight ahead, not knowing what to do with my hands. Noah is quiet, and there are dark circles under his eyes. He doesn't play any music, and I don't know if he's angry or if he just forgot, and when we get to school he doesn't move to leave the car. I lean down to get my backpack and put one hand on the door handle when he speaks. "My dad lost his job and started drinking again. I think my mom's going to leave." His hands are still resting on the steering wheel like he wants to be in motion.

"Noah," I whisper. Through the open windows I hear the bell summoning us to class, but I don't move. "I'm sorry."

"I hate being there." I feel him looking at me and I turn to face him, struck again by the intensity of his blue eyes. He looks like he's been crying. I'm not sure what to say. It hadn't even occurred to me that things weren't okay at home for Noah—he always seems so easygoing. But now that I think about it, there were clues. He puts on a good act, but he's pretending to be someone he's not, just like me.

On impulse I reach over and take his hand. He doesn't pull it away. "I won't tell you not to be sad," I say. "And if you don't want to go home, come to my house. I'm sure my parents won't mind."

He squeezes my hand. We just sit there quietly for a few more minutes and then go to biology. We're late. I don't think the teacher even notices—he doesn't turn around from the board when we walk in. Someone else notices, though, and I feel Nicole's glare on the back of my head for the entire class. She clearly likes him and I wonder: Does he like her, too? She is beautiful. But then I shake my head. Why should I care who Noah likes?

At lunch I head straight for the secret upstairs room.

Nicole is conspicuously absent. I'm not certain that this is related to seeing me walk into class with Noah, but I suspect it is.

Halloween is a few days away, and costuming is a constant topic of conversation. Chantal wants to be an angel, which everyone deems boring. "C'mon," pleads Leyla. "At least be a *zombie* angel."

Chantal looks horrified. "No way. Zombies are disgusting." She picks imaginary lint off her pale pink sweater. The rest of the girls crack up.

Madison and Piper are going to be Girl Scouts. "Dead Girl Scouts? Ax-murdering Girl Scouts?" Leyla asks, hopefully, but they shake their heads. "You guys suck! Halloween is supposed to be *scary*. What about you, Kailey?"

"Grounded, remember?" I remind her.

"Oh, right. Sad." Leyla pouts. "I really wish you could come to Dawson's party tonight."

"Yeah, it won't be the same without you," Piper says.

Kailey's friends are all going to Haight-Ashbury in the city to shop for costumes, but Leyla promises to look for something terrifying for me to wear. "Maybe Little Red Riding Hood? Only . . . she's actually been half eaten by the wolf?" I laugh, but I feel oddly worried for them. They have no idea that *real* monsters live in San Francisco.

I picture Cyrus's platinum hair and angelic face. The scariest thing about Incarnates is that we look just like everyone else.

That afternoon I stop by the antiques store. The owner doesn't want to hire a sixteen-year-old, I can tell. But after I correctly identify a Victorian Eastlake sofa, a turn-of-the-century Stickley chair, and an original Edison phonograph, he gives me the job and asks if I can stay for a shift immediately. At ten dollars an hour it will take a long time to have enough money to escape, but this doesn't bother me much. It's a start.

After work I eat dinner with the Morgans and we chat about the day. I'm still most definitely grounded, but I know they're proud that I've got a job. I tell them about the customers who came in—the rich lady who bought a painting of a dog, the zealous young homeowners searching for period-appropriate doorknobs for their old house, the man who collected antique lamps and didn't care if they were broken.

"At least someone appreciates old things." Mr. Morgan sighs dramatically. "As an antique myself, I can say that."

"You guys aren't old," I protest. I should know.

"I beg to differ," says Bryan. "They're certifiable experts on the one-hit wonders of the eighties."

"Hey!" says Mrs. Morgan. "We were very cool back then. I was in a band, I'll have you know."

Bryan groans. "Yeah, you sang Duran Duran covers."

"What's wrong with Duran Duran?" Mr. Morgan frowns.

Bryan and I crack up. "This calls for photographic evidence," he declares, heading to the bookshelf. He returns with a large, leather-bound photo album, and flips it open to a shot of Mrs. Morgan and her band. She's got a leather jacket with the sleeves pushed up to her elbows, immense shoulder pads, and poufy, feathered hair. My heart catches in my chest. She looks so much like Kailey.

"The epitome of cool," I assure her.

Bryan pokes me in the arm. "Listen to this one! You're just trying to get out of being grounded."

Mrs. Morgan sighs. "Bryan, you're so mean. I bet we can find some funny pictures of you in there. I seem to remember a certain phase when you wore a Power Rangers costume every single day."

"And *that's* my cue to leave," says Bryan, picking up his plate and carrying it to the sink.

I scoot closer to Kailey's mom as she leafs through the album. Photos of Kailey as a squalling, red-faced infant in Mrs. Morgan's exhausted arms. Kailey, at age two or three, with Bryan, shirtless and tan at the beach, their white-blond hair coated with saltwater. Kailey eating strawberries, red juice all over her face. Kailey, age seven, missing her front teeth, with her dad in front of a brand-new backyard tree house.

And more recent: sullen twelve-year-old Kailey, pouting

on a camping trip. Kailey wearing a black dress with purple hair. "Hmm . . . your Goth phase," Mrs. Morgan says. "We always let you do what you wanted, but I have to say that color didn't do much for you."

I laugh. I have to agree.

I've never had any photos of myself—Cyrus thought it was too dangerous to carry around any trace of who we've been—and I don't even remember what I looked like as a human. I remember my parents, though. My mom with her honey-brown eyes and dark tresses and my dad's square chin and easy smile.

Mrs. Morgan flips to a page filled with pictures of the whole family. Not one of them is technically perfect—Mr. Morgan has his eyes closed or Kailey is sticking out her tongue at Bryan and Bryan's giving Kailey bunny ears while Mrs. Morgan smoothes down his hair—but they perfectly capture how much this family loves one another.

There's a phenomenon that humans talk about, of seeing your life flash before your eyes in the moments before death. Of course, I have no way of knowing whether this is true or not. But I have the eerie sensation that, if it's true, I'm seeing what Kailey saw in those fiery, bloody, painful moments as she lay in the wreckage of her car.

"You know I'm going to miss you," Mrs. Morgan says, shaking her head.

My chest pounds. “Wh-what do you mean?” I stammer.

“College, Kailey. It’s coming soon.”

I force a hollow laugh. “That’s not for two more years.”

She pushes my bangs out of my face. “You’re young. When you’re my age, you’ll realize two years is nothing. Over in an instant.”

She kisses me on the forehead, and I give her a hug, feeling another wave of guilt. She’s right. Two years is a drop of water in the ocean. And Kailey will be gone from her life much sooner than that. I’m surprised to find I’m as sad for her as I am for myself at the thought of leaving—though I’ve only lived with the Morgans for a few days, in an odd way, they feel more like family than the coven ever did.

nineteen

I'm staring at the stars on Kailey's ceiling Thursday night when I hear footsteps in the hallway and whip my head toward the door. It opens a crack and Bryan pops in his head. "Get your stuff," he hisses. "I'm breaking you outta here!"

"Seriously?" I say, startled.

"Yes, get dressed!"

We drive into the Oakland hills, and the neighborhood goes from urban to forest astonishingly quickly. The house is a modern version of the forest cottage, all straight lines and glass walls, but somehow perfectly situated in an ancient redwood grove. Inside, kids are drinking beer out of red plastic cups and dancing to the pulse of electro music from Dawson's stereo.

Emerald City was the last party I attended—the jeans and plaid, pearl-buttoned cotton shirt I wear now are a far cry from my silk dress.

"Kailey! I thought you were still grounded!" Leyla wraps me in a tight hug, spilling a bit of beer on my sleeve. She's wearing a raspberry-pink eyelet dress over cherry-colored tights. Her hair is piled on her head, loose magenta-hued ringlets falling on her shoulders. She looks like a valentine.

"I am," I explain into her shoulder.

"I broke her out of the joint," adds Bryan, his gray-green eyes sparkling.

"You're like Robin Hood, bringing my best friend to me," Leyla tells Bryan, releasing me.

Bryan furrows his brow. "Did Robin Hood break people out of prison?"

Leyla shrugs, then takes a sip of her beer. "We're in the forest, aren't we? Let's get you two something to drink."

She takes Bryan's hand and leads him into the kitchen. He swivels his head and looks at me with an expression that says *This girl's crazy*, but I can tell he doesn't mind. I follow them to the keg, where someone places one of the red plastic cups in my hands, and a boy I don't know fills it with beer. "Hey, Kailey," he says.

"Hey." This is, I've realized in the few days since I've been Kailey, the most valuable word I know.

Bryan and Leyla are still chatting away, and with a trace of amusement I realize I am the third wheel. I can tell she likes him, and I suspect the feeling is mutual.

I sip the beer, enjoying the tingly path it clears through my belly. On the far side of the room, near the sink, I spot Noah. He's talking to a girl whose back is turned to me, but I recognize the long, shiny brown hair. Nicole. His gaze flits upward momentarily, as though he can feel me looking at him, and he smiles at me. He tucks a loose lock of his hair behind his ear, and I'm struck by how good-looking he is.

I'm surprised to feel my heart tug across my chest, like a needle scratching a record. I try to return the smile, but feel the unmistakable beginnings of a blush beginning to creep across my face, and I end up giving a curt nod before turning away. I try to appear occupied, studying the lip of my cup with great intensity. I don't see anyone else familiar in the kitchen, so I open the sliding glass door and step outside.

The backyard is nothing but wild forest, redwood trees leading the eye upward, beyond their canopy, to the stars beyond. A few hundred feet from the house, up a fern-lined path, is a huge fire pit. An acoustic band plays music that wouldn't have sounded out of place coming from a traveling Romany caravan. I approach the fire.

There's a girl playing the accordion, her dreadlocked hair pulled back in two pigtails on the side of her head. A fake flower is pinned to the strap of her suspenders. She has two bandmates: a boy wearing a battered cowboy hat is playing violin, and another boy with stretched earlobes and a shaved head is picking at a banjo. They're playing the Grateful Dead song "Friend of the Devil," but slowed down, and I realize the song isn't jaunty; it's a lament.

Set out runnin', but I take my time.

Amen, I think.

There's a huge fallen log nearby, and I seat myself on it, watching the fire. Chantal walks up to me, followed by Madison, and the contrast between the two of them makes me laugh. Chantal's hair is pulled back in a neat chignon, and she's wearing a spotless pale-blue wool coat. She sits gingerly next to me on the log, gesturing for Madison to sit next to her. Madison's shaggy hair hangs in her face; she tosses it back as she pulls a flask out of her leather jacket. She smirks at Chantal, who still seems uncomfortable.

"Just get into it, Chantal. It's okay to get dirt on your coat." Madison takes a swig from her flask, offering it to me.

"Shut up, Maddy," Chantal says affectionately. "The things I endure for a bonfire." She sighs.

Madison pokes her in the arm. "You're full of it. You just wanted to come out here to see if you could find Dawson."

She turns to me in explanation. "No one's seen him."

"Well, can you blame me? He's adorable," Chantal admits, patting her hair. Madison flashes me a smug smile.

I stop listening when Noah walks up to the fire, Nicole behind him. When she sees me, she grabs his hand. I pretend not to notice, watching the flames.

When Noah spots me he drops Nicole's hand. She narrows her eyes at me. "You're not supposed to be here," she says icily. "But we're so glad you made it." Her smile is insincere.

"Yes, I can tell just how glad you are," I say, smiling just as insincerely. I don't know what this girl's deal is, but I don't like her.

Nicole rolls her eyes and takes a seat on a nearby log.

I lean my head back and watch the tops of the trees. They sway in the darkness and I imagine them creaking and croaking in rusty tones. Oddly, these trees have been around as long as I have. It's a humbling thought.

"Can I see the violin?" I ask the cowboy-hatted boy, between songs. He agrees and hands it to me. Nicole looks incredulous.

I hold the base to my chin and draw the bow across the strings, playing a few experimental notes. "Whoa," says Chantal.

"I've been practicing," I explain, remembering the violin

in Kailey's room. I begin to play a song, the name of which I do not know. It's a traditional Irish lament, and reminds me of Charlotte.

The notes weave with the occasional snap of sparks from the fire, rising toward the trees on wisps of smoke. I keep saying the wrong things, and I'm happy to leave words behind for a little while. I finish the song, and hear a small click. I look up at Noah, who's holding his camera. Nicole looks ready to kill.

I hear clapping from the path. "Bravo, Kailey!" says Leyla, approaching the fire, Bryan at her side. "That was really beautiful. But also a huge downer. This is a party, not a funeral."

I laugh, and hand the violin back to the boy in the band. She's right. Leyla sits next to me on the log. "I have a very somber personality," I tell her.

"Yeah, right." She throws an arm around my shoulder. Chantal spots the elusive Dawson and heads off to speak with him, and Noah takes the empty spot on the other side of me. I'm not sure if I'm imagining it, but it seems like he's sitting very close. I can feel the heat of his body next to me, but I don't move away.

I feel strange, but in a good way. I almost can't believe I'm the same person who was ready to die only a couple of days ago. That emotion feels so far away now, like it belonged to someone else. I feel a smile playing across my lips. Could it be that I'm actually happy? I don't trust the feeling enough to call it permanent. But now, surrounded by people, by laughter—I don't care if it's fleeting. I grab hold of it, letting it buoy me like the friends who sit on either side of me, like the bonfire that heats my face, warming me to my core.

twenty

The next week passes easily. I still think of Cyrus and worry about what he might be doing to find me or how he's treating Charlotte. But as my daily checking of the Internet for mention of my car, Taryn, or the book yields nothing, I find myself slipping into the rhythms of Kailey's world more comfortably.

Noah drives Bryan and me to school every day. Whether it's rainy or sunny, foggy or brisk, we leave the windows down, and Noah turns up the music to drown out the sound of the VW's strained engine. I don't know any of the bands, but he tells me their names: Arcade Fire, Bon Iver, Fleet Foxes. The music has banjos and harmonies and a rawness that was entirely absent from Cyrus's incessant techno—he loved modern architecture with its cold geometry and music that was composed on computers. But there was something more human about an acoustic guitar and drums that were played with one's body. Riding in the backseat of Noah's car with the wind in my face and the songs in my head, I want the school to be farther away so the trip will be longer.

The following Wednesday is slow at the antiques shop, so I blast Billie Holiday records on the store's sound system and watch the rain streaming down the windows. I amuse myself by looking at a stack of daguerreotype portraits in brass cases. They're black and white, but some of them have intensely colored rainbowed edges, an artifact of the platemaking process.

All of these people have been dead a long time. There's one girl who looks a little like Charlotte, except her hair is far too orderly, parted severely in the middle and hanging around her face in perfect ringlets. I know it's not her, but I bring it over to the cash register so I can look at it while I work.

Thinking about Charlotte is painful. I miss her so much,

and I'm worried about her as well. Has she managed to keep her head down, to avoid Cyrus's wrath? I comfort myself with the knowledge that, above all, she's a survivor.

I set the portrait down and wander over to a piano, idly playing a few mindless notes. I haven't fully acknowledged a feeling that's been growing inside me, but I can feel it now, like a knock at the door, insisting to be recognized, to be dealt with.

"I wish I could just stay here." I whisper it softly. There's no one around to hear me, so I repeat myself.

I snap my head up at the jangling sound of bells from the front door. It's Noah, dripping wet and holding his camera in a plastic bag.

I can't help but laugh. "You don't have an umbrella, but you put your camera in a little poncho?"

"Priorities," he says, unzipping his sopping-wet black sweatshirt. "Plus, my folks were screaming at each other again. I didn't feel like going back in for an umbrella."

I take his sweatshirt from him and hang it on a worn oak coatrack. "You should stay here and keep me company," I say, standing close to him. I'm overwhelmed again by how tall he feels when I'm next to him, and feel a blush begin to bloom on my face. I look away, embarrassed.

Noah takes in the store. It's a jumbled, cozy place, warm

with an orange glow from the many Tiffany-style stained-glass lamps. There are rows of leather-bound books, racks of clothes, worn velvet sofas, out-of-tune guitars, and piles of old photographs. I show him the daguerreotypes, and he lights up.

"Today any old jackass can take a picture with their cell phone, but back then it was like having your portrait painted." I like the passion in his voice.

At the back of the store he stops in front of a display of old hats—elaborate women's felt hats, their feathers slightly dusty, and men's top hats and fedoras. He picks up a 1920s cloche with white silk flowers on one side and sets it on my head. I regard myself in the filmy mirror and giggle—I think I actually owned a hat like this back when they were in fashion.

Noah aims his camera and snaps my photo, but frowns. "I think you need to stop smiling," he tells me. "All those old-fashioned people are always so serious." I try to oblige, but a grin keeps working its way onto my lips.

"Nope," he says, looking at the photo on the LED display. "You'd never make it in the olden days. You're way too modern and smiley." This just makes me giggle more.

"Here, let me take a photo of you." I pick up a top hat and set it on his head. He hands me the camera, and I take a few shots. I inspect my work. His expression is far off, soulful. "Pretty good," I tell him. "But I think the T-shirt ruins it."

"Right," he says. "I think a hat like this needs a tuxedo."

The jangle of bells from the front door startles me, and I bump into a dresser covered with perfume bottles. One of them falls to the floor before I can catch it, and shatters.

"Damnit, Sera!" I sigh under my breath.

"Who?" asks Noah.

Panic grips me. "What?"

"You just said a name— Who was that?" He kneels over and starts picking up the glass.

"Um. Nobody. Be right back." I race to the front of the store to help the customer. There are two girls bent over one of the jewelry cases. "Can I help—?" I begin, but my voice catches in my throat when I see Nicole. The look on her face tells me she hadn't expected to see me either. I don't recognize the other girl.

"Hey, Nicole," I say, trying to sound friendly.

"Hey." Her voice is flat. Her eyes widen, and I look behind me to see Noah approaching. The smile fades from his face when he sees Nicole.

"Anyway, Kailey, I gotta go. Thanks for showing me

around. Good to see you, Nicole." He grabs his sweatshirt and is out the door.

The bells are still ringing when Nicole sucks in a deep breath. "I can't believe you, Kailey," she hisses. "You are so manipulative."

I'm taken aback. "Excuse me?"

"You know perfectly well what I'm talking about!" A flush rises beneath her freckles, and she tosses her hair back angrily. "First you tell me to stay the hell away from your brother—you tell me you couldn't stand it if one of your friends went out with him, and *then* you practically shove him toward Leyla."

"Um—" I don't know what to say, but she keeps going.

"And now you're toying with Noah, just because you know I like him! You've known him for years and you've barely given him the time of day—you wouldn't even talk to him at school. And now that he likes *me* you can't stand it! You *always* have to be the center of attention, don't you? But you only want what you can't have. It's completely obvious you're just stringing him along to hurt me."

I'm stung. I feel like she slapped me in the face. Does Noah really like Nicole?

"You don't need to say anything, Kailey," she continues, moving closer to me. "We're not even friends anymore, if we ever really were. So I don't care what you have to say. But—" Her eyes flash. "Stay the hell away from Noah. Or else."

Before I can respond, she turns on her heel and leaves, the bells swinging wildly as the door slams shut.

twenty-one

"Ow, Kailey, careful!" Bryan cries.

"Sorry!" I exclaim, realizing I was driving the point of the eyeliner roughly into his skin. I've been distracted ever since Nicole yelled at me in the antiques shop and laid claim on Noah.

"No worries." He looks at himself in the mirror and grins in delight. "That's disgusting. I love it."

I stand back and admire my work. "Gruesome." Armed with a palette of theatrical makeup and prosthetic pieces, I've made a horrific mess of Bryan's face. His forehead and nose appear to be rotting, and an eyeball springs out from one socket, melting into his cheek. I know Leyla will swoon.

"More blood?" he asks, furrowing his brow.

"I think you're good."

"Not even just a little bit more? Here, next to this gash. It looks a little empty." He cranes his head to get a closer look at the realistic-looking wound in his neck.

I sigh. "Okay, but then you're done. This is my masterpiece, after all," I remind him, dribbling fake blood down his neck. He watches with satisfaction as it stains the collar of his shirt.

"I'm lucky to have such a talented artist for a sister," he says.

"Thanks," I says softly, feeling a pang. "Have fun at the party. Say hi to everyone for me."

"I will," he promises.

We head to the living room, where Mr. and Mrs. Morgan are drinking cider and handing out candy to the miniature witches and pirates and princesses who ring the bell. I give Bryan a thumbs-up as he leaves, but I'm not feeling very festive.

In the backyard the night is cloudless and bright, the moon's round face peering down unabated and reassuring.

But the wind obliges the need for spookiness, stirring the wind chimes into a frenzy and urging the tree branches to claw at the sky.

The garden is strung with fairy lights and a strange, warm wind pushes me toward the redwood tree, dark and looming over the yard like a guardian spirit. I climb up into the tree house that looked so new in the Morgans' photo album, but now is rotting away. The roof has fallen away, but the base is still strong. I lie on my back and watch the sky, the stars only faint smudges next to the bright, beaming moon.

They say Halloween is a time when the veil over the world of the spirits is thinnest, when ghosts can cross over and whisper in our ears or touch us on the cheek. I want to believe this—and I don't. After all, I am a ghost myself. But I am also the creator of ghosts, the girl who can unpin your soul from its moorings and set it free to drift. But where do these souls go? I am no closer to knowing.

All the girls whose souls I've taken stream through my mind. I never knew most of their names. I picture each life I've led like beads strung together on a necklace to make me who I am, the sum of all these jewels. And each shiny bead turned to a puff of smoke, a necklace made of ghosts, one bead for one lost girl. *Where are you now, Kailey?* I snuggle into the collar of her peacoat—I can still smell the faint traces of her jasmine perfume. The idea that she's still here, watching me live her life, fills me with despair. I don't believe she is, but I whisper anyway: "I'm sorry, Kailey."

If Cyrus were here, he'd shake his head in disgust. He doesn't believe in an afterlife—that's just a fairy tale, he said, these existential questions are a waste of time. He would scorn Kailey's fantastical drawings, her magical creatures. For him, all magic can be explained by science.

Despite the warm wind that buffets the boards of Kailey's tree house, I shiver. The life that Cyrus gave me was unlike anything I could have dreamed, back in that torchlit garden. I am sad for that girl. I am sad for Cyrus, too. My bright, blue-eyed alchemist, who wanted nothing more than love and scientific truth. But something snapped in him when he became Incarnate. Something went wrong. The cruelty must have been there all along, but it was amplified by centuries of unchecked power.

I'm lost in my thoughts when I hear a board creak. I'm on my feet instantly, looking around in the darkness. I let out my breath when I see it's only Noah. "You scared me!" I say, sitting back down on the tree house floor. "You're way too good at sneaking up on me," I add.

"I'm sorry— Your mom told me you were out here," he says, with a rueful smile. "It *is* Halloween, though, so I think I should get a pass."

"You're forgiven," I say, relaxing slightly. He sits down across from me, his hands inside his sweatshirt pockets. The wind kicks up again, encouraging the garden's chimes to dance fitfully, their silvery peals drifting up toward us. I feel taut, like a violin's string.

"I thought you'd be at the party," I say, watching his face, the way the branches cast their moving shadows across his cheeks.

"I was. But it was stupid. I hate costumes," he says. "Just a bunch of people looking for attention."

"Was Nicole there?" I ask, biting my lip.

"Yeah." He looks away.

I take a deep breath. "She likes you, you know."

"I know." He fiddles with his shoelaces. "I think I may have accidentally given her the wrong idea. She's . . . not really my type."

"What is your type?" The words are out of my mouth before I can take them back.

At this, he looks up slowly, his eyes searching mine. He chuckles softly. "Well, until recently, I wouldn't say I had one."

My heart starts to pound. I want him to kiss me. I want his hands to tangle in my hair, to feel his beating human heart against my stolen one. The thought is unbidden, but I can't say it's brand new. I also can't say it doesn't scare me.

"What does that mean?" I ask quietly, almost in a whisper.

He smiles. "Kailey, it's pretty obvious."

"Is it?" I feel my mouth wanting to follow his lead, but I push the smile away.

He hunches his shoulders, digs deeper in his pockets. "We've been friends for a long time. Even though you haven't always been the nicest to me. It's okay, I don't care."

I don't take my eyes off him. "I don't believe you."

"Something's changed about you. Something . . ." His voice trails off, and he pulls his hands out of his pockets. "I can't stop thinking about you," he continues. "And I only hope I didn't just screw up our friendship by telling you that."

"You didn't," I say softly, finally returning his gaze. His eyes lock on mine, and the wind stops for just a few seconds. But sometimes seconds can last a very long time.

And then.

And then he kisses me, and my life slides into focus. Since I am strong, I do not worry about losing control like I did when I was trying to save Kailey. Instead, I close my eyes and picture the wind moving through nighttime flowers, the moon casting beams on his thick-browed turquoise eyes, the ever-present hood that hides his crow-black hair.

I feel his hand move hesitantly to my cheek, and I touch his arm. I may only be a spirit, but my lips are warm against his. The ancient redwood tree sighs contentedly.

I pull back and regard his face. It's different. I realize that his eyes are usually so sad, that his casual demeanor hides the sadness. But now they're not. He touches my cheek and says, "We have time," then lies back to look at the stars. I lie beside him, quietly, smiling in the darkness.

Time. *College, Kailey,* Mrs. Morgan said. Two years away. To an Incarnate, it's nothing, it's insignificant. But when you have people who care about you, who you're excited about, each day becomes significant.

Maybe, just maybe, I can stay here until then.

twenty-two

I wake up the next morning with a smile on my face. I want to stay in bed and think about Noah, but I go out to the kitchen and eat breakfast. Bryan's not here, and Mrs. Morgan reminds me he has early football practice this morning. That means it will just be Noah and me in the car. Little jeweled butterflies rise in my stomach, and I can't suppress my smile. "*You're* in a good mood," observes Mr. Morgan, amused.

I throw on my usual outfit of jeans and a sweater, but I'm not satisfied. I look boring, not like a girl who was kissed in the Halloween wind. In the back of Kailey's closet, I find a white crocheted dress that makes me feel like I ought to be making daisy chains in a soft-focus meadow. Better. I even put on lip gloss and mascara. I definitely don't need blush. I pick up the bottle of Kailey's jasmine perfume, but decide against it. That belongs to Kailey. I look up at the sound of the doorbell.

"Kailey!" Mrs. Morgan's voice drifts down the hall. "Noah's here!" I can hear her mix of confusion and glee—Noah usually just pulls up to the curb and waits for Bryan and me to run out. I peek out the window and see his car, but he's not in it. *Don't blush!*

I grab Kailey's leather messenger bag and force myself to walk slowly out to the foyer. Noah's standing awkwardly next to Mrs. Morgan, holding a cup from Peet's. Instead of the ever-present hoodie, he's wearing a corduroy blazer, which highlights his broad shoulders..

"That's a nice dress, honey," says Mrs. Morgan. "You should wear it more often."

"Yeah, you look pretty," says Noah, and I feel the first tingles of heat on my cheeks. He holds out the cup.

"Th-thanks," I stammer, accepting the coffee from him and taking a sip.

"Morning, Noah," booms Mr. Morgan, folding his newspaper under his arm and shaking Noah's hand.

"We should go," I say.

Mr. and Mrs. Morgan follow us out the door and stand

on the porch watching as we get into the car. Noah opens the passenger side door for me, and I start giggling. "You don't have to do that," I tell him.

"Right. You're one of those independent girls." He sits in the driver's seat and turns on the engine.

"Have fun at school!" calls Mr. Morgan, sporting a knowing smile.

"Drive," I tell Noah urgently, under my breath. "This is seventeen different flavors of awkward!"

We peel away and burst out laughing together. He glances over. "You are so red right now." This just makes it worse. He pushes play on his iPod, and music fills the car and the silence. I feel wound up and nervous, but in a good way. This is definitely new territory.

We get to school and climb out of the car, and I realize I'm expecting him to run off to class by himself like he usually does. But he's waiting for me. We walk a few steps when he takes my hand in his. His fingers are warm and dry and strong. At first we're out of step, but we relax into each other's pace.

"Good morning, Kailey *and* Noah," Leyla chirps with obvious delight, taking in the sight of the two of us holding hands.

Noah nods, a big smile on his face. The bell rings, so we don't stop walking, but I turn around to look at her. Her eyebrows are raised, but she looks happy for me. *Nice*, she mouths silently.

We pass Madison and Chantal, both of them beaming at us. I hear them erupt into discussion as we walk away.

Nicole spots us and glares, shaking her head. But not even her barbed comments or icy looks can penetrate my happiness. Noah isn't in love with her. He likes me.

We walk into the biology classroom and I stop in my tracks. I feel the blood draining from my face and my heart thudding thickly in my ears. I drop Noah's hand, feeling a cold sweat break out on my forehead, my chest.

There's a figure standing at the front of the room, his back to us. A familiar silhouette and platinum hair I'd recognize anywhere. He's writing something on the whiteboard.

No. It can't be.

The man turns around, and I feel my veins turn to ice. I am a butterfly, right at the moment it flies into a net. He straightens his tie and brushes off the forearm of his immaculate black suit. "Good morning, class," he says, with a brilliant smile. "I'm Mr. Shaw, your substitute teacher."

That smile, those eyes watching all of us, that sweep over me, calculating, watching, missing nothing. A smile I never thought I'd see again.

It's Cyrus.

twenty-three

Somehow, I make it to my seat. Despite my shock, my hands aren't shaking as they dutifully unzip my backpack and pull out my notes and textbook.

Cyrus waits patiently for the class to settle down, for papers to stop rustling, before he clasps his hands together and begins to speak. "The lesson plan for today is a discussion of the human brain." Students are opening their books to the corresponding chapter. Dazed, I thumb through my textbook, but none of the words make sense.

"Close the books, please," says Cyrus. "They are of no use to you today."

The students exchange curious glances with one another, but do as he asks. He clears his throat and approaches the whiteboard, where there's a detailed illustration of the brain, skillfully shaded and textured. "Cerebral cortex," he says, pointing to the board. "Hypothalamus. Cerebellum. Frontal lobe."

He walks away from the board. "You might think of this as a road map to the brain. But, like most road maps, it doesn't *really* tell you anything. You can memorize the names of the places and what they're famous for, but it's nothing like being there. No matter what those textbooks say, the brain is only partially understood. Some say space is the final frontier. But what about consciousness?"

He pauses, holding his chin in a cupped hand. "This may sound philosophical, but biology is the study of life. And where, in this mess of cells, does your consciousness reside? Is it a chemical reaction?"

I can't pay attention any longer, but I can tell by the expressions on my fellow students' faces that they're fascinated. I find it hard to believe this is happening, but I've been on this Earth long enough to know the difference between waking and dreaming.

What gave me away? I must have made a mistake, somewhere. I probably made a million mistakes. It was a mistake to go into that bar. It was a mistake to talk to Taryn. It was a mistake to leave the bag behind. It was a mistake to try to save Kailey—then try to live as her. And, I realize with a sinking heart, it was probably a huge mistake to report the car missing. What if the police called the man I'd bought it from? What if I didn't properly clear my browser history and Cyrus saw that I'd bought it in the first place?

How had I ever thought, for even a second, that Cyrus might not find me? He always gets what he wants. Always.

I'll find out soon enough if he knows it's me. I don't have any illusions about it—I betrayed him, and I will have to pay. I doubt he will kill me. After the note I left him, he knows that I don't want to be with him. He'd probably just lock me away, force me to swap bodies with innocents, and live with him for all eternity. Cyrus has always enjoyed meting out his particular brand of torture.

In all the years I've known him, Cyrus only had one true friend. Nathaniel joined our coven in the nineteenth century, when we lived in New York. Nathaniel was just as exuberant as Cyrus for the subjects of science, metaphysics, the chemistry of spirituality. But then one night Nathaniel told me he had fallen in love with a human.

"Ada," he replied. "She's so beautiful." His eyes were so serious. "I haven't told Cyrus yet, but I'm going to marry that girl, I swear."

I chuckled. Marriage took on a new meaning for an

Incarnate. "Till death do us part"—we understood the solemnity of that like few mortals ever could.

Later that night, I overheard Cyrus and Nathaniel arguing in the library.

"She's mortal! She'll grow old before your eyes. And it won't be long till you need a new body. What will you tell her then? You can't even give her children," Cyrus boomed.

"It doesn't matter," answered Nathaniel. "I will love her when she's old."

Nathaniel was gone the next morning. Cyrus didn't worry much at first. "He'll be back," he promised us assuredly. But the days turned into weeks and the first snows blanketed the city streets. Cyrus searched the whole island of Manhattan, combing the Five Points area, sure he'd find Nathaniel dead or hurt. But one day Cyrus finally admitted that Nathaniel was gone.

He was despondent. He sat for days in his library, reading books or just staring out the window, snapping at servants who brought him food. He dragged me out into the night with him, to gambling dens and bars, to smoky places where men fiddled frantic songs of love. One snowy night on our way home, we noticed a familiar man in front of us.

"Nathaniel!" Cyrus grabbed my hand and pulled me into the shadows, then forward, trailing the man for blocks and blocks.

"Cyrus," I whispered, "let's go home."

"No!" he hissed. "I just . . . want to talk to him. I miss him, Sera."

I obliged, keeping silent pace with him till the moment he stepped out from the shadows and confronted his old friend.

"Nathaniel." Cyrus sounded strong, certain.

Nathaniel whipped around. When he saw us, fear crossed his face. He took several steps backward. "What do you want?" he asked.

"Want?" Cyrus laughed bitterly. "Aren't we friends?"

"Cy—" Nathaniel began.

"How's the wife? Did you tell her what you are?" Cyrus took a step closer to Nathaniel. "Did you tell her about us?" Another step, and another.

Nathaniel shook his head sadly. "I didn't tell her anything. Cyrus, I'm sorry I left you. It was the only way."

The snow was falling so softly, thick upon the ground. It was white, then orange, under the dim light of the gaslights. I buried my nose in the fur stole, shivering.

"I loved you like a brother." Cyrus's voice snarled. "And you betrayed me."

His hand darted down to his boot, the boot where he always carried a very sharp knife, and in one swift movement he stabbed Nathaniel. I don't know where, probably his heart. I screamed as Nathaniel fell backward into the snow, his blood seeping outward in the pure white until it was just one big pool of red. His body evaporated into dust.

I'm pulled from memory by the realization that everyone in the classroom is staring at me, waiting for something. Cyrus must have called on me to answer a question, but I have no idea what it is. I swallow, then open my mouth. But before I can make an utter fool of myself, the bell rings.

Mercifully, the silence dissolves into the sounds of backpacks being unzipped, notebooks closing, and stools being shoved backward. I am halfway to the door when I hear my name.

"Kailey, right?" says Cyrus, peering at the seating chart. "Please stay a moment."

twenty-four

Caught. The word echoes in my head till it dissolves into nonsense. I glance down at Kailey's pretty white dress and worry, irrationally, about it being ruined when Cyrus begins punishing me. White dress, white snow, red blood.

I approach his desk. For a long minute he doesn't speak. He stares at my wrists. I cross my arms over my chest, willing him to say what he has to say. His gaze follows my hands. "Mr. Shaw?" I prompt, playing along with his game. I have no other choice.

"Right, sorry. I was just thinking." He smiles that

brilliant, icy smile, revealing perfect white teeth. "Kailey, what did you think of class today?"

Class? He's playing with me, like a cat with its prey. "I . . . thought it was interesting."

"Did you? Because you didn't appear to be paying attention." His tone is stern. "And if you don't find the material interesting, I'm not doing my job."

I take a deep breath. "I'm sorry, I—"

"No need to apologize. Truly, it's my fault. I promise that future classes will be far more engaging. But this isn't why I asked you to stay." He leans back in his chair and holds his hands together in his lap. His expression softens.

"The school administrators mentioned to me that there was a female student who had been in a terrible car accident recently. And naturally, I'm very concerned." His eyes—ice blue—watch me carefully for any reaction.

He's lying. I'm certain no one at the school knows about the accident. "Who was it?" I ask, my voice stronger now.

He sighs. "They didn't tell me. It's infuriating, really. Post-traumatic stress, even brain damage, can show up weeks after an event like that. I need to know who it is so I can be sure to watch out for signs of trouble." This strikes me as a strange thing for a teacher to say. But any other student would probably accept it at face value, would think he was perfectly caring and concerned. But I know him, and I sense the quivering rage lying just beneath the surface of his words.

But he really, truly doesn't know who was in the crash. This gives me strength. "I haven't heard about any car accidents," I lie smoothly.

"No? Perhaps the girl hasn't told her friends. I want you to think hard. Anyone been acting strange lately? Done things that are out of character?" He leans forward, watching, always watching.

I will my face to remain composed. I look up at the window, pretend to think. "Well, Nicole's been very sensitive lately. But I don't think she was in an accident."

"Nicole?" he asks, studying the seating chart.

"Nicole Harrison." I point out her name. "Long dark hair? Sits right behind me?"

"Long dark hair," he repeats. His expression brightens. "Yes, I remember her. Thank you, Kailey. You've done the right thing by telling me. It may be nothing, but I couldn't live with myself if I missed the chance to help a student." I feel a flash of guilt about offering up her name, but Cyrus will learn soon enough that she's just a regular high schooler. But it'll distract him, and what I need now is time—and to throw him off my track.

I glance at the clock on the wall behind him, but the time is all wrong. I pull out Kailey's iPhone to check the time. "I'm sorry, I've got to go," I say, smiling apologetically. "I'm late for English."

He doesn't say anything for a moment. He's looking at my phone. He chuckles. "Isn't it funny how we tell time with those things? No one wears watches anymore. Although it seems that you usually do?"

What an odd question. I look down at my bare wrist. There is a pale circle around it, visible in Kailey's golden tan.

"I really have to go," I repeat.

"Of course, of course. Please go to English. Thank you again for the information."

I nod, then pick up my backpack and head for the door, feeling his eyes on my back. I wait till I'm in the safety of the quiet hallway to exhale.

twenty-five

I spend the rest of the day in a fog, making mistakes in trigonometry and not hearing my—Kailey's—name called in history. After school, Noah drives me home and asks me if I want to join him on a walk through the neighborhood. I tell him no, that I've got to study. He tries to act like it's no big deal, though I can tell he's hurt. But I can't be around him right now. I can't be around anyone.

I go straight to Kailey's room and close the door. Cyrus may not know who I am now, but it won't be long before he figures it out. Either way, I've got to run. Tonight. I pull Kailey's backpack out from under her bed and start packing for an escape, my hands shaking. I throw in clothes and stop. I don't have anything I'll need—no fake ID, no cell phone. I think about taking Kailey's iPhone, but worry that will make me easy to track by the Morgans. I look in my wallet and count the cash I've made at the antique store: only $160. Kailey must have money somewhere, I figure, and start tearing apart her room. I find random twenties under her bed and hit the jackpot in a little box in the back of her closet. A bunch of birthday cards from her grandparents are stashed there, along with a roll of money—$360 in total. I wonder briefly what Kailey was saving up to buy; perhaps art supplies. Or maybe something related to why she was in Jack London Square the night she died.

It won't last long, but it will be enough to get me away from here. On impulse I grab the framed photo of Noah and Kailey from the dresser. When I realize I'll never see Noah again, my throat closes and my eyes grow thick with tears. I fall onto Kailey's bed and cry, staining the green silk coverlet with darker green splotches. I let out all the tears I never let myself shed, the tears that began gathering the night I ran away from the coven, the tears of being alone, being scared, having no one in the world I can confide in. I cry for Noah, the boy who was Kailey's good friend for years and years, who came to care for her—for me—as something more, who will lose her the next day. His family falling apart, and him with no one to talk to. No one to hold his hand.

I cry for Leyla: sunny, quirky Leyla, the girl who's always got a snappy retort, whose best friend will disappear. What will this loss do to her? I cry for Charlotte, who I've already lost. And I cry for the Morgans, who have been so kind to me. Who have, unknowingly, taken in the girl who failed to save their daughter's life and showed her what a family can be like.

The sobs grow stronger. I realize I can't remember the last time I cried like this; it may have been hundreds of years. I cry for myself, for the fourteen-year-old who caught the alchemist's son's eye, then died by the river. The girl who could live forever but never grow up. I cry for all the girls I've taken, the lost girls, the girls whose families never saw them again.

Finally, my tears are spent. I'm dehydrated from crying, so I go to the kitchen and grab a glass, filling it with water and gulping it down at the sink. I'm halfway through refilling it for another drink when I hear a voice behind me.

"Can you think of a five-letter word for 'giraffe relative'?" Mrs. Morgan is seated at the table in front of a crossword puzzle, tapping the eraser of a dull pencil thoughtfully against her lips. "Second letter is *K*. At least, I *think* it is."

"Let me see it." I glance at the puzzle. "Try 'okapi,'" I tell her.

She raises her eyebrows. "You're right. I don't think I've ever heard that word before in my life." She sighs, then looks up at me.

"Are you okay? Your eyes are all red."

"Must be allergies," I say, taking a sip of water. "You're home early." I change the subject.

"I know. My afternoon meetings got cancelled, so I left. I'm not sure what to do with myself. Hey, want to go shopping or something? I mean, if you have time." She's hopeful, but guarded.

Watching her, I realize she's used to Kailey turning her down. I doubt "hanging out with Mom" is high on any teen's list.

"Sure," I reply.

"Really? Okay, art supplies or clothes. Your choice."

I fear that I'd appear hopelessly unsure of myself at the art supply store. "Clothes," I answer quickly. "I'll go get my jacket."

This will be the last time Mrs. Morgan ever gets to hang out with her daughter, so I have to make every second count.

twenty-six

We drive to Fourth Street in Berkeley and wander among the boutiques and well-heeled shoppers. The air is crisp, carrying salt from the nearby bay. People say that there aren't seasons in California, but they're wrong. Seasons here are simply more subtle—a small shift I notice in the details. The angle of the sun in the sky, the dryness of the wind, the crispness of the leaves.

We pass a shop and I pause, struck by the display in the window. The mannequins are wearing normal clothes, but the scene around them is magical: a glittery forest that teems with color, small lights shimmering in the fake branches. On closer inspection, I notice that the mannequins have antlers growing out from their long hair, entwined with flowers.

I know Kailey would have loved it, this intersection of the real world and the magical. "You want to go in?" Mrs. Morgan asks, with a knowing smile. I nod.

The interior is softly lit, a kaleidoscope of soft fabrics and patterns, candles and locket necklaces, lace dresses and oxford shoes.

I'm immediately drawn to a lemon yellow tunic, but Mrs. Morgan shakes her head. "Cute, but that color won't look good on you." I glance down at my arms and laugh. She's right. I think it would have complemented the olive-hued skin of my last incarnation, but I don't have the eye for color that Kailey did.

She pulls a dusty-rose–colored dress from the rack and holds it up to me, nodding. I give up browsing on my own and follow her around the store, trusting her choices, till my arms are full of clothes. "What happened to automatically rejecting anything your mom suggests?" she asks playfully.

"Remember when I had purple hair?" I ask. "That was all me, right?"

"Good point," she answers.

A saleswoman tucks me away in a dressing room, and Mrs. Morgan waits outside on a damasked sofa under a twinkling chandelier. I pull on a deep green top that's softly gathered at the neckline, trimmed in gray embroidery. Suddenly Kailey's eyes look vibrant and sparkly. Stepping outside, I model the top for Mrs. Morgan, who nods with a satisfied smile. "I knew that would fit," she says.

Next is a scarlet dress, vaguely vintage-looking, fitted around the bodice with cap sleeves and pockets in its full skirt. I come out and Mrs. Morgan frowns. "I don't think you tied the back right," she says, stepping behind me to fix the sash. I watch her in a mirror.

"Mom?"

"Yeah?" I can feel her fussing with the dress.

"What was your relationship with your mom like?"

She looks up, surprised, and catches my eye. "Oh, that. Well. You already know the story." She finishes with the back of the dress. "There, now turn around." I do as instructed. "Hmm," she ruminates. "I think this one is a no. Any dress that your mother has to tie for you is too complicated."

I step toward the dressing room but turn around. "Will you tell it again? The story about your mother?"

She blinks and turns toward the window. "It was a long time ago." I don't move, waiting. "Okay, Kailey. As you know, I left home when I was sixteen. But I never told you that I ran away. I didn't think of it that way at the time—I was just going on a trip with my friends. My parents were so controlling, they never would have let me go. So, I just left."

I sit next to her on the sofa. She looks at her own reflection in the full-length mirror. "I was young. I wanted to see America. I wanted to get out of Milwaukee."

She turns to me. "And what I didn't realize is that my mother was out of her mind. She thought I was dead. She called the police, had everyone looking for me."

"And then?" I say softly.

"And then, while I was away . . . she died. She had a brain aneurysm. She never knew that I was okay." She reaches out and tucks one of my curls behind my ear. "And that's why I've always let you do what you wanted. Maybe it wasn't the best decision." Her gray-green eyes shine with unshed tears, and I feel my own grow wet.

"Do you ladies need any help?" The saleswoman's voice is annoyingly cheerful.

"We're fine, thanks," says Mrs. Morgan.

I stand up awkwardly. "I'll go get changed."

As I put my clothes back on, I feel a pang of sadness. Mothers and daughters. Is there any relationship more complicated in the entire world? I don't ever want to hurt Mrs. Morgan. The fact that, unknown to her, her daughter is already dead pierces my heart. Even though I know it's just the continuation of a fantasy, I want to let her live happily as long as possible.

Am I just trying to atone for my past? For the pain I

caused my own mother? I don't know. All I can think of is Cyrus's smug grin.

Mrs. Morgan pays for the clothes. Back outside, the light is failing swiftly, a quiet November twilight settling in over the shops and the restaurants. "Thank you," I tell her.

"You're welcome," she answers. "We should probably head home."

I feel tender and protective toward her as we walk back to the car. I'm lost in thought and barely hear when Kailey's name is spoken. Mrs. Morgan stops, looking curiously around. I follow her gaze, spotting the all-too-familiar platinum hair.

Cyrus is seated at an outdoor table in front of an upscale cafe. A half-drunk cappuccino is in front of him, and he's holding a book by Terence McKenna. "Good afternoon, ladies," he says, flashing his perfect smile.

I feel like there's a metal band around my chest, restricting my breathing. "Hi," I mumble. Mrs. Morgan has an expectant, confused look. "Mom," I tell her, "this is Mr. Shaw, our substitute bio teacher."

"Delighted," says Cyrus, taking her hand. "You must be Mrs. Morgan?"

"Nice to meet you," she says, and I cringe as she gives him a warm smile. He's too charming, when he wants to be, giving no hint to the monster that he really is. His victims never stand a chance. I want to get her away from here as soon as possible.

"I just found out I'll be teaching the class for the rest of the semester," he says, taking a sip of his cappuccino and somehow managing not to get a single bit of foam on his lip.

"What? Why?" I ask. "What happened to Mr. Roberts?"

Cyrus narrows his eyes at me. "He decided to take a sabbatical. He needed the time off." I know he must be lying. Why would Mr. Roberts leave without giving us any notice? I wouldn't be surprised if Cyrus killed Mr. Roberts. The thought makes me sick to my stomach. But I smile even wider.

"Well. Good for him. We were just leaving, so I'll see you tomorrow." I try to make my voice as carefree as possible, and start to walk away. "Come on, Mom."

"Great to meet you, Mr. Shaw," she says, reluctantly following me.

"He seems very nice," she says, as we buckle our seat belts.

"He is," I lie.

I'm reminded of how I used to play chess with Cyrus. It was his favorite game, and he was very good at it. I only won once, after which he smashed the board against the drawing room wall, splintering the wood and cracking one of the marble queens.

Suddenly, I am furious. There is hate in my heart, coiling

like a snake, wanting to strike. The more I think about Cyrus's smiling face and his perfect black suit, the angrier I get. In one day he's managed to threaten everything I've come to care about. I've lived for hundreds of years under his rules—trying to keep him calm, trying to appease him, to help him. All for nothing—it never stopped him from hurting people, from killing senselessly, from acting cruelly. And here he is again, ruining what little I have as carelessly as he would smash a plate against the floor.

He's so arrogant. He didn't even try to hide from me. He came waltzing in to Berkeley High in the same body that I last saw him in. He thinks he knows me so well—that I'd blush the second I saw him, stammer, or do something to give myself away immediately. Well, I didn't, and for that I am proud of myself.

He won't catch me so easily. I'm leaving tonight. If I go as soon as the Morgans fall asleep, I'll at least have a night's lead. When Kailey's parents discover me missing in the morning, they'll sound the alarm. I need to cover some ground before now and then. I am picturing the moment when I don't show up for biology tomorrow. Cyrus will definitely know it's me. He'll know that I won this round—that I got away before he could catch me.

Then I have a thought that sends me reeling: Cyrus *wants* me to run. Of course. That's why he didn't switch bodies. It wasn't just arrogance—it was a well-played gamble. If I run, he knows it's me, and he knows who to look for. My breath comes in little gasps of relief as I realize how close I came to playing right into his hands. He knows me too well.

If I stay, but play it cool, give my best possible performance as a normal teenage girl—I could win. He's already questioned me, and I must have answered well enough. If I can just wait it out, he might think I've already moved on or that I was never here to begin with.

I congratulate myself on figuring it out. Cyrus may know me better than anyone on Earth, but I know him, too. It's decided—I'll stay, and hopefully, not too long from now, he'll leave. In the meantime I can think about ways to convince him that Seraphina Ames was never here. If I plant a false clue somewhere . . . I'll think of something.

But one thing I know for sure: I'm done running.

twenty-seven

Noah doesn't look at me as I get into his car, and he spends the whole drive talking to Bryan about football. I know his feelings must be hurt. I feel bad about rejecting his offer of a walk yesterday.

Bryan runs off as soon as we get to school, and Noah starts to walk toward the building without me. "Hey!" I call. He turns around, but doesn't say anything. His face is expressionless. "I'm sorry about yesterday," I tell him. "I was in a bad mood, but it had nothing to do with you."

He shrugs. "You don't have to explain yourself, Kailey. If

you want to just forget about what happened on Halloween, that's okay with me. I get it."

I walk toward him till we are standing very close, then I reach out and take his hand. "I *don't* want to forget about it. I couldn't." I gesture for him to lean down, and kiss him on the cheek. "Nothing's changed," I murmur in his ear.

When I pull back, his face is relaxed again. He smiles. "You wanna hang out in the tree house later?"

I laugh. "Sure. Or, y'know, we could even go out on a date somewhere. Like grown-ups."

"How about I take you to the cafeteria for lunch?"

I'm amused. "Deal."

The overwhelming smell of formaldehyde hits me as soon as we enter the biology classroom, but it's the sight of Cyrus, in another beautiful suit, that makes me sick to my stomach. *Don't let him get to you,* I remind myself.

As soon as the class has settled down, Cyrus speaks. "Yesterday we talked about the chemistry of consciousness, about the mysteries that mainstream science has yet to explore. Today I want you to keep those questions in mind as we perform a dissection."

There's a collective groan from the class, and more than one audible "Ew!"

"We'll be dissecting rabbits," he continues, "and I agree,

it's unfortunate that our subjects are dead. It would be much more instructive if they were still alive while we cut them open." He pauses, taking in the shocked silence. "I'm kidding!" Nervous laughter fills the room.

Cyrus hands out dissection pans, gloves, scalpels, and finally, the preserved rabbits. I regard my lab partner, a boy whose name I can't remember—Mike or John or something equally common. He's nice-looking in a generic sort of way, tall and athletic, with close-cropped blond hair and a dimple in his chin.

"Before we do any cutting, I want you to notice the rabbit's structure," Cyrus instructs, wandering among the lab tables. "See its powerful hind legs—a rabbit is a prey animal, and its best chance at survival is to outrun its hunter. Sometimes escape is the best defense, better than any teeth or claws." He smiles at me, and I beam right back. I refuse to be intimidated.

"Okay, class, go ahead and make your first cut. We're going to remove the skin, then examine the musculature."

My lab partner picks up the scalpel. "I better do this part," he says gallantly.

"Go right ahead," I answer.

He turns the rabbit on its back and gently tickles its belly with the tip of the scalpel. His face is pale and slightly greenish. I watch him take a few deep breaths and then hold out my hand. "Let me do it," I say.

He looks abashed but grateful as he hands me the scalpel. I make a smooth slit from the rabbit's throat to its groin, then four additional cuts down each paw and hind leg. I've got the skin peeled back from the muscles before the rest of the class has finished their first cut. I've skinned plenty of animals in my life.

Cyrus walks by, examining my work. "Well done," he praises. "Very . . . precise."

"Thank you," I say curtly.

He clears his throat and speaks to the rest of the class: "I realize this is difficult for many of you. That in this modern society you do not often have occasion to come face-to-face, or hand-to-paw, as it were, with death. My advice to you is: Get over it!"

Everyone laughs. He always loved an audience.

My breath catches in my throat as Cyrus approaches Noah's lab table. He leans over Noah's shoulder, looking at his notebook. "These are beautiful diagrams you've drawn," Cyrus says with admiration. "You have a real eye for illustration. Are you an artist?"

Noah looks down, embarrassed. "Not really. I like to take photos, but that's not like being a painter or anything." He steals a quick glance at me.

Cyrus shakes his head. "Don't downplay it! You have a talent. And anyone who says photography isn't art is, forgive me, an idiot."

My lab partner says my name, and I realize he's been talking. "What?" I ask.

"I said, do you want me to fill in the diagram? Since you did all the dirty work."

"Sure, yes. Thanks." I strain to listen to Noah and Cyrus. There's something in Cyrus's manner with him that I've seen before, and I don't like it.

The bell rings, breaking me out of my reverie. My lab partner has cleaned up and the room is quickly clearing out. I am thankful to leave Cyrus's presence, and wait outside the door for Noah. I need him to reassure me, to make me feel safe again. But I hear Cyrus asking him to stay after class. *No,* I silently protest. *Leave him alone!* But what can I do? I head to my next class, a pit growing in my stomach. A feeling of dread—cold, like deep water that has never seen the sun.

twenty-eight

Noah is in good spirits as we wait to buy food in the cafeteria line. "Would the lady prefer the tuna sandwich on rye or the tofu dog?" he asks with a grin.

"Tuna. I don't trust fake meat," I answer.

"Very good choice."

Even though it's cold, we take our food outside, away from prying eyes and eavesdropping ears. Ever since I left him in biology class, I've had a tense knot in my stomach and my shoulders have been stiff.

"What did Mr. Shaw want?" I ask as soon as we're seated under an expansive oak tree.

"To talk about my photography. He was really encouraging—he said I should apply for art school. It was nice—I never thought of myself as an artist." He takes a bite of his sandwich.

"How can he talk about your photography when he's never seen it?" I ask. "I mean, it's nice of him, but he doesn't even know you." I know that Cyrus doesn't care about Noah's art. He's just flattering him. The same way he flattered Jared and Nathaniel before making them Incarnates.

"Kailey, I know I'm not as good as you. Your paintings are amazing." He looks deflated.

"It's not that—I just think it's insincere of him."

"Well, thanks for the vote of confidence," Noah says drily. "He also recommended some books for me to read—interesting stuff about quantum mechanics and metaphysical chemistry. I had no idea science class could be so fascinating."

"He should just use the normal textbook. That's what we'll be tested on." I feel a painful twist in my stomach and the beginnings of a headache. I hate this. I hate that Cyrus is trying to get his hooks into Noah. And I hate that it is causing us to fight. What does he want with him?

"What's the matter with you today? Is something bothering you?" Noah puts his hand on my shoulder, and I want nothing more than to confide everything in him. The idea is so tantalizing—to have an ally, someone else who knows the truth. To tell him my real name: Seraphina.

And then what? I ask myself. *Ask him to run away with you? What happens when he gets older and this body begins to fail you?* I've sworn not to kill again—this is my last body.

I swallow, pushing down the urge to tell Noah the truth. I can't open that door. "I don't trust Mr. Shaw," I say carefully, willing him to see my side. "I mean, where did he come from, anyway? Where's our teacher? When's he coming back?" I don't mention Cyrus's story about Mr. Roberts's "sabbatical."

Noah sighs. "Honestly, I wish Mr. Shaw was our permanent teacher. He's actually making us think."

"He is quite . . . charismatic," I agree. "But so are plenty of sociopaths."

Noah laughs, a deep warm sound. In spite of myself, I smile. I know I sound paranoid. A terrible thought occurs to me. "You didn't say anything to him about my car accident, did you?"

"Of course not." He looks puzzled, but also hurt. "I promised you I wouldn't say anything. And why would that even come up?"

"Sorry, I know. There's just something I don't like about him."

"Remind me never to get on your bad side," Noah replies. "Oh, and Kailey?"

"Yes?"

"In the immortal words of the Kinks, 'paranoia will destroy ya.'"

I laugh. "I don't think that's exactly how the song goes. But I get the point."

We spend the rest of the lunch period talking about other things: Noah's parents, the possibility of art school, where we should go for a proper date. But I'm only half there. There's a shadow hanging over my mind. There's more than one way for Cyrus to hurt me, I realize. Now that there are people here that I care about, I've made myself vulnerable.

I lean back against the oak tree. It's so strong, so solid. It's probably hundreds of years old, like me. And yet it could be cut down in a matter of minutes. I feel like everywhere I turn, Cyrus is there, anticipating my next move. It's a game I can't lose.

twenty-nine

The next afternoon, I get a text from Leyla:

art murmur tonight? i can pick u up.

I'm not sure what an "art murmur" is, but Google informs me it's an open art studios event in downtown Oakland. I text Noah, and he writes back immediately that he'd love to join us. On impulse, I pop my head into Bryan's room.

"I'm going to the Art Murmur tonight. You want to come?"

He groans. "Ugh, art and hipsters. I don't think so."

"You sure? Leyla's going to pick me up in ten minutes," I say casually.

"Oh? Leyla's . . . driving? Well. Um. Sure, why not." He grabs a pair of Chuck Taylors from his pile of shoes, and I make no effort to conceal the satisfied smile on my face.

Leyla arrives, looking embarrassed about pulling up in her old Honda. "My parents gave it to me," she explains to Bryan as he climbs into the front seat. "They said these things run forever."

"Reliable is good," says Bryan, adjusting the collar on his letterman jacket as he buckles his seat belt. "I'd take a boring ride with a strong engine over some weirdo car that will leave you by the side of the road."

Noah and I burst out laughing in the backseat.

"What's so funny?" asks Leyla.

"Nothing," I answer. "Bryan and his strong engine are right."

We park on Twenty-Fifth Street and wander over to the galleries. The atmosphere is festive. People fill the sidewalks and the streets, drinking out of plastic cups or bottles in paper bags. A group of boys rides by on bikes with brightly colored foil triangles woven into the spokes, like a fleet of pinwheels. There are tables set up where people are selling screenprints and jewelry, wallets made of duct tape, and knitted hats. We stop in front of a woman selling cupcakes, and Leyla asks what flavors she has.

"Pumpkin, lemon, and fried chicken," the woman replies, with a smile.

Bryan's eyes light up. "Did you just say fried chicken cupcake? Is this possible?"

"Seriously," Leyla agrees. "I'm afraid if I eat that, I'll realize I'm dead, because putting those two together could only happen in heaven."

Bryan buys each of them a cupcake, raising his in the air in a mock toast. Leyla plays along. "To the perfect combination of sweet and savory," she declares. "Clink!"

We walk through the galleries, looking at portraits painted on bowling balls, dreamcatchers made of electrical wire, maps of imaginary lands, and Art Nouveau mosaics made out of bottle caps. Noah is drawn to a series of black-and-white photographs of children in makeup for the Day of the Dead, little boys and girls in suits and dresses with painted-on skeleton faces. "That's seriously creepy," says Bryan.

We stop in front of some paintings that remind me of Kailey's work, lush watercolors of young girls lying in fields of patchwork or sleeping in a pool of stars. I wonder how these would look through Kailey's eyes. To me, they tell a story. But would she concentrate on the technique? Would she want to know how they were made? The artist approaches us, a girl in her late twenties wearing a ruffled plaid skirt. "These are beautiful," I tell her.

"Thank you," she says, looking at me more closely. "I think we've met before?"

"I don't think so," I stammer, turning to the others. "It's really crowded in here, let's go outside."

Out on the street it's cold, but we can move freely. We pass a guitarist playing folk songs, a puppet show, and a group of young men in baggy jeans and Oakland A's caps dancing next to a boom box. Their movements are sinuous, graceful, and there's an incredible sadness emanating from them, despite their claps and smiles.

Leyla spots a car shaped like a giant snail and pulls us toward it. We hear a murmur from the crowd around it as its antennae shoot flames into the sky. "Oh my God, I need to see this!" says Leyla, walking faster.

It's the color of antique copper, metal panels shaped into the spiraled shell that makes up the bulk of the car. A delicate cage of wire makes up the snail's head, and the orange flicker from its fiery antennae dances on the satiny finish. Dragonfly wings extend out from its sides, made of thin sheets of plastic that are painted to look like stained glass. Leyla pushes to the front of the crowd, where the artist is standing, wearing overalls and a fedora. "This is amazing!"

she exclaims, running her hands over the surface of the shell. "Kailey! Come over here!"

I join her, and the man asks if I'd like to control the flame, handing me the loop of leather that controls the gas. I pull it, and fire roars into the sky, to the delight of the crowd. My nose is filled with the scent of propane. "What's it called?" asks Leyla, taking her turn at pulling the control.

"*Fibonacci's Flight*," answers the artist.

Leyla frowns. "You should rename it *Fantastical Fiery Fairy Chariot*!"

"No, I think the name's perfect just as it is." He's not amused.

"Can I make it shoot fire again?" she asks hopefully.

"I think you're done," he replies with a stern expression.

She and I walk back to the boys, laughing. "I don't know what his problem is," she gripes.

"He's just cranky," I assure her, throwing my arm over her shoulder. "You didn't do anything wrong."

Bryan declares that he's hungry again, and we decide to get Korean tacos from a food truck. We're standing in line when I hear a familiar voice behind me. It's Nicole, with Chantal beside her. My heart sinks.

We get our food and huddle in a circle. Nicole and Chantal

join us, and I take a desultory bite of my taco, bracing myself for one of Nicole's trademark icy glares. But she's in good spirits, giving us all hugs.

"Why are you so smiley?" Leyla asks, wiping hoisin sauce from her chin.

"She's got a crush on the substitute biology teacher," Chantal informs us, smirking. "She won't stop talking about him."

"Shut up!" Nicole says, blushing down to the neckline of her low-cut T-shirt. "I don't have a crush on him—I just think he's really smart."

"Mmm-hmm," Chantal responds. "And you're so famous for your love of learning."

"He did offer to tutor me, one-on-one," Nicole admits, twirling a lock of her shiny brown hair. I can tell she's enjoying the attention, especially in front of Noah.

"Damn, girl. You're lucky. He's hot," Leyla says.

"Wait. Who is this guy?" Bryan frowns.

"He's a jackass substitute teacher who's already been here far too long!" I explode, and take another angry bite of my taco. Why does Cyrus have to ruin everything? I was having fun, almost managing to forget that I was here on borrowed time, on the wings of a great big lie—I was feeling normal, like this was my real life. Which it *is*—what other life do I have? Every time I manage to find the smallest shred of happiness, every time I turn around, Cyrus is there to ruin it.

"Kailey's not a big fan of Mr. Shaw," Noah explains needlessly.

Leyla's puzzled. "Really? I think he's pretty cool. And he's gorgeous, in that Viking sort of way. Tall and blond and cheekbones that could cut glass—"

Bryan scowls.

"If you're into that kind of thing," she finishes quickly.

I shiver in the gathering fog and press closer to Noah for warmth. I feel embarrassed by my outburst. I don't know what got into me. The others keep talking and laughing, but I stare into the distance. Thinking, calculating. I'm slightly worried about Nicole and her upcoming tutoring sessions—I don't think Cyrus will hurt her, especially once he figures out she's not me. But I can't be sure. He's so unpredictable when he's mad.

And now he's made a favorable impression not just on Noah, but on Leyla, too. He's getting too close to the people I've come to care about. What if my plan to lay low and wait it out doesn't work? What if he doesn't leave?

An idea occurs to me. A dangerous, stupid idea that just might get me killed. On Monday, after school, I'm going to follow Cyrus back to wherever he's staying in the East

Bay. I'll watch him, see what I can glean. If he catches me, my cover will certainly be blown. But I need to find out exactly what he knows about that foggy night in Jack London Square, the night of escapes and sedatives and blood and gasoline. The night that I left him behind and my real life began.

thirty

Monday morning I wake with a stomachache. It's gray and drizzly, wind shaking the trees. Still, I tell Noah I'm riding my bike to school. He's concerned, but I tell him I like the rain. "I'm not a witch—I won't melt."

In biology, Cyrus lectures on natural selection and the survival of the fittest. *I'm going to beat you*, I promise silently. As terrified as I am, it feels good to take action. At least I'm not just waiting for him to discover me.

After school I unchain Kailey's bike and wait behind a tree, a knitted hat pulled down low on my face, rain soaking my denim jacket. I don't even feel the cold. I watch as Cyrus leaves his classroom holding an elegant leather briefcase over his head. To my surprise, he heads for the bus stop. Cyrus—who owns cars worth more than a teacher's yearly salary, who could have a private jet waiting for him at the snap of his fingers—is taking the bus?

The streets are choked with traffic, and the bus makes slow progress down Shattuck, but I keep a few blocks behind it, just in case. I follow as it chugs through South Berkeley and crosses into Oakland, past coffee shops and cute restaurants on Telegraph. I dodge pedestrians and discover that the brakes on Kailey's bike need some work. At the corner of MacArthur Boulevard, he exits the bus. As he's waiting to cross the street, a shiny-rimmed car with thumping bass speeds by, splashing through a puddle that sprays Cyrus's suit with oily water.

He's on foot now, so I hurriedly lock the bike to a parking meter and take off behind him as he heads east on MacArthur. I hold an umbrella in front of my face like a shield, but he never turns around. He heads into the parking lot of a seedy-looking motel called the Fireside Inn. I'd wager my meager savings that there's not a working fireplace in the whole building.

Why, I ask myself, *is Cyrus staying in this dump?* He could have rented a beautiful house in the hills or a brand-new condo downtown. I realize I haven't seen Cyrus with any other coven member since he arrived. Would they condone what he's doing? I know that my leaving must have filled him with rage, and I wonder if there was a challenge to Cyrus's power. *He's here,* I realize, *because it's the last place in the world the coven would look for him.* I suspect they have no idea where he is. One thing is certain: Cyrus chose this place because no one would ask him any questions. It's completely anonymous.

I duck behind a Dumpster, feet slipping in the grime, and press my back to the stucco wall behind me, its surface digging into my shoulder blades. I'm breathing hard, my sodden hair plastered to my cheek. I roughly shove the lank curls underneath my hat and will myself to become part of the stucco, to be invisible, to have the patience of stone.

The November twilight falls even faster in the storm, and it's soon dark. I wait and wait, eyes trained on door number seventeen, the second-floor room into which Cyrus disappeared.

I almost miss the moment when he walks out, distracted by shouts coming from the street. There are two men, both looking quite drunk, yelling at each other. But my senses are heightened by danger, and the small movement from Cyrus's door catches my eye. He's still wearing one of his expensive suits, and couldn't look more out of place. He glides down the exterior staircase, avoids parking lot puddles, and is gone.

I pull my hat low, put on gloves—can't leave fingerprints—and crane my neck around the wall, watching him stroll up MacArthur, take a right, and disappear from view.

Scrambling up the concrete staircase, I nearly fall, but just bang my knee. His door is locked, as I knew it would be. Luckily, I know how to pick locks, and the motel is old enough that there's no electronic key-card system to contend with.

I grab a hairpin from my pocket and coax the lock open in less than a minute. I slip inside and close the door quickly behind me. The cloying scent of pine air freshener assaults my nostrils, and the room is dingy and dark. Nothing here is to Cyrus's extravagant taste; nothing is as he would have chosen.

But nonetheless, I sense his presence strongly. I can smell the soap he uses, vetiver and cedar, underneath the mustiness emanating from the polyester curtains. I can almost believe in ghosts, the ghosts of the living, as I imagine him here, coming home to this room night after night, fueled by his desire for revenge.

I hear what sounds like a gunshot outside, and instinctively fall to my knees. But it's only a car backfiring. In the eerie echo that follows, I ache for the normalcy of traffic sounds. But I am caught in silence, its thick, cottony web, only barely able to make out the clatter of rain on the roof. I turn around and silence trails after me, curling up my arms like a living thing.

In front of me is a bulletin board, covered with paper, hastily nailed to the wall, cracking the plaster in miniature canyons. I approach through the gloom to get a better look, my knees going rubbery as I realize what I'm seeing.

It's a collage of mistakes. The mistakes I made on a foggy night, three weeks ago.

There are two parking ticket notices, dated October 15, the night I ran away, from Minna Street in San Francisco. The place I had parked my car while I was at the party at Emerald City. Photos taken from a distance of a man who looks familiar—it takes me a moment to place him. It's the man who sold me the car. There's a newspaper clipping of the police blotter article that mentions the crash, the date highlighted. I pull down a stack of stapled e-mail printouts and sit on the saggy bed, my face crumpling.

There are e-mails that I wrote—the correspondence I had with the Craigslist seller, under an account I created just for that purpose. Cyrus must have hired a hacker to trace all the activity on our IP address. Of course I never thought to use a public computer instead of my own. . . . In my original plan, it wouldn't have mattered. There would have been nothing left of me to find. I can only assume that Cyrus found out the police were looking for the car because I reported it stolen, and maybe was even able to trace the call to a pay phone outside Berkeley High.

I return the e-mails to the board, taking in the rest. It doesn't seem as if he knows about Taryn yet, or the book. But there's a request for hospital records that came up empty. *Thank you, patient confidentially*, I think. At least Cyrus didn't get Kailey's name. But everyone has a price, and Cyrus will find the right person to bribe. . . .

There's one more newspaper clipping, this one yellowed with age. I peer closely—it's a group shot, with many girls I don't know. But Kailey's in it, standing between Nicole and Leyla, an exhausted smile on her face and a number taped to her chest. The caption reads: "Berkeley High School Annual Breast Cancer Walk." They're all holding their hands up in the air, wearing identical silver bracelets. The hairs on the back of my neck stand on end—the image chills me for some reason I cannot explain.

Sinking back on the bed, I try to think and suddenly feel exhausted. Out of the corner of my eye, I see a flash of light in the dim room. I examine the bedside table. There's a copy of the Berkeley High yearbook. And tucked halfway underneath it is something shiny. Something silver.

A young girl, maybe sixteen, with tangled blond hair and a silver bracelet around her tanned wrist.

A tug, then a metallic snap as I pull Kailey from the car. I hope I've not broken any more of her bones.

Cyrus, staring at my hands.

No one wears watches anymore. Although it seems that you usually do?

I pick up the bracelet, the same one that Kailey's friends wear. It has a small circular charm on it, one side engraved with an image of a ribbon. And on the back, the engraving 2010 BERKELEY HIGH SCHOOL ANNUAL BREAST CANCER WALK. Gooseflesh covers my arms as I realize where I first saw it: Kailey was wearing it when she died. I examine the pale line on my wrist from where the bracelet had lain. It must have fallen off during the accident, and when Cyrus went to investigate the intersection where a car was stolen and a girl got into a car accident, he found it there, in the crabgrass along the side of the street. A little white line, a road on a map, leading Cyrus straight to me.

No, not quite. I pick up the yearbook and thumb through it. In thick black marker, some of the faces are crossed out. Piper, Chantal, and Madison are all crossed out, along with plenty of other girls whose names I can't recall. Nicole's is also crossed out. I touch the line—the ink seems fresh. But over Kailey's face is a garish question mark. The sight of it makes my blood feel thick and cold. But even worse is the second question mark, over another girl's face. Leyla's.

He's going through every female student of driving age until he figures out who was in that crash. I'm not surprised that he's suspicious of me. As clever as I think I've been, a small part of him must have recognized me. But Leyla? She has no idea of the danger she's in.

I snap my head up at the sound of footsteps on the stairs. They grow louder. Cyrus. He's home. The jangling sound of keys being pulled from a pocket fills me with terror. Hastily, I put the yearbook and bracelet back on the night-stand, hoping he won't notice if they're slightly out of place. I roughly rub my eyes, trying to clear away my tears so I can see clearly.

I look around the room wildly, hearing more rustling sounds from outside the door. The bathroom. It's my only way out. I run into the small, mildewed room, trying to step softly. The window is shut firmly but I wrench it open, cringing at how loud it is. It will only open halfway, but it's enough. Barely. The sound of a key sliding into its lock spurs me on. I push myself through the window, feeling a rip of pain as a loose nail rakes my thigh.

I land hard on the concrete walkway below, but scramble quickly to my feet and take off running. I don't look back and don't stop till I'm back to the spot where I parked Kailey's bike.

It's only now—legs pumping furiously, unsure if my vision is blurred by tears or rain—that the implication of my findings sinks in. I pull the bike over and take shelter under a storefront awning. I sink down on my heels and lean back on the window, holding my head in my hands, sobs wracking my body.

It's clear to me now. I need to leave. Cyrus is so close to figuring out who I am. But I'm not the only one at risk. He's suspicious of Leyla and he's trying to gain Noah's loyalty. I led him here—if I go, he'll follow.

thirty-one

I don't go home, but stay huddled there against the storefront, using Kailey's iPhone to research the logistics of buying a new ID. I've never had to worry about these practical details before; Cyrus always took care of them for me. At first I thought it was kind, thoughtful. But really, it was just another way of controlling me. But it can't be that difficult—kids do it all the time to buy beer for parties.

There are a few places in East Oakland that look promising. It's too far to bike, so I leave it locked up outside the store, then head to the nearest BART station. When I get off at Fruitvale, the rain is coming down harder, and there aren't many people out and about. I'm thankful for this. The few people that I do pass shoot me curious glances. I catch sight of my blond curls in the rippled reflection of a *lavanderia* window and understand why: Kailey looks a bit out of place in this neighborhood.

I finally find the place I read about and go inside. The market is small and jumbled, tall metal shelves leaning unsteadily over the aisles, and no customers in sight. I'm overwhelmed with the smells of cooking meat and cilantro emanating from the rear of the store. I look around uncertainly, then notice a counter near the front.

"Yes?" says the man sitting behind it, idly thumbing through a magazine. He sets it down on the counter, and I'm surprised to see he's reading *Vogue*.

I take a deep breath. "I'm looking for Lucia?"

The man smiles, deep creases showing around his eyes. "Of course you are." He hops off his stool and comes around the counter to lead me to the back of the store.

Lucia comes out from the kitchen—she's younger than I expected, maybe midtwenties. Her lips are very red, and her hair is pulled up in a severe bun.

"What you need, sweetie? *Mica?* No . . . a license?" She nods to the man, and he walks away.

"Yes," I say. "My favorite bands are always playing twenty-one-plus shows. Can you help?"

"Mmm-hmm." She raises her eyebrows. "You got cash?"

"How much?"

"Seventy-five. But it's legit. You can scan it and everything." She crosses her arms over her chest, and I nod okay.

"Right, let's go for a walk." She pulls a raincoat off a peg on the wall, and we head out to the street. We walk a few blocks, and she offers to share her umbrella, but I shake my head no. "Come on, now," she says, looking at me ruefully. "You're like a drowned bird. You want to look pretty for your picture."

We stop in front of a photo studio, its display windows full of glamour shots in elaborate gold frames, all soft focus and dreamy expressions. The inside of the studio is dim and smells faintly of mildew. There are an assortment of backdrops and a rack of frilly dresses. I run my fingers over them, but Lucia heads straight to a door and leads me into another room, with a plain blue screen. I recognize the hue as the background for the California driver's license headshot.

A man wearing dark sunglasses comes in, his bald head gleaming under the studio lights. He murmurs to Lucia in Spanish: "You sure she's cool?" I can't hear Lucia's response, but he seems reassured.

She brings me a towel to dry my hair. "*Gracias,*" I whisper. I give her my money, and the man takes my photo, then leaves.

"It will be about an hour," she tells me. "You can meet me at the taqueria."

"Can I stay with you?" I ask her. I'm hungry.

"You're pretty new at this, eh?" She laughs at me, but agrees.

As we walk back to the market, I'm lost in thought. Kailey's hospital records are a problem. Every hour will count when I make my escape, and I can't risk him finding out who I am before I'm well out of town.

At the taqueria I order two carnitas tacos and sit at the counter on a stool. Lucia cracks open a mango Jarritos soda and slides it over to me. "On the house, sweetie."

I take a grateful sip. "Hey, Lucia," I begin. "I have another . . . request. Do you know anyone with computer skills?"

"What, you need help buying concert tickets?"

I smile. "I need to make some information disappear. There's a hospital visit and a police report that I don't need my parents finding. They'll kill me." I feel my face grow hot and take a bite of the taco, spilling onions onto the paper plate.

"Ah, I see. I do have a friend who's a total genius with this stuff. I can ask him for you."

She pulls out a cell phone and disappears into the kitchen. I strain to overhear, but can't make anything out. After a few minutes she comes back.

"You probably won't want to pay. He can do it, but he wants a thousand. And he says he can't make anything on the Internet disappear." She leans against a refrigerated case of beer and clicks her nails, waiting for my response.

My face falls. "I only have three hundred."

Lucia studies me for a moment, chewing her lip. Then she returns. "Okay. Just this once he'll do it for three hundred."

"Thank you, thank you, thank you! How did you do that?" I breathe. It will wipe out my cash, but there have to be other ways to replenish it. Perhaps Bryan has money, or I suppose I could find something in the Morgans' house to sell. The thought makes my stomach churn, but I am desperate.

Lucia shrugs. "He owes me."

I pull out my wad of cash and count out three hundred dollars, then hand it over to her. She gives me a piece of paper, and I write down the details of Kailey's accident: date, location, and the name of the hospital she was taken to.

Just then the bald man from the photo studio appears and hands me an envelope. I open it and am staring at Kailey's face on the new ID. My new name is Jane Smith. I look at the man questioningly, and he shrugs, the smallest hint of a smile playing on his lips. "You didn't tell me what name you wanted, so I picked it out."

I thank them both, resisting the urge to hug Lucia. I tell her she's a fairy godmother, and she laughs and waves me out.

thirty-two

"Good morning," I say brightly to Mrs. Morgan on Tuesday as I glide into the kitchen, punctuating my greeting with a kiss on her cheek.

Mr. Morgan looks up from his newspaper. "Uh-oh. Last time you were this happy, Noah came to the door acting suspiciously like your boyfriend. What's next? Are you two engaged?"

"Ha-ha." I swoop down and kiss his cheek as well. "I'm just in a good mood. It's a beautiful day." I hope I don't sound as fake as I feel. Come tonight, their lives will change irrevocably. They will know there was a *before*—a time when they had two happy children—and an *after*, when they are left with only one. They will look back to before and wonder how they failed to savor every moment. They will wonder why they ever let petty problems bother them, why they didn't realize how good things were. I can't spare them the grief they'll feel, but I can try to leave them with good memories.

"I've got to go," says Mrs. Morgan, finishing her coffee in one big gulp. "I promised I'd be in the office early."

"I'll leave with you," says Mr. Morgan, pushing back his chair.

They're halfway to the door when I clear my throat. "Mom and Dad?"

They turn, expectant. "I just want you to know that I love you. Don't ever doubt that." My voice quavers.

They look surprised, but touched. Mrs. Morgan opens her arms, and I fly into them. "Not as much as we love you," she tells me.

When they leave, I return to Kailey's room. After this morning, I won't be back here again. I pull Kailey's backpack from its hiding place under the bed, then sit on the lime-green bedspread.

I look around the room, taking in Kailey's things: her paintings, the photos of her and her friends, her clothes, her perfume. I want to thank her for letting me stay here, for letting me live her life, if only for a short time. This room, the color of peacock feathers, is quiet. It's listening to me. It's Kailey. What would I say to her, if I could?

Kailey, I never met you, not really, but I know you. I slept in your bed, I wore your white dress. I hope you are free and happy, that you are the color of water—turquoise water, like the walls of your room. That the wind is warm and you are part of it. That you finish your paintings—the sky is your canvas—and you show them to the other ghost girls. That you make more wind chimes, but this time you use the silvery starlight for your bells, that you string them up on soft green vines that never stop flowering. I wish you peace.

I pick up the bottle of jasmine perfume, turning it over in my hands. It feels warm. I hold it to my nose and inhale its sweetness. I add the bottle of perfume to my bag—Kailey would understand.

I stand and leave, closing the door softly. I walk down the hall.

Bryan's at his computer. He rips off his headphones when I poke my head in.

"Hey," he greets me. "Is it time to go?"

"No, not yet." I pause, then simply say: "You should ask out Leyla."

He blushes. "Yeah? I thought I wasn't allowed to date your friends."

I walk over to him and ruffle his hair. "Life is short," I tell him. "Live a little."

thirty-three

By late afternoon the fog lies thick over Berkeley, covering everything with its white fingers. But the colors I am able to see are so vivid against its blank backdrop. The light wanes quickly, and by 5:30 it is completely dark. The lamplight inside the antiques shop spills out onto the street like gold. I don't want to leave. I know what lies ahead of me: cold, swirling mist, the avoidance of well-lit places, the fugitive's need to keep to the dark. I need this fog; it makes it much easier to disappear.

Noah texts me to let me know he's on his way to pick me up. I turn off all the lights, all but one—a stained-glass lamp in the window—and lock up the shop. The cash I took from the register—close to five hundred dollars—weighs heavily in my pocket. I promise to send the owner the amount in the mail as soon as I find a new job.

I wait outside, letting the lamp cast its blue-green shadows on my face. The VW's headlights reach through the fog to me like a path or a hand I could take hold of. Inside the car, Noah is blasting the heater.

"I missed you," he says.

His words hit me hard, but I force a laugh. "It's been, what? Three hours?"

"Where do you want to go?" he asks. "We could have a nice dinner."

"I want to go to San Francisco. Let's get takeout and sit on the beach." I never expected to set foot in that city again, but there's nothing more for me to fear there, now that Cyrus is in Oakland.

"The beach? It's freezing, Kailey."

"I'll keep you warm," I tell him boldly, arching an eyebrow.

We head into the city, taking it slow across the Bay Bridge. It's oddly free of traffic, but the fog is even thicker as we drive over the bay. The lights from downtown are smudged and diffuse, and I'm reminded of fireworks, how July in San Francisco is no guarantee against an overcast evening. Revelers on the Fourth, wrapped in warm jackets, with nothing to cheer except muffled booms and the brief suggestion of color in the misty sky. Cyrus hated that. He loved fireworks, but to me, they were too loud, too much like real explosions.

In the Richmond, we get dinner from a Thai restaurant and walk toward the beach. The closer we get to the water, the more deserted it feels, like we're in some sleepy tourist town in winter. The pedestrian traffic and honking horns of downtown feel very far away. We pass apartment buildings and motels that were built in the 1960s, with cheesy names like the Beachcomber and Mermaid's Cove. The sidewalks grow gritty with sand.

At Ocean Beach, we find the remains of a bonfire that some optimistic person must have built, hoping for a nice evening. Noah disappears for a few minutes and returns with an armful of driftwood.

"I have triumphed," he informs me. "You shall be warm." He hunkers down next to me, and we eat coconut rice and stir-fried chicken with spicy chiles and basil, then lean back on one of the logs, bellies satisfied and warm.

I watch his profile in the orange light from the fire. His dark hair grazes his chin, wavy in the damp air and salt. He pushes it back to reveal his strong jaw, his thick brows. *My sea prince*, I think, remembering those hours I spent on the ship from Barbados to New Amsterdam. How close I came to jumping overboard, to chasing a fickle sunbeam down into the deep.

I don't plan on going into the water. But everyone will need to think I did.

I shiver, and Noah puts his arm around me. "What's the matter? Someone walked over your grave?"

Yes, I think. *I did.*

A thought occurs to me, a question I need to ask. "Noah, would you still like me if I looked like someone else?"

He sits up and looks me in the eyes. "What do you mean?"

"I don't know—like if I had a completely different body. If I looked like Leyla, maybe. Or Nicole. But I was still me."

He cups my jaw. "This is a really weird conversation. But okay." He thinks for a moment. "I'm trying to imagine you with a different face."

I gaze at him serenely, but he starts laughing. "I can't do it, Kailey."

"Okay, fine." I pretend to pout.

"You want me to be serious? I'm going to be serious. I've known you almost my entire life. I probably know your face better then my own. But you have a spark that I'd know anywhere." He pauses. "So yes, even if you looked different, I'd still love—"

He breaks off, embarrassed. "I can't believe I just said that."

"Do you mean it?" I ask, my heart thumping.

He looks down, but I put my hand to his cheek and tilt his eyes back toward me.

"This is no time to leave things unsaid." Maybe I'll never have a moment like this again. It isn't fair to him, I know. But I can't help it.

He's staring in the direction of the water, distant waves breaking like static. He won't look at me, but he takes my hand. It's enough. It's a sweet dream I can pull out and examine in the lonely days I know I have ahead.

"You don't have to say anything," I allow. "Let's walk. I want to go look at the Golden Gate Bridge."

Walking warms us up, but the top of the bridge is whipped by chilling wind. It doesn't seem to affect the fog, though, which curls around the orange metal structure in wisps. "It's so far down," I observe, shivering. I wrap my arm around Noah's waist.

"Not like you can see anything through this fog," he adds. Droplets of mist cling to our hair. He shivers. "Let's go home."

I take a deep breath. It's time.

"You can go. I think I'll stay awhile. I need some time to myself." I try to make my tone casual, like this was the most normal request in the world.

"What? No. It's not safe. I'll stay with you."

"No, really, Noah. I want to be alone. I'll be fine."

"What if something happens to you? No, it's crazy." His tone is firm.

"I come out here all the time by myself. Seriously. It's safer here than it is in Berkeley." I try to sound confident.

"How will you get home?" he worries.

"I think I know how to call a cab," I say drily. "I'm a big girl."

"I don't know. It doesn't feel right to me, leaving you here with no one to take care of you." His voice is uncertain now. I sense a crack in his armor.

"I don't need any boy to take care of me," I say sharply. "Do you think I'm really that weak?"

"No, of course not." He smiles. "That's one of the last words I'd use to describe you."

"Then let me do what I want. I promise I'll be safe."

"Okay . . . I guess, if you really want to be by yourself. But you have to text me the minute you get home so I know you're safe." He pulls me close to him, and I bury my face in his chest. I listen to his heart.

In a tiny voice I whisper the words that I want to say. "I love you, too." His arms tighten around me, and I feel one small tear threatening to escape my eye, but I blink it back.

I feel his hands on my shoulders, and I look up. I find his

lips and kiss him. "Go," I tell him, tearing myself away.

"I wish you were coming with me," he says.

I do, too.

"I had fun tonight, Noah."

"Text me," he repeats. "As soon as you're home."

"I will," I lie.

He reluctantly walks away, leaving me alone on the bridge. I have to bite my lip to keep myself from calling out to him, to keep myself from crying. *Please don't leave me.* But he honors my wishes, and I watch him disappear in the fog.

thirty-four

I wait for a long time before taking action. I need to be sure Noah's far away from the scene of Kailey's death so there's no chance he'll be implicated.

I walk near the railing and listen for the sound of the water below. I imagine falling for real, the welcoming arms of the water as it would pull me under, down into the world of shipwrecks and silvery, silent fish.

Don't be silly, I tell myself. There would be nothing soft about that water at all.

But maybe if I jump, the wind will catch me up like a bird, or I'll sprout wings and fly, like Kailey in the portrait of herself as an angel. It's almost time for me to send my message to Kailey's mother. But not yet. I close my eyes and wait, thinking about the one person I know who actually can fly: Amelia.

It was in Brooklyn, 1913. Cyrus took me to the circus. I held my breath as the tiny blond acrobat leaped from a swinging trapeze and landed on the high-wire tightrope, strung at a neck-craning distance across the tent's ceiling. The crowd erupted in applause as the ringmaster cried out, "The beautiful, the amazing, Lady Amelia defies death! See her fly without wings!"

"I wish he would shut up," Cyrus murmured next to me.

"Yes. What if the noise makes her fall?" I worried.

"Impossible," Cyrus said breathlessly and with admiration. "She really is a bird."

As if she could hear us, Amelia coiled her muscles, jumping off the tightrope and spinning backward in the air before landing on her feet. I squinted—she did have feathers in her hair, jewel-toned peacock plumes pinned at each temple, as well as gathered at her tiny wrists.

After the performance, Cyrus dragged me through the dusty fairgrounds till we found her trailer, its side decorated with a painting of a winged woman reclining in a giant nest. She answered our knock wearing an iridescent silky robe that shimmered between purple and green, and I could tell by the way she coyly cooed Cyrus's name that they had met before.

From a distance I had first mistaken her for a child. She couldn't have been more than five feet tall, with impossibly slender limbs and fine, pointed features. Her white-blond hair hung around her face in a feathery shag. I reached up and touched my own smooth chestnut hair, which was carefully styled in pin curls. I felt too coiffed, too earthbound. She was a wild thing, and I wanted to be like her.

She flitted about the trailer fixing us drinks that tasted like melon, with a hint of bitterness. Cyrus leaned back on a pile of beaded shawls and regarded the two of us. "Amelia," he said, "Sera loved your performance today."

Amelia was perched on top of a trunk, her slim feet pulled up under her robe. She cocked her head at me and smiled sweetly. "Thank you," she said, "that is so kind."

"It was amazing. It really seemed like you could fly. How long have you been an aerialist?"

Her face fell. "Too long. I'm getting old. I won't be able to stay with the circus much longer—then what will I do?"

Cyrus smiled. "That's why we're here, Amelia. We don't want you to grow old, either." He unbuttoned the top two buttons on his shirt and pulled out the vial that he always wore on its silver cord. "You can come live with us, Amelia. And if you choose, you can be young forever."

The look on her face said she wanted to believe it was possible. "How? Magic?"

"No," said Cyrus, opening the vial and taking a whiff. "Alchemy."

I rouse myself from my memories. Enough time has passed. Noah has probably made it home by now. I shake my head to clear it from the ghosts of the past. I take out Kailey's iPhone and call a cab to take me to the bus stop, where I'll set off for Texas, then maybe try to cross the border into Mexico. "I'm waiting in the parking lot of the Golden Gate Bridge," I tell the operator. She replies that a car will be there in five minutes.

I hurry to the middle of the bridge. There are cameras, but I know the fog will obscure any recording. I take off my jacket, shivering, and put Kailey's ID in the pocket before draping it on the railing. Then I pull out the phone again to compose a text message to Kailey's family.

> Mom, Dad, Bryan—I've been living a lie. I'm so sorry, but I can't keep pretending. Believe me when I say I'm in a better place and I love you all. —K

I'm about to hit send, but I hesitate. Does it say enough?

I want it to be better. I want it to convey the love I truly do have for them. The sorrow that I share. I glance at the time. Only two minutes before my cab arrives, and I still need to get down to the parking lot. I sigh. It will have to do.

But before I can press send, a message appears from Leyla.

A chill runs up my spine to the roots of my hair.

The message reads:

Mr. Shaw is dead!

thirty-five

My knees grow weak and stars swim in my vision as I sink to the wet ground. I feel like I've been punched in the solar plexus and can barely breathe. Cyrus, dead? Could it be true? Or has he simply jumped into a new body, to disguise himself as he tracks me down? I don't know what to believe.

I leave Kailey's jacket on the railing and run toward the parking lot, sneakers pounding on the walkway. My good-bye message to Kailey's family is still unfinished, but I can always send it on the way to the bus station. A couple minutes won't make a difference. I spot the cab, bright yellow dodging in and out of view through the mist. It's about to leave. "Wait!" I yell, ribs aching, breath frantic. It does.

"Well, well, well," the cabbie says as I slide into the backseat. "Here you are!" He's an older man wearing a dark green suit and his dashboard is covered with fake flowers.

"Here I am," I agree breathlessly. "Can you take me to the bus depot?"

He frowns, no doubt taking in that I don't have a bag or even a coat.

"I travel light," I say sharply, pulling out my phone and calling up the *San Francisco Chronicle* website on its Internet browser.

He nods and turns up the heater. I flash a grateful smile. The glow from the phone's screen lights up my face. It takes an eternity to load. "Come on!" I whisper urgently, shaking the phone. Finally the site loads. And there, at the very top, is an article about Cyrus.

> OAKLAND — A Berkeley High substitute science teacher was shot to death this evening in an apparent robbery on the shore of Lake Merritt. After suffering multiple gunshot wounds, the victim fell into the water. His body has not been recovered. Multiple eyewitnesses claimed to have witnessed the killing. A San Francisco man, 19, who spoke to the *Chronicle* under the condition

> of anonymity, said that three or four young men had accosted the victim, demanding his wallet. According to the witness, when the victim gave it to the muggers, one of them pulled out a gun and shot him. "It was terrible—I saw him die in front of me." Another witness, a 22-year-old woman from San Francisco, corroborated the story. "He didn't even have a chance," she said. No arrests have been made.

I set down the phone and lean back. Is it possible? If he really did die, they wouldn't find his body. It would have disintegrated into dust the second he hit the water, like Nathaniel's did when Cyrus killed him. But I can't believe that Cyrus has actually fallen victim to such a mundane act of violence. He'd lived for six hundred years. He was a survivor. He must have taken a new body. And yet . . . an inkling of doubt, one I don't dare to encourage, takes root in my heart.

Multiple eyewitnesses. It was possible that he had been mugged. Random crimes like this occur all the time. I pull out the phone and reread the article. "Multiple eyewitnesses." The phrase echoes in my brain. Witnesses who saw him get shot, who saw him die. The more I consider it, the more plausible it seems. It feels morbid to think it, but could I be so lucky?

"Miss, I don't mean to pry"—the cabbie makes eye

contact with me through the rearview mirror—"but you seem troubled. You sure you want to go to the bus stop?"

His deeply lined face radiates kindness. "No," I admit. "I'm not sure."

"Take your time," he says.

I pause, considering. There are only two ways to go. And if I leave, send the suicide note, I know I can never go back. But if Cyrus is dead, I don't have to. I tap the phone to life and reread the article. I think back to when I was hell-bent on killing myself, how every action I took toward that end was thwarted. Now I sense that invisible hand again, steering me to the correct path.

But if he didn't die, if it's all a setup, he could be at the Morgans' right now.

"You know what?" I say. The cabbie looks up. "I changed my mind. Will you take me to Berkeley?"

"Of course." He executes a screeching U-turn.

We get off the freeway in Berkeley, and I direct him to the Morgans' house, tapping my foot impatiently the whole time. If anything happens to the Morgans, I will never forgive myself. We pull up in front of the driveway, I pay the fare, and rush inside.

Relief courses through me as I see the whole family is curled up on the couch, sleeping. A movie plays, unwatched, on the TV screen. Mrs. Morgan is snoring loudly. "I'm home," I say softly. Bryan mumbles something and shifts, pulling a blanket up over his face. I turn off the TV and walk softly into Kailey's room.

I lie on the bed, pulling the coverlet over me, my mind whirling. Does the fact that Cyrus isn't here mean he really, truly is dead? Did he get so arrogant that he forgot how dangerous the world is? As I stare up at the stars on Kailey's ceiling, I dare to believe it's true.

I find Kailey's phone and delete the message I composed earlier on the bridge. It seems so long ago, like another life. Even though sand still fills my sneakers, even though I'm still cold and damp from the fog. I send a text to Noah:

home safe & sound. see u tomorrow. <3

Could it be, I think as I drift off to sleep, *that this is the life I was meant to have?*

thirty-six

It's the same nightmare that I used to have, back when I lived with the coven. An endless walk up the gallows steps, a scratchy rope looped around my neck. *Don't I have wings?* I think, frantic. *Someone told me I could fly. If I could only remember who said that, I could run away.* At the top of the structure stands the police officer who arrested me for truancy. He's holding a stack of printed e-mails, shaking his head. *But I tried to save her!* I try to scream, to explain what happened, but no sounds come out. I try again and again, my mouth open in a desperate, silent cry. The force of effort finally wakes me up, and I gasp, choking, my hand to my throat.

A small clock on Kailey's nightstand illuminates the room: 2:13 AM. I sink back onto the pillow, so glad to be awake. I turn over and close my eyes again, when I have a terrible realization: Cyrus's room is filled with evidence. The article about my crash, the e-mails, the photos. The bracelet. The police may have decreed his death a textbook robbery-homicide, but how long before some intrepid detective decides to take a closer look? The evidence may not lead directly to me, not yet, but it will raise questions.

I need to go down there and remove it. I swing my legs out of the warm bed and throw on jeans, a long-sleeved undershirt, and a heavy wool sweater. Moving softly, I slip out of the house. Kailey's bike is still chained up downtown, so I grab Bryan's instead, wheeling it slowly out to the street, stepping as lightly as possible.

The night's fog is still thick as I ride down the street, mist clinging to my eyelashes and hair. I pedal quickly and fly through stop signs and red lights. I race through Berkeley's deserted downtown, all shuttered windows and locked doors, through North Oakland's Temescal neighborhood, squinting my eyes against the damp air, till I reach my destination: the Fireside Inn.

Again, I stash the bike behind a Dumpster and cautiously enter the parking lot. As I approach Cyrus's room, I am inexplicably sad for him. I imagine his last moments—the final fleeting emotions of a boy who never expected to die, who had seen so much—had witnessed such a stretch of human history, lived through wars, through the birth and death of countries. He must have been terrified. And now, where was his soul? Dissipated into the ether? Or hovering close by, watching my every move, but unable to affect the world any longer, tormented?

I shudder. I hope he lets go, so he can be set free. As much as I hate him, I can't wish that kind of torture upon anyone.

Despite how much I've done to be rid of Cyrus, I feel lonely now that he's gone. He was with me for six hundred years. He was the only other person on Earth who could truly understand where I came from. Who knew my mother, my father. Who was by my side through lifetimes, many more lifetimes than anyone should be able to live. I have my clean slate now, I realize. It's what I wanted, what I needed. But it's also overwhelming.

You're not alone, I remind myself as I ascend the staircase. *You have Noah, Leyla. You have Kailey's family.* And now that Cyrus is dead, I might be able to get word to Charlotte, let her know I'm safe. The idea fills me with hope as I quickly pick the lock, open the door, and step inside.

As before, I am overcome with his presence. I can smell his soap, the lingering traces of his leather briefcase. I flick on the light and see the room's been completely scrubbed clean, emptied of all its evidence. All of Cyrus's things, his elegant suits and polished shoes, his bulletin board—gone. I sigh. Nothing I can do about it now. I'll just feign ignorance if the police come asking. It won't be the first time I've had to put on a performance lately.

I pull Kailey's phone from my pocket and check the time. It's nearly four o'clock—I need to get back. But I sit on the bed for a minute, running my hands over its scratchy, faded polyester surface. I am reminded of when I addressed Kailey's spirit this morning as I sat on her bed.

"Good-bye, Cyrus," I whisper, knowing he probably can't hear it. But it doesn't matter. Kailey wasn't listening, either. "I'm not sorry I left you. But I'm sorry you died like this, afraid and hurting. I hope the pure light of the planets calms you down, that the anger you always carried is released into the air and dissipates like smoke. I hated you. But I loved you once. Now that you're gone, I am free. I hope you are too."

I stand and walk slowly around the room. It's time to

go. I pause in front of the desk, running my hand over its dented oak surface. It's covered in gouges and burns, drips of candle wax and random nicks. I feel a vibration from the phone in my pocket and pull it out. There's a message on the screen: "Words with Friends—Your move with Noah."

He's up late, I think as I tap through to the game board.

When I see the word he has played, my fingers involuntarily clench around the phone. I stare at the letters, willing them to rearrange themselves, to form any other word.

No.

My hand starts to shake and I drop the phone. It seems to fall to the floor in slow motion, and I close my eyes.

Cyrus used to love to play chess. I'd lose pawn after pawn, bishops and knights, as he advanced on my king. How his pupils would dilate, his breath quicken. He was so good at laying traps. But that was a game, and this is real life, and the consequences of mistakes can be deadly. How could I have been so dumb?

He's not dead— He must have switched bodies. The witnesses were mistaken, or they were bribed.

I've lost the game. I don't cry, not yet. That will have to come later. The room swims and blood roars through my ears like static.

The word on the screen is "alchemy."

Can't wait forever to discover what happens next?

Turn the page for a sneak peek of

THE IMPOSSIBILITY OF TOMORROW

the breathtaking sequel to

The Alchemy of Forever.

In 1812, there was an earthquake in the unlikely location of New Madrid, Missouri. It was so violent and ruptured the ground with such force that the Mississippi River temporarily ran backward. Cyrus and I were living in Manhattan at the time, and I remember what he said to me as we strolled through the market: "It takes an earthquake to alter the course of a river. What does it take to change the course of a life?"

I wish I didn't know how easily it is done. I wish I didn't know that sometimes, a life pivots from its intended path in the wake of the tiniest thing.

Sometimes all it takes is one word.

Alchemy.

It can be uttered by a platinum-haired boy as he pulls out a vial of potion dangling on a silver chain. Or delivered the modern way, electronically, the brightly backlit screen of a cell phone belying the dark message it displays.

I sink to my knees on the musty, stained carpet of the motel room. Kailey Morgan's iPhone lies in front of me, unharmed from when I dropped it. Just carpet, after all. I want to smash that stupid phone. But I don't. I pick it up, coaxing it back to life with trembling fingers, and stare blankly at the Words with Friends screen, as the last droplets of hope evaporate from my soul.

It's still there. *Alchemy.* The word was played on Noah Vander's phone. It must have been typed with Noah's fingers. But it couldn't have come from Noah. Only one person in Berkeley knows what that word truly means.

Cyrus.

My longest companion, my greatest enemy, who would cage me like a bird. Who used alchemy to make me what I am now: an Incarnate, a wandering soul that takes up residence in human bodies. When I ran away from the coven several weeks ago, it was with one vow in my heart: that I would never again take another life. I was ready to die. I only took sixteen-year-old Kailey Morgan's body by mistake, when her car crashed right in front of me, a fiery display of gasoline and cracked glass.

I look upward, at the bare bulb that illuminates Cyrus's motel room, suddenly feeling exposed. I shove the phone in my pocket and dart to the light switch, flipping it off. The room disappears into a velvety, choking darkness. I blink, waiting for my eyes to adjust.

I don't think Cyrus will kill me for leaving him. In his own sick, twisted way, he loves me too much for that. But one way or another, he'll make me pay. He's already made me pay by taking Noah.

A volcano of pain erupts in my heart. A hurt that heaves from white-hot to glowing orange courses through my veins. A sob rises from deep inside me as I picture his beautiful face, his strong jaw, his smiling lapis-lazuli eyes as he holds up his camera, his hand pushing his reckless crow-colored hair out of the way. The next time I see him, his face will be transformed by Cyrus's soul, a hideous change that will be invisible to everyone except me. The thought of Cyrus inside of Noah's body, of Noah's soul shoved out into an uncaring foggy night, is almost unbearable.

A loud peal of laughter sounds from outside the room, from the direction of the parking lot, followed by a heavy footstep on the stair. My heart starts to thud. Whoever's making those footfalls is big—much bigger than me. And suddenly I realize that the message on Kailey's phone means so much more than Noah's death.

It means Cyrus knows who I am. And, even worse, *where* I am. He's probably right outside, waiting for me to emerge.

The image of the rabbits we dissected in Cyrus's biology class flits through my mind. *A rabbit is a prey animal*, he said. *And its best chance at survival is to outrun its hunter. Sometimes escape is the best defense, better than any teeth or claws.* But I have been running for way too long. I have lost this game, and it's time to face him. My pulse hammers in my ears as I turn the knob and open the door. A blast of damp air meets me.

But the man on the stairs isn't Cyrus at all. He's tall and thin, with deep brown skin and a neatly trimmed goatee. He's carrying a woman, whose head is tipped back. She's giggling softly.

He looks up at me. "Well, hello there," he says, somewhat gallantly, though he's slurring his words. The woman laughs louder.

"Put me down," she demands. "I'm too heavy for you."

"Yeah, right," he answers, shifting her weight. "You're drunk, baby. You'll fall down these stairs." He leans over and kisses her cheek.

"We just got married!" the woman exclaims to me, punctuating her statement with a small hiccup. "We're a family now!"

At the word *family*, a coldness that has nothing to do with the night's mist settles upon me. A slow realization, an icy chill that hisses at it laps in my veins. It's not just Noah who was in danger. And not just me, either.

Kailey's family, who I've come to love, is utterly defenseless against Cyrus. Her mother, her father. Her brother, Bryan, who I think of as my own. Cyrus could be at their house, right now.

I squeeze past the couple on the stairs and sprint to the Dumpster, where I stashed Bryan's bike earlier. The woman calls after me. "Hey! Aren't you going to congratulate us?"

"Congratulations!" I call, tears pooling in my eyes as I hoist myself onto the bike. "Hold on tight to each other. While you can," I add under my breath. All my time on Earth has shown me that love is a rare and fleeting thing.

The road looks flat, but the burning in my legs and my ragged breath tells me it's uphill. I pedal faster, away from Cyrus's motel room, squinting as the cold, damp air blasts my eyes, coaxing tears from their corners.

I throw the bike into its highest gear and swerve to avoid a pile of crushed glass from a car's shattered window. I gulp air, ignoring the pain in my exhausted muscles as I steer the bike to the center of the lane.

I coast through a red light without bothering to look for cars. There's no one else out at four AM on a Friday morning in November. No one to witness the immortal disguised as a young girl pedaling furiously along the road that leads back to the Morgans.

Cyrus wouldn't hesitate to kill Kailey's family in order to punish me—and to give me a warning never to run away from him again. I can picture him now: his ice-blue eyes, his falsely angelic face. *See what happens when you disobey me, Sera?* he'd say. *People die. Innocent people. And I know how much you hate that.*

The others in our coven—Jared, Sébastien, Charlotte, and Amelia—they wanted what Cyrus offered. Perhaps this is why they never felt guilty for what they did, why they only laughed when I described us as monsters. Because that's what I think I am—a monster, a predator, a killer. Whenever I said those words to Cyrus, he just smiled, like he enjoyed it. He must have loved taking Noah's body.

I bite my lip to keep from crying. *Oh, Noah*, I think, blinking back tears. *I am so sorry.*

The boy I love is dead. But the Morgans might be alive. There's a chance I can save them, and I cling to that thought. I know I won't be able to beat Cyrus in a physical fight, but I can placate him by leaving with him—and take him far away from Kailey's family.

North Berkeley flies by as I near the Morgans' neighborhood, a blur of restaurants and vintage houses presided over by redwood trees and Japanese maples. My legs have finally, mercifully, gone numb from the exertion.

I wish I could say the same for my heart.

I turn off Shattuck and enter a leafy expanse, coming to a stop in front of the Morgans' house, a Craftsman bungalow with an unwieldy, storybook garden. My heart slams in my chest, but Cyrus, wearing Noah's body, isn't outside waiting for me as I expected.

For a moment I just stand there. It feels as though I'm watching myself from outside my body: a small, solitary figure in the middle of an empty, lonely road. The silence is as thick as the fog, and in the early morning gloom, I feel obvious. A beacon. Hunted. But no, I remind myself. I'm the hunter now. I wish I really believed it.

Dismounting from Bryan's bike, I tug it over the root-broken sidewalk and leave it inside the Morgans' chipped picket fence. Across the street, Mr. Vander's Lexus is parked at the curb. It looks fairly new but is marred with dents and scratches, missing a side mirror. Noah's father is a drinker. Noah's bedroom window is dark, just like the rest of his house. Keeping to the shadows, I watch, looking for the smallest movement, the tiniest shift in the curtain that will reveal Cyrus's presence. But there's nothing.

I turn and walk up the Morgans' slick wooden steps, adrenaline coursing through my veins. When I try the doorknob, it opens easily. I suck in my breath. Did I leave it unlocked? I left in such a hurry that I can't remember.

My scalp prickles as I step into the foyer. I pause, allowing my eyes to adjust to the darkness, dreading the unspeakable carnage I fear I will see. But surprisingly, nothing is out of place. Mrs. Morgan's leather purse hangs from a large brass hook, and several colorful umbrellas are folded into a wrought-iron stand. In the living room, two pillow-laden velvet couches slump on faded Persian rugs. The refrigerator hums in the kitchen, and I can hear the faint sound of Mrs. Morgan snoring from the hallway that leads to the master bedroom.

I move softly in the opposite direction. Bryan's door is open a crack, and relief settles over me at the sight of him, tangled up in his sheets, his chest rising and falling with reassuring regularity.

At least I don't have their lives on my hands. Yet.

Cyrus will come for me before the night is over to take me back to the coven. He'll force me to switch bodies and keep me on a closer leash than ever. I won't go down without a fight, though. I have no illusions—I'll probably fail. He's stronger than me, more ruthless, and altogether more deadly.

But I need to try.

I tiptoe through the living room and stumble into a stool at the kitchen counter, wincing as it hits the ground with a loud crash. For a long, panicked moment, I wait for the Morgans to stir or for Cyrus to leap out from behind the curtains to grab me. But when no one emerges from the darkness, I grab a knife from the wooden block in the kitchen, then pad back down the hallway.

The shadows are long and the hardwood floor groans under my weight, no matter how lightly I try to step. I hear a noise from the bathroom and cock my head, holding my breath. But it's just the water that always drips from the old faucet. In Kailey's room I look around quickly, expecting Cyrus to be sitting under her window or sprawled out on her bed. But it's empty. I latch her door and the window. Flimsy locks, both of them. They won't stop Cyrus. But they'll buy me precious seconds.

I crawl onto Kailey's bed, my hand still wrapped tightly around the knife, and lean against the wall. I'm ready.

Let him come.

There's a loud bang on the door to Kailey's room.

"Kailey—is your door *locked*? Are you okay?" Mrs. Morgan's voice is stressed.

I blink my bleary eyes, trying to understand what's happening. My neck is painfully stiff and I'm still gripping the knife. I must have fallen asleep.

"Can you hear me? You're going to be late for school," she calls. "Open this door!"

I try to speak, but my throat is dry. "I'm . . . I'm up. Just a second." I unwrap my fingers from the knife's handle, ignoring the stabbing pain that courses through my hand.

After hiding it underneath Kailey's pillow, I open the door.

Mrs. Morgan is ready for work in crisp wool trousers and a green blouse that matches her eyes. Her wheat-blond hair is pulled back in a low ponytail. Concern flickers across her face as she takes in my appearance. I'm still fully dressed in yesterday's jeans and sweater; I even have sneakers on.

"Did you sleep in your clothes?" she asks, narrowing her eyes. "What's going on in here? Why did you lock the door?"

"I fell asleep reading," I lie. "And what's wrong with a little privacy?" I try to approximate a casual teenage surliness.

"Okay, Miss Cranky. There's nothing wrong with privacy—you just had me worried." She frowns. "It's not like you to lock the door. You better get ready for school. Bryan had an early practice, but Noah will be here any minute to pick you up." She closes the door with an exaggerated flourish.

I'm numb—and confused. Why am I still here? Why didn't Cyrus come for me?

In a fog, I drag a brush through my chin-length dark blond hair, wincing as it pulls at the tangles. Noah and I ate Thai takeout on the beach last night, and salt and sand are still crusted in my hair. I finally give up, pinning it back with barrettes that I find on Kailey's vanity.

I pull on gray cords and a black button-up shirt in slow

motion. Glancing dully at the getaway bag I packed just last night, I take out my few belongings and place them in Kailey's backpack. My hands hit something solid and heavy—the bottle of Kailey's jasmine perfume, the scent so indefinably her.

The room swims, and I collapse at Kailey's desk. Her room is colorful with its peacock's palette, its evergreens and violets, as colorful as I imagine Kailey's own personality was. And here I sit, a drab grayness, an absence, sucking the life out of the jewel-toned walls just as I sucked the life out of Kailey's body the night she died in Jack London Square. I feel so empty. A husk. A body without a soul inside.

When the dizziness subsides, my eyes focus on one of Kailey's paintings. A vaguely familiar girl with shaggy brown hair stands on top of a cathedral, balanced between two sides of a roof that pitch steeply away. She has a guitar strapped to her back like a quiver of arrows. From the lift of her hair and the sway of her feather earrings, it's clear that the wind is blowing, but she looks so surefooted. In the sky above her floats another girl with blond hair and wings that glint in the setting sun's light.

"Kailey! Noah's here!" Mrs. Morgan calls from down the hall.

Game time.

The kitchen knife is too unwieldy to hide in my bag, so I

rummage through Kailey's desk for the Swiss army knife I saw there last week. It's pathetic, but it's something.

My resolve has not changed. Cyrus has come to drive me back to San Francisco, where he'll lock me in our condo for as long as it takes to break me, to make me his again. But with any luck, we won't make it farther than the Bay Bridge. I will attack him the first chance I get.

In the kitchen, Mrs. Morgan is murmuring to the boy she thinks is Noah. He's wearing an argyle sweater that I've never seen before and his hair is neater than usual. I try to lock my grief in a glass box deep inside me. But looking at Not-Noah—at his broad shoulders, the hands I held just yesterday, the lips that I kissed—creates hairline fractures in its walls. Even now I find him beautiful. I grit my teeth and ignore the way my stupid heart tugs at the sight of him.

"Hey, guys," I say carefully.

Mrs. Morgan looks up. "We were just talking about that teacher who was killed last night. It's all over the news. Awful, absolutely awful."

His eyes are as bloodshot as mine. "I couldn't sleep. I kept thinking about Mr. Shaw."

"Yes. Poor Mr. Shaw." There is just the slightest hint of bitterness in my voice. Mrs. Morgan would never detect it. But Cyrus does, and his jaw tightens.

He picks up his backpack and tilts his head toward the front door. "We should go."

My heart starts to pound and I hug Mrs. Morgan tightly. "Bye, Mom. Love you."

"Be careful out there," she says into my hair as she kisses the side of my head. "It's a dangerous world."

"I know." I hold on to her as long as I can, knowing this is likely the last time I will see her.

I'm grateful to Cyrus, at least, for not breaking into the Morgans' house last night. For not causing a scene or punishing them, too. By pretending to be a boy picking up his girlfriend for school, Noah Vander and Kailey Morgan can simply disappear. It's tragic for their families, but it's better than the bloody scene I'd imagined. And with Kailey's mysterious past and Noah's unhappy home life, they will likely be labeled runaway lovers.

My throat grows thick, but I swallow hard. I need to stay numb. The only emotion I can allow is my hatred. Hate keeps me strong. Hate will let me exact revenge.

Outside, the sun strains to break through the clouds, the rays too bright for my sleep-deprived eyes. I squint at Noah's car and touch my pocket, feeling the outline of the knife.

Cyrus's hand is at the small of my back, urging me forward. I glance at him, but he's looking everywhere but at me—at the rippling sky, at the shocking orange blur of

California poppies that shiver in the Morgans' garden. Entering a new body is intoxicating for Incarnates. Colors are more vivid, the breeze is delicious, and the body thrums with a vitality that most humans will never know.

I hope that the beauty of the world will distract him as he drives. I only need him to falter briefly. Then I will strike.

Cyrus opens the car door for me, playing the part of the perfect gentleman, but I feel like I'm climbing into a hearse. The VW that used to feel like home is suddenly stifling, claustrophobic.

As he pulls away from the curb, I watch out the window. The hundred-year-old houses slide by, the sky half cloudy, half clear. I want to remember every detail—the young bearded father with a baby strapped to his chest, the UC Berkeley students with their messenger bags, the old man who sweeps the sidewalk outside the organic cheese shop. I feel tears in my eyes as I realize how much I'll miss this neighborhood, this life.

"How did you find me?" I say softly.

"It wasn't *all* that hard," he says with a hint of a smirk.

I look at his profile, his wavy black hair, the shadows underneath his cheekbones. *It isn't Noah*, I remind myself.

Silence reigns until I can no longer stand it. I reach forward and turn on the radio.

". . . and police have no new information on the death

of Jason Shaw, a popular substitute biology teacher at Berkeley High. Bereaved students have already started an online memorial . . . ," a newscaster intones. I snap the radio off.

Cyrus shakes his head. "It's so odd. Everyone is mourning Mr. Shaw, but no one even knows who he really was or that he came to Berkeley to find his true love," he murmurs, smoothly changing lanes to avoid a bicyclist. "They met when they were just kids—she was fourteen, and he was a couple of years older. It was at a masquerade party."

I close my eyes, remembering that night, almost able to smell the pomegranate wine, the smoky torches, the roses' heady perfume. I can recall every detail—the way my mask made it difficult to see, the cool air pouring over my face when Cyrus asked me to remove it.

"He knew that night that he had to be with her, always. That it was meant to be. They ended up running away together. They left their homes, their families, everything. But it didn't matter. They had each other."

Oh, it mattered. I remember sobbing like the child I was when I realized I could never return to my parents. That they thought I was dead, and I couldn't even comfort them while they quietly wept at my funeral. I feel my throat grow thick, and I wonder why he is telling me this, why he's making our life into some sort of dark fairy tale.

"They traveled the world together until one night, she left him. He didn't understand why."

It's a parable, I realize. A lesson. He's treating our life like a story because he doesn't know how to speak to me directly. He's telling me how badly I hurt him, how much he loves me.

He brings the car to a stop at a red light. "He was sure she came to Berkeley. He came here to find her."

I wrap my fingers around the knife in my pocket, pulling it out with a jerk. Fury makes my fingers tremble. I drop my hand down between the passenger seat and the door so he won't see.

The light turns green, and to my surprise, he doesn't turn right, toward the freeway. As I watch him, trying to figure out his plan, I slide the blade open in my right hand. I run one finger along its edge, never looking away from him.

"How does the story end?" I whisper.

He guns the engine. "How do you think?"

I am shaking. I am shaking so hard that I drop the knife. My heart sinks—I've lost my chance.

But then he makes a sharp left, and I realize where he's taking us.

Berkeley High.

He jerks the car into an open spot, yanks the keys out of the ignition, and sits quietly. He won't look at me. The sun has finally won its battle with the fog and I stare at the motes of dust that twist in the air and settle on the faded dash. All around us kids stream into school. I can see them laughing, but it's like watching TV with the sound turned off.

I fight the urge to throw open the car door and run. I wouldn't make it ten feet.

"Why are we here? At school?" I ask, my pulse wild, my breath rapid. Anything is better than this suspense, this not knowing what comes next.

He leans back in his seat and drapes his wrists over the steering wheel, tucking his chin to his chest. "It does feel a little ridiculous, doesn't it?"

"To say the least."

"Today is a day to be with friends." His voice is rough. It drags over my heart like wheels on gravel. He meets my gaze. "You never know—it could be the last time you'll see them."

Finally, I understand. He's going to give me one day to say good-bye. Perhaps he's remembering how devastated I was to leave my mortal family with no farewells. He's trying to be kind. But what can I even say to my friends here? What can I say to Leyla, to Bryan? Nothing.

And I can't say good-bye to the person who matters most. I picture Noah, the last time I saw him. Only last night, walking away from me on the Golden Gate Bridge, disappearing into fog. If only I could touch him one more time. It's not till I taste salt that I realize I'm crying.

The boy who looks like Noah strokes my hair. He finds my hand and squeezes it so hard I feel my bones sliding against each other. I want to pull back, but I force myself not to move. I pretend I am a statue. A statue doesn't care what happens to it. A statue doesn't flinch.

I know he wants me to forgive him. Killing Noah wasn't enough for Cyrus. He still thinks, after everything that's happened, that I will love him. He wants me on my knees, crawling back to his familiar crushing embrace.

"Come on, Kailey," Madison Cortez pleads in our art class. "You're the best artist I know. It can be whatever you want—I don't know, ice fairies? Snow queens? Deer? You love antlers." She fixes me with her brown eyes, shining beneath the heavy line of her blunt chestnut bangs.

I force a laugh, despite the hollowness I feel, knowing my time here is quickly ticking away. I can only hold on to the fact that with me gone, my friends will be safe. "I'm just *busy*. I have a job and—"

"And Noah. I know. Hey, why don't you paint Noah for

the mural? Two birds, one stone. Make him into a snowman, whatever."

The mention of Noah makes me want to scream. Cyrus has barely left my side all day, appearing outside each of my classes to escort me to the next one. He stopped short of actually grabbing my elbow to steer me along, but his meaning is clear. *Don't even think about running, Sera.* Not that I plan to. I have nowhere to go, no one to run to.

Madison snaps her fingers. "Kailey? Hello? The mural for the dance? Will you do it? Please say yes. I need to cross it off my list."

This has been going on for the entire class. Normally art is quiet, but the whole classroom has been abuzz, unsettled and loud. Madison is fixated on the dance, but I know what everyone else is talking about: Mr. Shaw's death. When I got to my biology classroom this morning, there was a makeshift shrine set up outside the door: candles, flowers, science books, all laid out in mourning for Mr. Shaw. It made me sick. Cyrus, who has murdered hundreds of humans, being grieved? When he's not even dead? All day, my rage has been growing, glowing in my belly like a hot coal.

"I'll be your best friend . . . ," Madison tries.

I was taken aback to hear that Madison is the chair of the winter dance committee given her rock-'n'-roll bad-girl vibe. I would have pegged her for one of the kids that smoke pot in the parking lot and wouldn't be caught dead at a school dance. But I guess even after six hundred years, people can still surprise me.

The other girl who shares our table speaks up shyly. "She's right, Kailey. You should do the mural. It would be good for your soul to honor the solstice." I don't know if I've ever heard her speak before, and I struggle to remember her name. Enid? Erica?

She watches me for a few seconds, her eyes outlined in a thick stroke of silver eyeliner that stands out from her dark skin. It mimics the shape of the vintage cat-eyed glasses that constantly slip down her nose. She's wearing neon blue high-waisted bell bottoms and a T-shirt that reads I ♥ without the initials of any city that would traditionally follow. Metallic gold clogs peek out from the hem of her pants.

She's bent over a piece of leather that she's painstakingly engraving with a blade and an awl. I watch what she's doing for a bit, until her thick curtain of braids falls in the way. She's got yarn and ribbons and feathers braided into her hair. I wonder how she washes it.

Madison sighs, running her fingers through her shaggy brown hair. "Does this mean you'll do it? The mural?"

"I'll . . . consider it," I deflect. I'll either be dead or back with the coven by the time the dance rolls around. But even if, by some miracle, I *am* in Berkeley on December first,

I still wouldn't want to do it for one small, yet significant reason: I can't draw. At all. A fact I've only been able to hide thanks to a long ceramics unit.

"Class, may I have your attention?" We're interrupted by Mrs. Swan. She stands at the front of the studio with hands clasped, next to a boy I haven't seen before. He's wearing a vintage-looking vest over his white button-up shirt, closed with cufflinks at the wrists, and striped wool trousers that remind me of the 1930s.

Mrs. Swan smiles, tucking a lock of long gray hair behind her ear and smoothing her ankle-length skirt around her hips. "Please welcome Reed Sawyer to our midst. He joins us from Sonoma, where he worked on his family's vineyard." She beams, and the class makes a collective rustling sound.

The boy is good-looking, though not my type. He's got very short brown hair that looks freshly attended to with clippers, and he turns a fedora over and over in his hands. I wouldn't call myself an expert on high-school fashion, but he looks like he's wearing a costume.

Mrs. Swan deposits Reed at our table before disappearing in a cloud of her tuberose perfume. He catches my eye and smiles, revealing large white teeth.

"Hey," he says, sitting on the stool across from me. "I'm Reed."

"I'm Kailey," I answer listlessly. It feels so pointless to meet a new person when I'm about to disappear.

"Kailey, huh?" He gazes at me for a second, then smiles. Two deep dimples appear in his tanned cheeks, darkened with a fledgling beard. "You look familiar. Have we met before?"

"I don't think so," I say, though I suppose he could have met Kailey.

"Have you ever spent time in Sonoma?" he presses.

"Nope." *Not in this body, at least.*

"Maybe you know each other from a past life," Enid-or-Erica says in her musical voice as she looks up from her project. "Way more common than you'd think." She offers her hand to Reed. Her long fingers are covered with at least six silver rings.

"I'm Echo," she tells him. Ah, so that's her name. Like the nymph.

"I'm Echo," he responds.

She throws her head back and laughs, the sound like a carillon of bells. "You know," she says, looking at him more closely, "I haven't actually heard that one before."

"Probably because people have no idea who Echo is," he replies. "No one studies Greek mythology anymore."

Echo smiles, looking pleased, and Madison introduces herself as well. Her lips have somehow acquired a coat of cherry-red lipstick that looks like fresh blood against her pale complexion.

"It must be kind of a weird day to be starting here," she says apologetically, batting her eyelashes, which are coated with several layers of black mascara. "You know, with Mr. Shaw and all."

Reed flinches, looking down at our table. "Yeah," he admits. "My parents are freaking out. People don't get murdered in Sonoma. Like, ever. They were ready to pack up and leave when they watched the news this morning."

"We definitely need some healing energy," Echo says. "I brought some sage to burn at lunch," she adds, patting her canvas backpack.

"And as we all know, sage fixes *everything*," Madison says drily.

Reed ignores Madison and smiles at Echo. "It's not a bad idea. Herbs are more powerful than people think."

"*I* think we ought to get back to discussing real issues," Madison sniffs. "Like the mural Kailey should be painting for the school dance."

Damn, the girl is persistent.

The rational piece of me realizes she's just dealing with Mr. Shaw's death in her own way, but still, I'm losing patience with her. My entire life is falling apart, crumbling like an old bridge over choppy waters, and I'm losing my ability to pretend everything's fine.

But before I have to answer, the bell rings, and I scoop up my sketchbook and my backpack. "I guess we'll have to continue this conversation later," I say, darting for the door.

Cyrus is already outside. He is leaning against a wall of lockers, arms folded over his chest. Even though I know it's Cyrus, the sight of Noah's body brings me, as usual, a fluttery feeling. I walk toward him slowly, wanting to bask in the illusion, wanting to pretend that it's really Noah. That last night never happened.

"Everyone's eating outside," he says. "Since it's such a beautiful day." But then he smiles—Noah's smile—and leans close to me. Close, closer. His hands are in my hair, his hands are under my chin. And then his lips—Noah's lips—are on mine, kissing me. I kiss him back. I am dizzy, flames licking the side of my body. Fire and ice. Ice and fire. His passion is real. Mine is, too, but it's misplaced. It's almost like kissing Noah. Almost isn't enough.

I force myself to pull away. It's nearly impossible, but I do. I shove the fire down, inside the extinct volcano of my heart. What if Noah's soul is nearby, watching this? Seeing his body being used as a puppet? Seeing that puppet kiss the girl he loved—the girl who got him killed? Or is Noah's soul long gone to some other dimension, some peaceful realm far away from here, where everything is starlit and joyful and earthly problems have lost all significance? I cannot pretend to know.

That's the thing about Incarnates. We know everything about being alive and nothing about death—except how to cause it, over and over and over again.

The wind has picked up, warm and dry, the kind of wind that means fire danger for California, no matter how much rain has fallen recently. In the south they call them Santa Anas—up here it's the Diablo wind, picking up ferocity as it screams through narrow canyons to the ocean. Saint or devil, the result is the same. The whole state is tinder.

It seems like the entire student body is outside for lunch, taking advantage of the sun. The oak tree we're standing under shakes and small dried leaves fall around us like little dead wings. I am surrounded by Kailey's friends—*my* friends, now, though I still feel a tinge of guilt for thinking of them that way.

The atmosphere is misleadingly festive as we watch a group of students play an acoustic version of "Amazing Grace" in memory of Mr. Shaw. The song is uplifting and I love the soft jangle of banjo and violin, but I hate that they're playing it for Cyrus.

I recognize the band members from the party in Montclair that Bryan brought me to just days after I became Kailey. The girl with blond dreadlocks isn't playing the accordion this time—she sits with a conga drum clutched between her knees, her flowing mauve dress the same color as the fake flowers she has pinned in her hair. The boy with the violin is wearing the same crumpled cowboy hat he had on at the party, a shock of golden hair peeking out at his tanned neck. His eyes are trained on the banjo player's fingertips as they move up and down the metal strings.

They've drawn quite a crowd. As I watch the violinist, I smile in spite of myself, remembering how I borrowed his instrument at the party, how I gave myself over to the music. I loved that night. A bonfire, and redwood trees creaking in the wind. Bryan helping me sneak out of the Morgans' house. The first time I felt comfortable with Kailey's friends. Noah, standing in the kitchen, giving me a smile that made my pulse race . . .

Stop it, I remind myself. *Don't think about him.* I swallow hard.

When the song ends, a low murmur of voices ripples through the crowd, rising above the muted applause. Like in art class, Mr. Shaw's name is on everyone's lips.

"I just can't believe he's gone. It doesn't feel real," Leyla Clark, Kailey's best friend, murmurs next to me.

It's not, I want to tell her, but I bite my lip. The boy who looks just like Noah is on my other side, his fingers firmly laced through mine.

Leyla's dressed in purple down to her scuffed lavender high-tops. A knit cap is tugged low over her ears, and her dark, magenta-streaked hair spills out the bottom. The wind keeps blowing into her mouth, where it sticks to her grape-scented lip gloss. On the other side of her is Bryan in his letterman jacket, his sandy blond hair gelled into spiky submission and immune to the wind. She shifts, leaning into him as he puts his arm around her shoulder.

"I heard he was trying to buy drugs," says Chantal Nixon, who is, as usual, perfectly composed and ladylike in a headband and blazer.

Leyla scoffs. "No way. He was a teacher. He just got mugged. It can happen to anyone."

"Remind me to stay out of Oakland," sniffs Nicole Harrison, who wanders up to the group with Madison in tow. Nicole looks uncharacteristically chaste in a black turtleneck under a cable-knit sweater. She doesn't have on any makeup, and her red, puffy eyes suggest she's been crying.

"Don't be such a priss, Nicole," Chantal retorts, which is odd coming from a girl wearing pearls. "Lake Merritt isn't exactly the hood. There are worse neighborhoods in Berkeley."

"I heard they didn't find the body yet." Madison's voice is dull, her face half swallowed by giant sunglasses. Her dark hair sweeps behind her in feathered tangles and the sun glints off the small diamond stud below her lip. Her hands shake as she fiddles with a lighter. She's much more somber than she was in art. Her best friend, Piper Lindstrom, isn't here and won't be for months—according to a text she sent Madison, she has mono. Without Piper to gossip with, new boys to charm, or dance business to occupy herself with, I suppose Madison has no choice but to face death, just like the rest of us.

Cyrus tightens his grip on my hand. "The police are still looking?" he asks. "For the body?"

Madison nods. "They're going to dredge the lake."

Bryan's brows knit together. "Seriously? Lake Merritt isn't even ten feet deep. It's not like the muggers pushed him off the Golden Gate Bridge."

"Maybe someone moved the body," Cyrus says. "Or maybe the detectives working the case are completely incompetent."

Or maybe the body is nothing but dust, I think pointedly.

"There's going to be a candlelight vigil," says Leyla. "We should all go."

"I'm in," Nicole offers, pushing her shiny curtain of brown hair back from her freckled cheeks. "I heard he didn't have any family. There might not even be a funeral."

Cyrus catches my eye, shooting me an unreadable expression. "If only he had found Seraphina," he murmurs.

I stiffen, a spark of rage shooting through me. He's playing with me, gloating.

"Who?" Leyla asks.

Cyrus's eyes glisten in a perfect replica of human emotion. "No one."

I refuse to indulge Cyrus. I keep my mouth tightly shut as the band strikes up another song. They're covering my favorite Beatles tune, "Blackbird," about a bird who learns to fly, broken wings be damned. I concentrate on the music, letting it momentarily stanch my anger.

What am I going to do? I can't run, obviously. I don't have the advantage of being in disguise anymore, and the only way I will switch bodies again is by force. I need to think of a plan more foolproof than my Swiss army knife, but nothing comes, and Cyrus's firm grip on my hand makes it impossible to think clearly.

The smell of sage cuts through the air, and I see Echo

holding the promised smudge stick, sweet herbal smoke greedily snatched by the wind. It reminds me of the warehouse raves Cyrus used to drag me to in the 1990s, electronic music pushing baggy-pants-wearing dancers into a delirious trance. Techno was Cyrus's passion, not mine, but I've always loved to dance, to forget myself in the rhythm and the crowd.

A chorus of applause erupts as the band finishes the song. I rip my hand away from Cyrus's grasp to clap loudly, and the boy with the violin catches my eye, a sunny grin spreading across his face. His ice-blue eyes crinkle at the corners, and he tips his hat at me. I feel a blush rise in my cheeks and I steal a glance at Cyrus. I don't want this violinist paying any attention to me—Cyrus's jealousy has proved deadly before.

"Nice," says Cyrus warmly, summoning his immortal charm. He's not mad, I realize. Why would he be? He won, after all. He's captured me.

"Thanks." The boy's eyes flick between Echo and Leyla as they drift away across the quad; the music over, the crowd has begun to disperse.

"'Blackbird' is one of my favorite songs," I say tentatively to the violinist.

"It's a classic," violin-boy says, his eyes bright. "It's nice to meet another Beatles fan."

"Oh, we met before," I correct him. "At Dawson's party in Montclair. I borrowed your violin."

He cocks his head.

"Are you guys talking about the party in the hills?" The tiny girl with the blond dreadlocks sets her conga drum down on the grass and throws an arm around her bandmate's shoulders. "Because Eli here was high as a kite that night. Seriously, he almost fell into the canyon. Don't believe anything he says about that party."

Eli chuckles, holding up his hands. "In that case, I plead the fifth." But I barely hear him.

Almost fell into the canyon. The phrase ricochets through my mind. An idea takes hold suddenly, and I know how I'm going to kill Cyrus. Well, perhaps that's too optimistic.

I know how I'm going to try.

I reach for Cyrus's hand. I tug on it and he gives me his full attention.

I gaze into his deep blue eyes, making my face into a contrite mask, lifting my lips in a veneer of love and obedience. "I have an idea," I say, ignoring the nervy ball of dread that sits in my stomach. "Let's go hiking tonight in Tilden Park. Before we go home." The word *home* feels false in my mouth. The coven's San Francisco condo will *never* be my home. As long as Cyrus is there, it can only be my prison. "Just you and me," I add.

He looks at me for a long moment while my heartbeat thuds down to my toes. But he pulls me close, wrapping his arms around me. "That would be really great," he murmurs into my hair.

A flock of birds lands on the concrete, then takes off, one by one, dipping and swooping in the air, aloft on invisible streams. And free, like I could be if I succeed.

"Not right after school, though." I make my voice confident, breezy. "I have a few things to take care of first." I need it to be dark when we set out on the path. I don't want any witnesses to what I intend to do.

I pull away and smile at him. "That's allowed, right?"

"I suppose so," he says, cupping my cheek with his warm hand. Behind us, Eli's band launches into another song, a traditional ballad that reminds me of something my mother used to sing, a mournful tale of love and loss.

I turn away from Cyrus and set my lips grimly, watching Eli's fingers dance over his violin strings. Cyrus agreed readily—perhaps *too* readily—to my plan. Perhaps he has no intention of taking me back to San Francisco, and I just set the scene for my own murder.

I can't think like that. I've been losing to Cyrus for centuries, but this has to be the one game I win.

You're a killer, Sera. That's what Cyrus always says. *Now act like it.*

I can't stop staring at the girl's hair. She sits with her back to me, headphone wires trailing from her ears, plugged into a sleek laptop. She has no idea I'm here, hunched low in the library's poetry section, but I've been watching her for close to an hour, the minutes ticking by far too quickly. When I leave here, I will meet Cyrus, and I am scared. No—*terrified*.

The girl's hair is wavy, rippling down the back of her faded green sweatshirt, and veers between auburn and scarlet and brilliant persimmon, depending on the angle of her head beneath the fluorescent lights.

From behind, she looks exactly like Charlotte, my best

friend for two hundred years. But then she twists and bends to her side, pushing down her knee sock to scratch at a mosquito bite on her pale ankle. Her profile is nothing like Charlotte's—her nose is strong, rather than pert, and she's missing Charlotte's light smattering of freckles.

The illusion broken, I glance at the clock that rests on a sagging shelf of reference books—4:25 PM.

Reluctantly, I leave the safety of the library and make my way outside. The wind shows no signs of stopping. It lifts my hair, whipping it harshly around my face. The gusts are warm and dry, but the weather reminds me of *le mistral*, a freezing wind that rages across the south of France. In 1349, right after he made me into an Incarnate, Cyrus and I fled to Les Baux-de-Provence. *Le mistral* was in full force, ripping tiles from the roofs of houses. Local legend said it brought ill spirits and bad tempers, but I loved it. I loved the way it threw my long, dark hair above me like a banner. The way it blew away memories of my childhood in foggy London, of my mother and father. Losing them was too painful to think about, but the wind scrubbed me clean.

Oh, California wind, please do the same.

I reach our meeting place, the gnarled oak tree now backlit in the rapidly setting sun. Cyrus sits with his back against the trunk, his knees pulled up to his chest, poring over a thick text. My heartbeat thunders like a herd of wild horses across packed earth, but I force my face to remain impassive, to pretend that this is a normal afternoon. To pretend that isn't the afternoon when either Cyrus or I—or both of us—will die.

"Hi there," I say, a sweet smile on my face.

He looks up, surprised, acting as though he wasn't aware that I was standing in front of him. His expression is a lie, just like mine.

"Are you ready?" he asks, his eyes steady and flecked with gold in the dying sunlight. Static electricity bridges the air between us.

"As ready as I'll ever be," I say.

He stands, swinging his backpack over one shoulder. I am struck by how tall he is, how hard he will be to overpower.

We walk toward the parking lot, arms brushing. I wish I could put some distance between us, but he has to believe I've forgiven him. If I am to avenge Noah, if I am to save those whose bodies Cyrus will eventually steal, I have to play this exactly right.

There are only two cars left in the lot. Noah's, and an Oakland police cruiser a couple of spaces away. A man sits inside the police car, leafing through a notebook.

He rolls down the window. "Excuse me," he calls. His gravelly, world-weary voice is a contrast to his youthful face.

He's got a shaved, tan head and a dimple in the middle of his chin. Mirrored sunglasses hide his eyes. "Do you two go to school here?" His lower jaw works on a piece of gum.

Cyrus turns to me and raises his eyebrows. "Yes," he answers the cop.

The officer rolls up his window and climbs out of the car. He's holding his notebook open to a page that is, I notice, covered in coffee stains and surprisingly elegant, cursive handwriting. "I'm Officer Spaulding," he announces, walking closer to us. I can smell the spearmint from his gum. "I'm investigating the murder of a teacher here—Mr. Shaw—did you know him?"

The hairs on my arms stand on end. Cyrus's posture straightens and he fixes his eyes on the cop. "Yes," he answers. "He was our biology teacher. Are there any developments in the investigation?"

Officer Spaulding takes off his sunglasses. His eyes are a light green color that I can only describe as feline. "I can't answer that," he says, "but there were some *irregularities*, let's say." He smiles, revealing very white, very straight teeth.

"What kind of irregularities?" Cyrus presses, narrowing his eyes. He must be worried that he made a mistake, left behind some pieces of evidence that won't add up. Officer Spaulding doesn't reply. Instead, he looks at me. "How about you? Did you know Mr. Shaw?" He reaches up to his head, as though to push back a mane of hair that's no longer there, and awkwardly pats the back of his neck.

"Yes," I answer quietly. "He was the biology teacher, like Noah said." It feels absurd to use Noah's name.

"And did you ever notice anything strange about his behavior? The way he interacted with female students, for example?" The cop narrows his eyes, studying my face.

Cotton blooms in my mouth. Does this mean that the police found Cyrus's yearbook? The one with *X*s through the faces of the female students he had ruled out as being me? What other evidence might they have?

"Absolutely not," answers Cyrus. "What are you trying to imply?" He sounds angry. He nods his head to me, reminding me to stay in line. "Did Mr. Shaw ever act weird around you?"

"N-n-no," I stutter. "Of course not. He was a great teacher. I still can't believe he's dead."

"Sorry, kids. I've got to follow up on every lead. It's my job." Officer Spaulding tucks his pen behind his ear, where it perches precariously. He smiles again, no longer chewing his gum. I wonder if he swallowed it. "Thanks for your time. Please give me a call if you remember anything—anything at all—about Mr. Shaw. Especially," he adds, looking at me, "if your girlfriends have anything they want to say."

I shiver and take the business card he's holding out. I wish I could tell him that Mr. Shaw was nothing but a mirage. That the man who "killed" him is standing right in front of his squad car. And that if I succeed, that killer will finally, *finally* meet his own end at the base of the canyon in Tilden Park.

"I got you something," Cyrus says when we reach the trailhead, and holds out his hand. He is smiling shyly, as though we're any human couple on a date.

It's only five in the afternoon, but darkness has fallen quickly, like a curtain on a stage. The first cold needles of starlight shine above us, piercing the faded azure sky. I was on edge the entire drive to the park, the road winding around the Berkeley Hills. Cyrus drove fast, taking the turns with practiced speed.

I force myself to smile, to say, "What is it?"

He opens his palm and reveals a necklace on a silver

chain, pooled in the center of his hand. He holds it up so I can see the small birdcage charm that hangs from it, complete with a tiny bird inside. It glints in the light of the full moon that rose when I wasn't looking.

A bird, caged in silver. Like me.

It's the silver cord that binds your soul to your body, Sera, Cyrus said to me when he made me what I am. *This potion is unraveling it. You'll soon be free.*

Free. Nothing could have been further from the truth.

"I love it," I lie. He gestures for me to turn around and I oblige, lifting my hair from my neck so he can fasten it. The chain is like ice against my skin.

The wind shakes the eucalyptus trees that grow here, releasing their minty oils into the air. Cyrus wraps his arms around my waist, and I feel heat, the sun of six hundred years' worth of summers.

"Should we walk?" he asks softly. "Don't get me wrong. We can just stand here if you want. I kind of like it." I can't see his face, but I know he's smiling. He tightens his grip on me, but I pull away.

"Let's go," I answer, turning to him, a smile painted on my chapped lips. As I move forward along the path, I have the sensation that I'm leaving one world for another, from a dream to waking life. Two places with different logic, different rules.

We set off, and I match the speed of my steps to his. I don't like having him behind me—I don't trust him. *It's been too easy to appease him*, my brain tells me. *He knows what you're going to do*, it says. *He always knows.*

So what if he knows? I argue back, fiddling with the knife in my pocket. *One way or another, this ends today.*

The trail tangles up the hill in front of us, littered with eucalyptus leaves and thick strips of its flammable bark. I hear a rustle in the trees ahead of me. I stop abruptly, a chill raising goose bumps on my arms.

"What's wrong?" he asks.

"Didn't you hear that?"

"No," he replies, cocks his head, listens. "There's no one else here—the parking lot was completely empty."

"Are you sure?" I say. I don't need any heroic witnesses trying to save the life of someone who should have died centuries ago.

"I'm sure."

We wait, but there's nothing except the breeze working its way through the forest. "Do you want to go back?" he asks, his eyes trained on the trees.

"No, it's okay," I say, setting off again. I walk faster, determination tensing my muscles.

We reach the cliffs, breathing hard. The whole Bay Area is spread out below us in a shimmering sprawl, like a topographic map brought to life. We can see the Golden Gate Bridge, arcing toward the Marin headlands. The cities of Berkeley and Oakland twinkling in the clear air. The Bay Bridge, just a ribbon of light cutting across the choppy blank water.

"It's beautiful," he says, taking my hand.

Below us, the land falls away sharply. I let go of his hand and edge closer. "Come see," I say, only a few feet from the lip of the drop.

"That's okay," he says. "I'll stay right here."

I shrug my shoulders and move closer, closer, till I can see down. The moon bathes the chasm in milky light. There are rocks at the bottom. I close my eyes, just for a second, and picture Noah's body lying at the bottom, twisted and broken.

No, I remind myself. *You won't have to see it. He'll turn to dust as soon as he hits.*

"I want you to come here with me," I say, my voice unwavering.

He waits, then appears to come to a decision. "Okay, but only for a second." And then he's at my side. I watch his profile in the moonlight, half lit and half dark. Like Cyrus himself. Half passionate alchemist, seeker of truth. Half killer.

"Look at San Francisco," I say. "It doesn't seem real. It's a toy town."

"I'd rather look at you," he says. I feel his hand on my cheek. It's rough and warm. I take a shaky breath. "You look so pretty." I feel heat rising to my face, and curse myself for being so weak as to blush at a moment like this, when I'm supposed to be an avenger.

"I thought you didn't usually like blondes," I say lightly. His weakness is long chestnut hair.

"That's idiotic," he says. "I like *you*. Beauty is a fringe benefit."

I take another step toward the cliff, pulling him with me. We are only a foot away from the lip of the canyon. I can do this. I can. I will take the fall with him if need be. We will turn to dust together, two old souls with too much blood on our hands.

"Thank you for coming up here with me," I say, wrapping my arm around his back, trying to find the best position for my hand. I raise my elbow behind his back, for leverage.

"I really needed to get away," he whispers.

I coil the muscles in my legs. But just as I am about to shove, he turns to me. I suck in my breath when I meet his lake-blue eyes. They stop me cold. I'm not sure why at first. They are the color of water when shards of sun hit the bay.

They are *Noah's* eyes.

But this is *Cyrus* . . . isn't it?

I hesitate. I hesitate again. I'm reeling. I'm muffled in

cotton. *Dear God, forgive me if I lose my chance. But I need to be sure.*

"When . . . did your feelings for me change?" I ask.

"You already know that," he answers, stroking my hair.

Doubt creeps into me. It tingles, like I'm waking up from anesthesia.

"Tell me again," I say urgently, grasping for something—for someone—that my brain tells me is gone. But another part of me, maybe the illogical part, isn't so sure.

He laughs. "Okay. Right after your car accident. Something was just . . . different. It started that night that I found you sneaking out of your house."

"And what happened right after that?" I press.

He puts his hand thoughtfully to his chin. "I seem to recall you acting really weird. Kind of like now. And then you went back inside to go to sleep. Wait." His voice grows tense. "Are you having some kind of concussion relapse?"

It's not possible. It's not possible. There's no way Cyrus could know that. "No," I whisper. "The other night—you played a word. On our game."

"Yeah. And you never played your turn."

"Why," I ask slowly, "did you play that word?"

"Because I had the letters for it, genius." His brows are furrowed, his confusion clear.

"Tell me why," I say.

He sighs. "And because I had just found out about Mr. Shaw. Okay? I know you didn't like him. But he was teaching me stuff before he died. About . . . I don't know, esoteric stuff. He used to talk about alchemy all the time." His voice grows sad.

The wind buffets me, but I am granite. I am listening.

"And I was just sitting there, upset, thinking about him," he continues. "And I don't know why, but I pulled out my phone. I think I was trying to distract myself. And I was staring at my letters—and the word just jumped out at me. Alchemy. I mean—it was like a *sign*, like he was *okay*. It was like . . . his ghost was telling me not to worry about him. So I played it. And I felt better."

I am silent. It's him. It's Noah. My Noah.

He steps backward, pulling me with him, away from the edge. Away from a death that only happened in my mind. He envelops me. A bird leaves its cage.

My mouth finds his with windswept urgency, my fingers tangling in his hair. He kisses me back. All the years I've lived have led me here, to this place, to the lip of this canyon, to Noah's lips.

"I'm so sorry," I breathe.

"What for?" he answers.

"For being so crazy today," I say.

"It's a crazy day," he answers. I feel his hands on my

shoulders. I feel his lips on my neck. "But everything's going to be okay. Better than okay," he murmurs.

We stay for a while longer, not speaking. Just being. And when we leave, I almost skip down the trail.

It's only when we reach the parking lot and see the briefest of red flashes—taillights of a car pulling out, their scarlet gleam bouncing off the asphalt and the trees—that a darkness edges against my euphoria.

Even though I'm away from the cliffs, I'm still in danger. I could still fall. I could still lose everything. Because there was no other car there when we arrived. Someone followed us. And if Cyrus isn't Noah, who could he be?

Before Cyrus made her immortal, Seraphina Ames was a normal fourteen-year-old girl living in London in 1349.

Turn the page—*and turn back time*—to see the beginning of Seraphina's forever-life. . . .

london, 1349

I must be dreaming. But the dream is so wonderful, I don't want to wake. My eyelids flutter, and I steal a glance at the boy's face. Cyrus, the apothecary's son, is carrying me in his strong arms. His silver-blond hair shines in the moonlight, and his face looks worried. I can't imagine why. I let my eyes close. Where is he taking me? *It's my wedding night*, I decide, snuggling closer to his chest.

My father always said I would marry Edmund Stuart, one of his business partners. But somehow it is Cyrus that I'm marrying instead. My father probably realized the mistake he was making, giving his daughter to the old widower who had children her own age. For some reason I cannot recall the actual ceremony, but I remember my gown: the white silk panels threaded with gold. My servant told me it was for the masquerade ball, but she must have been wrong. I am sure my mother will have words with her later. I cannot picture my veil, my mind substituting a mask instead, shaped like a butterfly and sparkling with jewels.

The summer night's breeze moves over my face, carrying with it the usual stench of the city streets, where sewage and offal and old ale flows. But it doesn't bother me. It is simply the smell of life, of many people living in close quarters. I am jostled as Cyrus sidesteps the filth, the rats that scurry on the stones.

Dimly, I hear Cyrus speaking to his gatekeeper, whose rough voice registers disgust. "Filthy beggar," the gatekeeper hisses. "Probably has the plague." *Who is he talking about?* I wonder. *Tell him I'm your bride, Cyrus.*

I hear Cyrus's answer as though I am underwater. I can't understand his words, but his imperious tone is laced with threats. The gate is swiftly opened. I feel the heat of torches flicker across my face as Cyrus crosses the stone-walled courtyard and enters the front door.

He's carrying me across the threshold, I think happily.

I open my eyes again as he climbs the stairs, this time glancing at my body. My heart grows cold at the sight: I am wearing layers of filthy, ragged wool. My hands are crossed over my stomach, but they are gnarled and rough. *What happened to my hands? Where is my wedding gown?*

My mind rebels. This must be a nightmare.

"Shh," Cyrus murmurs to me. He kisses me on the forehead, and I relax. Soon, I'll wake up, and everything will be right. I'll be with my husband.

I feel Cyrus setting me down on a bed, the fine velvets grazing my cheek. I keenly feel the loss of his warm arms. "Come back," I whisper.

"I'm not going anywhere," he says, and I sigh contentedly at the sound of his voice, the love that I can hear in it.

He moves around the room, and my nose soon recognizes the scent of burning lamp oil and candle wax. I hear movement as Cyrus settles into a chair next to the bed, and I inhale vetiver as he puts his mouth near my cheek. *He must be admiring the roses that are woven into my hair*, I think happily, thankful to my servant for remembering to include them.

"Just rest, Seraphina," Cyrus murmurs.

I'm startled by the thud of heavy footsteps, the door to the room being thrown open, the wood banging against the stone wall. But this is not nearly as alarming as the voice that follows, that bellows loudly at my feet.

"Cyrus! What have you done?" I recognize the voice as

Johann von Hohenheim, the apothecary, Cyrus's father. He sounds furious, and I keep my eyes squeezed tightly shut.

I hear a scraping sound to my right, as Cyrus scrambles out of his chair.

"What else could I do, Father? She was going to die!" There is an edge to Cyrus's voice, a challenge that I would never allow to creep into a conversation with my own father.

"Who is she?" Johann demands. I can tell by the coolness on my face that he is standing at the foot of the bed, blocking the heat from the lamps. All my senses are alive.

Cyrus sighs. "Seraphina. Lord Ames's daughter."

"We discussed this, Cyrus." Master Hohenheim's voice is urgent. "That you would not use the elixir without consulting me. Alchemy has been forbidden by the crown. If anyone finds out, we can be tried for sorcery, or worse. And there cannot be a race of Incarnates preying on London. I won't be responsible for it!" Johann's voice rises in volume as he speaks.

"I know what we discussed. But there was a thief. She was stabbed. She was going to die!" Cyrus cries.

Who was stabbed? Is he talking about me? That's impossible. Except . . . I can imagine it happening. I can picture it clearly in my mind. The woman suddenly behind me, her dagger in my back, turning my white gown red with blood. *No*, I think. *No, that never happened.*

"How many others have you made without my knowledge?" Johann asks. "Tell me."

"None!" Cyrus swears. "It's the truth. She's the first one. I . . . I had to. Father, please understand." I hear his voice crack, a shuffling sound as he sinks into a chair. "I love her!"

I open my eyes. Cyrus's head is in his hands, and he is quietly weeping. His platinum hair picks up the candlelight, the paleness in stark contrast to the embroidered black tunic he wears.

Johann still stands at the foot of the bed, regarding me with alarm in his eyes. They are shadowed under the wide purple beret that covers his head, the same rich color as his belted tunic. He looks nothing like Cyrus—Cyrus is pale, but Johann's complexion is a warm olive. Cyrus's eyes are ice blue, and Johann's are a deep brown, almost the same color as his glossy black hair.

I pull myself up to a sitting position. Cyrus is smiling at me, though Johann's face remains cold. I gaze around the room. Upon one wall a piece of linen has been thrown over a painting. Except . . . it's not a painting. I can see light shining between the loosely woven threads. I know what it is.

A mirror.

I rise to unsteady feet and cross the room. Neither of them stops me. I stand in front of the linen. I reach out my hand.

"Seraphina!" Cyrus yells. "No! Don't touch that."

Too late.

I pull the fabric away from the mirror. I see myself.

And I begin to scream.

My open mouth shows brown, stained teeth. Several are missing. I am wearing rags. The face that gazes back at me is that of a much older woman, possibly close to thirty, but deeply lined, ruined from too much time in the sun. My hair is lank and greasy. I am sure it's crawling with lice.

It's not me.

And yet, when I scream, she screams. When I put my hand to my face, she does the same.

In a flash, I remember everything. Meeting Cyrus at the masquerade ball, being accosted by the thieves on the bridge, the burning elixir he placed on my tongue.

Cyrus, forcing me to kiss the repulsive woman who had stabbed me only moments before. Opening my eyes in her body.

"What did you do to me?" I moan over and over as I scratch at my new skin.

Cyrus appears behind me, pulls me away from the mirror. "It's okay, Seraphina, don't worry. You will be beautiful again."

Johann shakes his head sadly. "The girl must be sedated," he says firmly, then nods at a servant, who had rushed in when I screamed. She ducks out the doorway.

But I can't stop yelling. I'm terrified. My throat is raw, ragged. The sound of my voice is foreign to me, lower-pitched than it used to be, and this only makes me scream more. The servant girl reappears, carrying a silver tray. Cyrus hastily grabs a goblet and forces it to my lips. I taste chamomile, violet, and something else. Something dark and musty. It dribbles down my chin. "Drink, Seraphina," he urges me, stroking my filthy hair with a heartbreaking gentleness.

I do. Almost immediately my eyelids flutter closed and I sink into his arms. I vaguely sense him putting me in the bed, turning down the lamps, and leaving with his father. Through the open window, the late June air crawls inside. The last thing I hear is a bird's unearthly song coming from the courtyard. *It must be a nightingale*, I think as I am pulled down to sleep.

A shaft of sunlight beams through the open window, pooling on the stone floor. It slowly creeps up the bed where I am sleeping till it falls upon my face and wakes me. My whole body is sore. For a long moment, I do not know where I am, but when I look down at my aged hands, it all comes rushing back. It's not a nightmare. Or if it is, it's the most realistic and longest nightmare I've ever had.

A sense of panic envelopes me as I watch my hands. The sunlight is cruel, reflecting off the aged skin and illuminating every line, every mole, every detail that tells me I have been changed, irrevocably.

At least my hands are clean, the filth removed from under my nails, which are filed and buffed. I am wearing a fresh linen shift, and an experimental swipe at my head tells me my hair's been washed. I smell like lavender and rose, but no amount of flowers or herbs can cover up the stench of my fear, which emanates from deep inside.

"You're awake." Cyrus's voice is soft as he steps into the room, sunlight falling on his shimmering hair. I catch my breath at the sight. He reminds me of the paintings in the chapel, the ones of saints with their circular halos.

"Where is my mother?" I ask, willing myself not to panic at my unfamiliar voice. "I demand to see her." Perhaps if I speak with enough authority, it will happen, like when my father commands our household servants to bring him a bowl of cream or a tankard of ale.

"You know that's not possible," he says, not unkindly, as he sits next to me on the bed. My pulse races at his proximity. I briefly close my eyes, remembering the times that Cyrus and his father would visit our house, bringing salves and ointments and herbal remedies when we fell ill. I recall the dazzling smiles he would shoot my way when my father wasn't looking. He always made me feel beautiful.

A rueful glance at my sinewy arms, at my wrinkled hands, tells me that I am no longer that beauty. That I have been cursed somehow, made old and ugly.

"I know nothing of the sort," I retort. "In fact, I know . . . nothing at all. What happened to me, Cyrus? What did you do?

"I will explain everything to you," he promises, reaching out to touch my cheek. To my surprise, he doesn't recoil at its rough surface. He doesn't appear to be disgusted by me, even though I am disgusted by myself.

"Can you change me back?" My voice cracks, and I abandon the pretense of strength.

He sits there for a long moment, gazing into my eyes, until I feel my cheeks flush and I look away. The bed shifts as he stands and walks toward the window, an immense emptiness filling my heart the farther he strides from my side.

In that moment, I know the answer to my question without him saying it aloud.

"In some ways I think my father a complete fool," he begins softly, staring out to the courtyard. "But he is a brilliant man. A scholar and a philosopher. Probably the most intelligent person I've ever known." He runs his finger down the length of the drapery that frames the window.

"He was born in Vienna," Cyrus continues. "But he studied at Oxford, where he learned about theology and mathematics, about astronomy and everything in the natural world. He became obsessed with the idea that the human soul has physical properties. And after he completed his education, he traveled widely—to Paris, Prague, Florence—where he studied further. In Spain, he met a translator who told him about alchemy, and a mysterious substance called the Philosopher's Stone. It was said to be an elixir that would grant immortality."

As he speaks, a shiver runs through my body, beginning at my shoulders and working its way downward, till I am chilled to the bone, despite the sunlight that still plays over my face. My eyes drift to the colorful artwork on the walls. One tapestry shows a unicorn in a forest, surrounded by roses. Another shows an elephant, a creature as exotic as the unicorn, surrounded with abstract designs that appear foreign to my eye. Johann must have collected these on his travels.

"My father has never been a pious man. He always says that the Church is simply a political tool to control the people. That the popes are liars, and Christianity holds no more truth than the ancient pagan myths."

I suck in a breath at this—it's unspeakably blasphemous. Johann would be burned at the stake if his beliefs were known. "That's heresy," I say, shocked.

"Yes," Cyrus agrees. "Which is why he makes such a show of attending Mass, why he appears to pray more fervently than anyone else, and especially why he donates large sums of money to the Church."

I'm shaken, but I don't reply. This conversation feels dangerous.

Cyrus resumes his story. "My father eventually settled in Caffa, where he met my mother, Sofia. I was born there, and lived there till I was fifteen—two years ago."

I nod, searching my memory, trying to picture the large map of Europe that hangs in my father's library. Caffa is a Genoese settlement on the Crimean peninsula, on the shores of the Black Sea. It's surprising that Cyrus has only lived here since I was twelve years old. It feels like forever that I've secretly watched him. But then, two years sounds like a very long time to me. At twelve I was still a little girl, but now I am at the age where I'm expected to be married.

"What happened to your mother?" I ask quietly.

"I don't know much about her, except that she was devoutly religious and her family came from Italy. Genoa, to be exact. She died giving birth to me. My father refuses to speak of her." His voice is measured as he delivers this information, no trace of bitterness or sorrow.

"I'm sorry," I say anyway.

To my surprise, he chuckles softly. "No need to be sorry, Seraphina." My heart skips a beat as he pronounces my name. "She's been gone my whole life. I have nothing to miss. And besides, she's with God now—according to my father, that's what she always wanted. Of course, he believes God is nothing more than a fairy tale."

My heart closes like a fist. I wish he would at least whisper such profanities. The open window makes me nervous, as though the king himself might hear Cyrus speak.

"Six years ago the Mongols laid siege to Caffa. Food was still shipped in, but we were trapped. We lived that way for several years. I was just a child, really, and ready to accept any reality as children do. It was completely normal for me." Cyrus's jaw tightens, and I realize he's lying—his casual attitude is a façade. It must have been ghastly.

"And then one day, our enemy had a brilliant idea. A way to bring us down, though they could not have known the true extent of the damage they would cause. They had no way of knowing that they were about to unleash a wave of death over all of Europe when they hurled the corpses of their plague-infected dead over the city walls. My father was one of the first victims. I still remember the day that I came home and found him in bed with red sores covering his neck. He was feverish, crying out in pain. It wasn't long after that his fingers turned black."

"The Black Death," I whisper. The signs are unmistakable. Everyone knows the symptoms that accompany the plague that's been raging through London for the past year. When they thought I was asleep, my mother and father would murmur in low tones about the hundreds of corpses that are burned each day. But fortunately my family has been unaffected.

"Yes," Cyrus says. "The plague. And his imminent death is what drove my father to experiment upon himself. He'd been trying to develop the elixir of immortality ever since he heard about it years before. Puttering in his laboratory till all hours of the night, mixing potions and meditating on the Philosopher's Stone. He thought he had perfected the formula and tried using it on horses and dogs, but they always died soon after. It wasn't until he was sick that he thought to use it on himself."

Cyrus takes a shaky breath. I am completely sucked in by his story, so caught up that I almost forget my hideous face, my ruined hands, my missing teeth. Almost.

"I remember that last day in Caffa so well," he says. "The way my Greek tutor was impatient with me during our lesson. The way the sunlight sparkled on the surface of the sea. I remember entering my father's bedchamber and hearing nothing but silence. The most chilling silence you can ever imagine. And then I saw his body laid out on the bed. Completely lifeless. I fell to my knees."

I feel my throat grow thick. I want to pull him into my arms and comfort him. At the same time I imagine my own father, dead. I don't know which thought makes me weep more.

"And then I heard a voice. 'Cyrus, my son, I've done it. I've cheated death.' I whirled around." As he speaks, he moves his head, reenacting what happened. "My father's servant was sitting there, in my father's favorite chair. My hair stood on end."

As does mine now. "It was Johann?" I whisper.

"Yes," he says. "It was my father. He knew things that only my father could know. It didn't take long for me to believe him completely."

His father, speaking to him out of a foreign mouth, from a body that was not his.

Like me.

"We left that night for London, leaving everything, *everyone* behind," he continues, and I sense the first hint of bitterness in his tone. "He was terrified that the servants would suspect us of witchcraft, that we would be accused of sorcery. He was unreasonable, completely terrified."

"People have been burned at the stake for much less," I say quietly.

"He's a paranoid old fool!" Cyrus spits. "He lives his entire life in fear of the crown and the Church. I will *never* be like him."

He lifts his chin, defiant, and pulls himself up to his full height. Fire flashes in his eyes.

"So you used the same dark magic on me," I say finally, to fill the silence.

"It's not *magic*, Seraphina," Cyrus corrects gently. "It's science. It's based on the physical laws of the natural world. It's not a thunderbolt from heaven." He begins to pace, raking his hands through his platinum hair.

"Whatever you choose to call it, you used it on me," I allow wearily. "Am I dead?"

"No," he says fervently, hurrying to my side. "Nothing could be farther from the truth. You will *never* have to die."

"But my body. My old self. She's gone forever?" My voice rises in pitch.

"Yes," he replies. "Forever."

"Do my parents know?" A pit of dread collects in my stomach as I wait for his response.

He looks down to the floor. He won't meet my eyes. "Your body was found several days ago."

"Several days? How long have I been asleep?" I gasp.

"Four nights," he admits. "I gave you an herbal preparation to keep you asleep. I thought it would be easier for you to accept if you had a chance to rest."

I throw back the heavy covers and swing my legs over the side of the bed. "Four nights?" I repeat, an edge of anger entering my words. "They must be out of their minds with worry. I must go to them."

He puts his hand on my arm. "Seraphina, they're not worried. They're grieving."

His words hit me like a slap across the face. "They think I'm dead." I say it like a statement, not a question. Because I already know the answer.

He closes his eyes, the sun hitting his long, golden lashes. "Your funeral is this afternoon, at All Hallows by the Tower," he says, naming the oldest church in London, built seven hundred years ago.

I shrug off his hand and stand on the cold stone floor. I have the feeling that it is always cold, no matter how much sun shines on it. "I'm going," I say firmly. I summon the most authoritative tone I am capable of. "And you're taking me. Now."

Cyrus holds my hand as we hurry through London's warren of twisting streets, attracting more than one curious glance. I'm certain the people we pass are wondering what this beautiful young man in a well-made velvet tunic is doing with a coarse servant.

I'm wearing a scratchy gown made of wool and stiff leather shoes that are too small and pinch my feet. My attire is worlds different from the silk gowns I usually wear, the shoes that are supple and not made for running. But I am grateful to have anything between me and the unpaved streets that run with filth.

The houses go from stone and slate roofs to cheaper wood, covered with thatched straw, as we leave Cyrus's neighborhood and enter one of the poorer districts. My father's grand estate on the Strand could not feel farther away. Stray pigs wander amongst the crowd and noxious fumes from the dyers' vats sting my eyes. We hurry past the market, where bright silks and woven carpets twist in the breeze next to spice sellers and swordsmiths. I see more than one plague doctor with the trademark bird's-beak mask and long black robe.

The tolling of the church bells tells me we're close. I feel each low gong thrumming through my whole body.

The procession has already made its way to the churchyard. A low stone wall surrounds it, thronged with dozens of beggars, hands out for alms. I recognize my father's guards blocking the entrance, their chain mail glinting in the afternoon sun, my family's crest on the flags that fly above them.

Cyrus stops in his tracks, but I tug on his hand. "We must get closer," I say, urgently. I stand on tiptoe and catch a glimpse of my mother and father, close to the casket, which is draped in white. My mother looks beautiful in a black gown with full sleeves. Her deep chestnut hair is elaborately braided, hanging down beneath her silk hood. Tears run down her face, in stark contrast to my father, who shows no emotion. His face could be one of the stone angels carved on the doors of the cathedral. Though I know this is how men grieve, somehow this hurts me more than the sight of my own casket, where my true body lies, my long brown hair and once-rosy cheeks stilled by death.

The crowd shifts, and my view is suddenly obstructed. "Why are there so many beggars?" I ask Cyrus, gazing at the masses.

"Your father is a wealthy man, Seraphina," he explains. "They're expecting a handout."

It's true, my family is very rich. Only the most fortunate can afford funerals, especially now, with the plague bringing London to its knees, a place where corpses are buried by the hundreds in mass graves each day. This display of the Ames family's wealth is impressive, heartbreakingly so.

Especially because their daughter isn't even dead. If only I could get closer, I could explain, like Johann did to Cyrus. I could tell them that I am alive, through the wonders of science. My mother would stop crying, my father could dismiss the friars that swing censers of incense around my casket.

"I'm going to them," I say firmly.

"I don't think that's a good idea." Cyrus squeezes my hand.

"Then why did you let me come?" I say, beginning to panic. My parents are *right there*. I must talk to them.

"I thought," he says in a low tone, watching the ground, "that if you came here, you might accept the truth. That there's no going back."

"You thought wrong." I stamp my foot and drop his hand. He looks at me helplessly. After a pause, he nods, but makes no move to join me. Let him stay here. I don't need him. I have my family. My mother and father, who will take me home and summon our servants to dress me properly. Who will hug me and kiss me. *How wrong we were*, they will say. *You're alive and well and we will never let you go again.*

I shove my way through the crowd, nostrils assaulted by the reek of London's poorest citizens—unwashed bodies crawling with lice, urine, beer, and sweat. No one gives me a second glance. Despite the fact that I've been bathed and my dress isn't ripped and full of holes, they think I am one of them.

When I get to the front I stand on tiptoe, straining to see beyond the impossibly tall shoulders of my father's guards. The casket is flanked by monks in brown robes belted with hemp ropes. One of them stands at the head, a large wooden cross carried aloft in his arms.

I can bear it no longer. "Mother!" I scream. "Father!"

Their heads lift, but they don't turn toward me. I remember that my new voice is unfamiliar to them. That must be why they don't look.

I take a deep breath. "Lord and Lady Ames!" I yell at the top of my lungs, willing my voice to echo throughout the graveyard, to rise above the clamor of the crowd. "Your daughter is not dead!"

This gets their attention. My mother looks startled, like a deer I've stumbled upon in a winter forest. She glances around, not making eye contact with me. But she takes a few tentative steps in my direction before my father yanks her back. I'm dismayed to see Edmund Stuart, the old man I was betrothed to, at her side, weeping quietly, as though he's lost the love of his life. It makes me furious. He was never in love with me—I was the prize that my father wanted to give, a reward for a long and successful business partnership. He's only here now to curry more favor with my family.

My mother back at his side, my father meets my gaze, staring at me for what seems like an eternity, before nodding to his manservant Reginald.

Reginald nods back, turns and begins to walk toward me. My heart lifts. The world will be right again. They heard me. They understand that they've made a mistake. That all of this can be explained away. That death is something that happens to other people, not to their young daughter, not at a masquerade ball where she had roses entwined in her hair.

And then Reginald is in front of me. He gestures to the guards and they step aside. I wait for him to offer his arm, to lead me to my parents. To summon the carriage that will take us home.

Something cold presses into my palm. I look down. Reginald has handed me a coin. "Lord and Lady Ames wish to thank you for your kind words, lady," he says gruffly, the way he pronounces *lady* suggesting he thinks I am nothing of the sort. "They know that their daughter is not dead, for her spirit lives on in Heaven."

"No," I say, "you don't understand—"

"Now get away from here," he continues, his voice lower now, more menacing. He grabs my shoulder, hard. Pain shoots down my arms. "You got what you wanted, beggar. Now stop preying upon this family in their time of grief, you filthy parasite." He gives my shoulder a hard shove, and I stumble backward.

"But—" My voice is too small, too quiet. He departs, and the hungry crowd pushes against me, the appearance of the coin churning them into a fervor. I am swept backward by the movement, like water, like wind, like nothing I could possibly control.

It's not till I feel Cyrus's hand reach for mine that I realize how far I've been pushed.

"Look what you did!" I scream at him. "Look what you did to me—what you took from me! *Who* you took from me!"

"Sera—" he begins, but I throw the coin at his face. It strikes him on the cheek.

I turn and run away from this nightmare. In my worst dreams, I couldn't have conjured a more potent terror: my own parents not knowing who I am. My feet pound on the packed earth, one two, one two, like the syllables that rage in my skull: *beggar*, *filthy*. I can barely see through my tears, and the wails that escape my lips are a stranger's.

At some point I slip, the slick leather sole of my shoes failing to find purchase in the muck of the lane, and I fall to my knees. "Move!" yells a man on horseback, and I scramble to the side. I lean my head against the wall of the building—from the delicious scent of hot bread, it must be a bakery. I see people walking by, looking down at me in pity and disgust, and I drop my head to my chest.

I am nobody. I am nothing. I am worse than nothing. I am a filthy parasite.

Soon I sense a presence in front of me. I open my eyes. I'm staring at well-made leather boots, worn over clean men's stockings. Cyrus kneels in front of me, his ice-blue eyes full of concern, full of feeling, possibly full of regret. They are glassy, like the spring sky viewed through a rain-dampened window.

He wraps his arms around me and pulls me close.

"Change me back," I whisper.

"Shh," he murmurs, stroking my hair. "You know that's impossible."

"Your father, then. He must have some way. Please, Cyrus." I pull away. My lips are covered with my own salty tears. I meet his gaze. "I never asked you to make me into . . . *this*." I don't even know the word for what I am, and this makes me cry harder. "Make me what I was."

He wraps me again in his arms. "You'll never be what you were, Seraphina. But I can try. Not exactly the same, but close."

I'm not even sure what this means, but it's better than nothing. It's all I have. "Yes," I answer. "Please." I allow myself to surrender to his embrace. His large frame shelters me, protects me from the cruel streets and my crueler memories.

"I will," he swears. "I'll do whatever it takes."

That night Cyrus sends for me, and I meet him in his father's garden, a small slice of paradise in the middle of the city. The unmanicured space explodes with life, hundreds of varieties of flowers and herbs gone wild. Climbing roses drip from the archway through which I walk, and everywhere there are ceramic pots of lilies and foxglove, nasturtium and primrose, all sheltered beneath the willows that brush the earth. Johann must cultivate these plants for his apothecary work.

A girl sits on a stone bench. The warm glow of torchlight flickers across her hair, which tumbles down her back in chestnut waves. She's wearing a long-sleeved wool gown in dark scarlet, simple and unadorned, though obviously well-made. Its waist comes to a deep V below her navel, emphasizing her slender form. A silk veil covers the crown of her head and wraps around her neck and shoulders. Her hands are hidden, buried in the folds of her dress.

In a word, she is beautiful. She is young, possibly seventeen at the oldest. I touch my hand to my own weathered cheek. She is everything I used to be. Everything I lost. If I were her, perhaps my family wouldn't turn their backs on me. Wouldn't call me beggar. They'd listen to me and know I was Seraphina.

Though the night is warm, she shivers when she sees me. "Who is this woman?" the girl whispers to Cyrus. "Where is the doctor?"

"The doctor is coming," he murmurs to her in a reassuring tone.

"Sit, Seraphina," he commands me, and I sink in the wooden chair across from the girl. He walks slowly behind her back and stands there, a foot's distance between them. "You remember what I told you? That your soul is not bound to your body?"

I think back to the night that my world was destroyed. "The silver cord that binds my soul is unwound," I say dully. "It is free. That's what you said."

"Yes," he says meaningfully. "So the body you have now is not the only one you may occupy. If it doesn't please you, you can choose another."

The girl shifts, confusion covering her face. "Sir?" she murmurs, turning her face to Cyrus. "The doctor?"

"Soon," he promises her. "Don't speak."

She nods, uncertain but trusting.

"I can choose another body," I repeat.

"Yes, Seraphina." Cyrus smiles at me.

"Like hers," I whisper. The first flush of fear comes over the girl's face.

"Yes," he says again.

"But what happens to her?" I ask.

"She dies." He says this firmly, without hesitation. At least he's not lying to me. "But she will die anyway."

The girl opens her mouth, perhaps to scream, but Cyrus claps his hand over it. He's wearing gloves, I notice.

"I won't do it," I say, shaking my head. "'Thou shalt not kill.'" I know the commandments by heart.

The girl thrashes in his hands, her eyes wide and alarmed now. "Please," he implores me. "I cannot bear to see you so unhappy. You need to do this."

"No." I raise my chin. "She has a mother, a father. Just like me."

He sighs. "No," he says, reaching for the silk that covers

her neck. "She doesn't. They're dead. Just like she's going to be, with or without your help." With that, he rips away her veil, exposing her neck, at the same time yanking her hands out from the folds of her gown.

Her neck is covered with large red boils, and her fingers are black at the tips, already gangrenous. Her face isn't flushed from anger, or fear, or desire for Cyrus. It's the fever, I realize.

She has the plague.

Cyrus is right—she'll be dead in two days, if that. "But I don't want to become a sick girl. Those horrible boils . . ." I shudder, imagining them on my own neck.

"Your soul will heal this body, just like it healed the beggar's wound; she cracked her head open when I knocked her over," Cyrus says. "You won't be sick, I promise."

I take a step toward the girl. "How do I—?" My voice falters. I don't even know what I'm asking.

"Put your mouth on hers," Cyrus instructs me, removing his gloved hand.

She wrenches her face toward his, her eyes flashing with betrayal. "You said you had a doctor here who would make me well," she pleads.

"There, there," he says gently, running his glove down her shining hair. "I said I knew someone who would take away your suffering. And I wasn't lying."

“Her?” the girls asks, jabbing a black thumb in my direction. “Where’s her mask?” Plague doctors stuff herbs inside their beak-shaped masks to protect them from the sickness.

“She has a different kind of mask, but don’t worry,” he answers. “She’ll make the hurting stop.”

“I am in so much pain,” she whispers.

Another step. She’s right in front of me. Her breath hot on my face.

“Seraphina, end her pain. Do it now.” Cyrus’s face reminds me, briefly, of my father’s this afternoon, the stoic, impassive stare of a man who will not falter, will not show weakness.

The girl’s lips are soft and yielding. My body takes over and a hunger asserts itself, one I did not know I possessed. I think of my mother’s hands, the sure way they embroider cloth or pluck a harp in our garden, the notes high and sweet. Sweet like the taste that now floods into my mouth, like violets and honey and summer breeze. I feel powerful, holy, celestial. Funeral church bells toll in my mind, yet I want to laugh. Who has died? Not me. Not me.

The sweet taste ends, and I feel a twisting movement, deep inside my body, like a rose being ripped loose from its stem. I am separate, entirely alone, adrift. Abruptly, the sensation ceases, and I expand. I could zoom out of the garden toward the distant stars. I feel an overpowering sensation of love, of oneness with all things. I picture showers of sparks raining over the city in benevolent beauty. It makes me want to cry, but I have the strangest thought that I no longer possess eyes. The idea almost terrifies me, but I am so content, so happy, that nothing can dim my joy.

And then it comes: the feeling of compression, twisting, folding, being stuffed into a small space, like when I was younger and would hide in the trunks in my bedroom to surprise my nurses. Every part of me is under pressure.

"If you could only see how lovely you are," I hear Cyrus murmur.

I find my eyes and open them, inhaling deeply. The garden is stunning, the distant melody of a nightingale more achingly exquisite than any song I've ever heard. The night-blooming flowers call to me, beckon for me to trail my fingertips along their velvety petals. The breeze caresses my hair like the finest silk.

I drag my eyes to Cyrus and momentarily see two of him, one light and one dark. I shake my head and my vision steadies itself until there is only one Cyrus.

His pale blue eyes are luminous by torchlight, staring at me like I am some rare work of art, some special flower that blooms only once a year. The intensity of his stare is overwhelming, raw.

The air between us crackles, and I am suddenly sure he wants to kiss me. But I am not sure I want him to. Not yet. His eyes are fiery, and I fear he will consume me, burn me, break me. Before he changed me, I had never even touched a boy before.

"You look . . ." He trails off, shaking his head in wonder. "Someday I'll know what you're experiencing."

"You've never switched?" I breathe, the night air heady and intoxicating around me.

"No," he answers. "Though I could. My father gave me the elixir, in case I need to leave my body quickly. I hope you'll be with me when that day eventually comes."

A warm feeling comes over me. Cyrus wants to be with me, just as I've always secretly dreamed of marrying him. He takes a step toward me and takes my hand. This time I am ready.

"Cyrus! What did you do?" Both our heads fly up at the sound of Johann's voice, his sharp tone quavering with barely restrained anger. I didn't hear him approach, and judging from the nervousness in his posture, neither did Cyrus.

I look where Johann is pointing, toward the ground at my feet, where a pile of gray dust swirls in small eddies.

"What do you think I did, Father?" Cyrus's voice is weary, carrying a bitterness that should belong to a man much older than he is.

"Are you trying to get us all killed?" Johann steps forward, his jaw jutting. "Because that's what will happen if the servants start to gossip. If this girl's family comes looking for her. We'll all be tried for witchcraft. We'll all burn."

Cyrus sighs. "The girl's family is in a mass grave. We're in no danger."

"You have *no idea* what you're talking about," Johann hisses. "Come with me, son. There are some things we need to discuss."

"I'm not leaving her!" Cyrus stands up, defiant, and I realize he towers over his father.

"You will do exactly as I say, or I'll kill you myself," Johann swears. Cyrus flinches, but follows his father away anyway, back toward the house.

Within moments I am alone in the torchlit garden. I know I should be worried for Cyrus and perhaps for myself, too. But euphoria from the transformation still courses through my veins, making it difficult to focus. And as I touch my fingers to my new lips, I can't help but smile. I just almost shared my first kiss with Cyrus.

In the end, I decide to follow them inside. Each step back to the house takes an eternity, a wondrous eternity. As I walk, jolts of pleasure rise up through my feet, as though the ground is kissing me. I pause under the trellis of climbing roses. The petals are dewy and soft, but even more amazing are my fingers. They are unmarred, smooth, perfect, all traces of the plague's blackness gone.

I follow the candlelight down the hall and stop in my tracks when I see a full-length mirror, the same one I avoided when we arrived home from my funeral, not wanting to see my stooped posture, my ruined cheeks.

But now I stand before it, a smile lighting up my face.

My skin is creamy and youthful, my hair lustrous and thick. Deep brown eyes stare back at me, framed with long black lashes.

The girl I have become is beautiful, and I cannot deny that vanity plays a small part in my delight. But the true reason I am so happy goes far beyond a narcissistic appreciation for my new countenance.

I look very much like my original body. My new self is a few years older, with wider, mature hips and a full bust. But we could still be sisters, with the same hue to our cheeks, the same glossy dark hair, the same brown eyes.

This new body, it gives me hope.

Hope that my parents will see *me* inside. That I can calmly explain to them what happened, just as Johann explained it to Cyrus that day in Caffa.

I have no illusions that it will be difficult to convince them. But I know things that only Seraphina knows—the songs that my mother used to sing to me, that my father's favorite horse is named Fourthwind. In time, they'll believe me, I am sure of it.

I am reluctant to leave the mirror, but giddy at the prospect of reuniting with my family. I tear myself away, hurrying down the hall to tell Cyrus where I am going.

Perhaps, I allow myself to think, Cyrus can speak with

my father. He could ask for my hand in marriage. After all, he is the reason I am still here.

The voices grow louder as I continue down the hall. Through the open door to the library, I see Cyrus and Johann in the middle of a heated discussion, flames leaping in the fireplace. Behind them are tables laden with texts and scrolls, and to their left, a pedestal holding a single bright blue book. Cyrus is seated in a high-backed wooden chair as Johann paces in front of him.

". . . should never have trained you as an alchemist. You clearly weren't ready for this knowledge. You've shown no caution, no intelligence. You're acting rashly. Changing bodies in the *garden*? Where any of our servants could have seen? Not even trying to keep it hidden?" Johann is frightful in his anger, slashing the air with his hands as he makes his points, but Cyrus doesn't appear to be intimidated. If I had been sitting where Cyrus is now, I would be cowering, shaking. But his chin is held high, his eyes level, his skin absent of any flush of rage.

"I promised Seraphina that I would make her young again," Cyrus says simply. "She would have gone mad in that beggar woman's body."

"Gone mad," Johann repeats incredulously. "That's *exactly* why you should never have changed her in the first place. Don't you see, Cyrus, how easily we could lose control of this situation? What if she ran through the streets, raving that the von Hohenheim household had placed a curse on her? This city is a pile of kindling, just waiting for the spark that will burn it to the ground. The king would be happy to burn a pair of heretics, if only to distract the people from the plague."

I flinch, remembering how I threw the coin at Cyrus's face, how I screamed at him at my funeral. They *are* heretics. Not that I want them to burn at the stake or be thrown into prison. But Johann's meaning is clear: I am a threat to him. And he seems the kind of man who would extinguish such a threat without a second thought.

"But she would have died," Cyrus replies calmly.

"Of course she would, stupid boy! But our elixir is not medicine. It's not a herbal preparation to administer to the sick. It's not soothing an ailment—it's forever." My mother used to tell me she'd love me forever, and I remember the way it made my heart would swell with happiness. I felt safe, content, sheltered. But Johann says the word so differently. *Forever.* He makes it sound like a curse.

Cyrus is quiet for a moment. "But—" he begins, then falls silent. It's the first crack I've seen in his composure. "But," he tries again, "she's special. To me."

His words make me feel light, like ash floating away from a fire.

Johann begins to laugh, bitterly, mirthlessly. "Don't tell me you love her," he spits. "You don't even know her. That's the most irrational thing I've ever heard. And no love can survive immortality."

The room is quiet, filled only with the crackling of the fire, and suddenly I don't want to hear Cyrus's answer. What if he *doesn't* love me? What am I without him by my side? Some strange creature that no one believes exists, some freak of nature, some threat to the reassuring rhythms of normal life.

Finally, Cyrus speaks. "All I know is that I'm drawn to her. You always told me that there's no such thing as destiny, and I believed you. I still do. But she makes me wonder. If I could love anyone forever, it would be her. When I'm with her, I feel complete."

A chill runs up my spine at this reminder that I will never be whole again. That I am just a spirit without its true body. But this notion is tempered by the sweet feelings that open inside me at Cyrus's words.

Johann lets out a low sigh as he walks toward the fireplace, gazing into its swirling miasma of flame. "There's something you should know. About your mother, and how she really died." He won't make eye contact with his son.

"She died in childbirth," Cyrus whispers, but there's an uncertainty to it.

“She went mad, Cyrus. Insane. ”

Cyrus’s expression is pained, his hands straying toward his ears, as though he wants to stop hearing this dreadful story. “Father—”

“Let me finish,” Johann hisses. “I will never forget the day the soldiers came for her, with an order signed by the doge himself, accusing her of being a witch. They *burned* her.” At this, Johann’s voice finally cracks.

Cyrus looks ill, and a part of me wants to rush to his side, to comfort him. But my fear keeps me rooted to the shadowy spot.

“Your mother was no witch—she was sick. But they killed her anyway,” Johann spat. “That’s the world we live in. That’s what Seraphina’s presence could bring upon us, all over again,” Johann’s voice grows hard at this last part, grows sharp, like a blade. My blood feels cold and slow, trudging through my veins.

Cyrus snaps his head up. “What are you trying to say?”

“The girl is a problem. She can’t stay here. She knows too much. And yet, we can’t cast her out. Don’t you see? It would be better for everyone if she simply . . . disappeared.”

I should leave. I should run. But my limbs feel thick and heavy. I may as well be sinking to the bottom of the Thames, rocks tied to my ankles.

“I won’t kill her.” Cyrus closes his eyes.

"You won't have to," his father says softly, kindly. "If you can't face it, I—"

"No," Cyrus says quietly, uncertainly. His eyes flick toward the pedestal holding the blue leather book, then back to Johann. I wish he would scream at his father. I wish he would defend me.

Johann approaches his son, lays his large hand on Cyrus's silvery hair. "I'll give you till the morning to do what needs to be done. If you can't, I'll take care of her myself."

Take care of her. How chilling his choice of words. My mother took care of me when I was a little girl, rocking me to sleep in her arms. And yet I know exactly what he means. If Johann has his way, I will be dead by morning.

I need to get out of here, to melt away into the shadows like I was never here—like this never happened. Except as I move backward, my footstep echoes in the hallway, and both their heads swivel my way. Cyrus leaps from his chair in a graceful motion that only serves to increase my terror.

I do the only thing I can. I turn and run.

"Stop her!" Johann's voice thunders behind me. I hear a sickening crack, flesh against bone, before his threat cuts off abruptly, and I can only assume that Cyrus has hit his father. I don't hear anything else but the pounding of my heart as I fly down the hall, through the stone courtyard, and emerge on the street, running for my life.

I say a prayer of thanks that my new body is young and strong, far stronger than my mortal self ever was. I feel almost borne by the wind as I run west through the streets toward my family's estate on the Strand. I am grateful to see people everywhere—it must not be curfew yet—and I know I must reach the gate at the city walls before nine PM, when it will close for the night, keeping me trapped in here with at least one man who wants me dead.

Each step forward is a promise that I can have my old life back, that I will be safe and secure in my family's house, protected by my father's guards. I dodge a wealthy bishop in a furred robe dripping with jewels, noting what a target he is for thieves. Better him than me. A group of young men-at-arms run their eyes over me as I stream by, but I pay them no heed. Judging from their foul scent, they are already quite drunk and headed for the taverns and brothels of Southwark, across the Thames.

As I run, I cannot help the horrible thoughts that arise in my mind from the story of Cyrus's mother, burned at the stake. Her madness scares me, the idea that someone could suddenly lose her sanity, her grip on what is real. Because if I had been told that someday my soul would be leaping from body to body through some trick of science, I would have called that person mad. And yet, here I am, believing it. Am I insane? Have I lost my grip on what's real?

Oh? Then where did your pretty scarlet dress come from, Seraphina? I ask myself. *Or your pretty new face? How do you run so strongly?*

With each step I put between myself and the von Hohenheim household, the more fantastical the story sounds, like a tale a nurse might sing to put children to sleep.

Luckily the gate is open, and I attract no notice as I hurry through it, leaving the stench and smoke of the inner city behind me. I slow as I reach the grand estates along the Strand, the Savoy Palace's sprawling gardens lit with torches and lanterns. I am almost home. I pause to smooth my gown and adjust my veil over my hair, allowing my body to cool and the redness to leave my face. My heart still pounds—not from exertion, but fear. I won't feel safe from Johann till I am behind my father's walls, but I know I must be completely composed to make it past the gatekeeper.

Old Henry stands guard at the gatehouse, just as he has every night I can remember. Deep shadows fall on his familiar grizzled face. He's been Old Henry since I was a little girl—even when his skin was smooth, his beard free of gray.

"Good evening, sir," I say with confidence, banishing the fear I feel inside. "I am here to see Lord and Lady Ames. They're expecting me."

He narrows his eyes at me. There is no glimmer of recognition in them. "I was not notified of this," he says, with a coldness that he's never used with me before. My heart sinks. He can't deny me entrance. He simply can't. If I am forced to stay out here, it's a death sentence. Johann will find me.

I hear a noise and cock my head—is that the distant pounding of hooves, drawing near? Is it Johann? No doubt he has guessed my destination.

I force myself to smile and look into Old Henry's eyes. "Lord and Lady Ames must have forgotten in their grief." I look down. "Such a tragedy. Lord Stuart's heart is broken," I continue, naming my father's business partner, the man I was betrothed to.

"Lord Stuart, did you say?" Old Henry's face relaxes at the familiar name.

"Yes, of course. I bear a message from him." I draw myself up, squaring my shoulders.

"Why not send his usual messenger? A young girl like you shouldn't be out at night. It isn't safe."

"No," I say softly, thinking of Cyrus's father. "It isn't. I'll thank you for escorting me to the house, then. We wouldn't want a repeat of what happened to Seraphina." I shudder, and it's only half false.

His eyes flicker, sorrow falling over them like a veil. "Of course, lady," he says in the gruff voice I know so well. "Follow me."

My heart lifts when the gate swings shut behind me, when I am standing on my father's property, and the bar that will hold Johann out is firmly set in place.

Reginald meets us at the front door and a chill runs down my spine. My house feels strangely imposing. It's never seemed so in the past, but as my new eyes flash upward at the crenellated turrets that loom over me, I feel as a newcomer might. Reginald's dagger hangs from his waist, and it has never looked sharper.

"She has a message for Lord and Lady Ames," Old Henry explains.

"From Lord Stuart," I add. "It's a matter of some urgency."

Reginald stares at me for a moment, calculating, judging. I cringe inwardly, remembering how his face contorted with disgust the last time I saw him. How he called me a filthy parasite.

It's not his fault, I tell myself. *He didn't know.*

I won't reveal myself to him, though. I learned my lesson. I must speak only to my mother and father. They know me better than anyone in London. They'll believe me.

Then Reginald steps back, leading me inside. The customary fire crackles in the center of our great hall, smoke racing toward the roof. He deposits me in the sitting room where my parents receive guests.

It's disorienting, being treated like a stranger, even as I sit on the pillows I embroidered when I was eleven years old, even though I know the tapestries on the walls as well as I know my own face.

My original face, that is.

Purposeful footsteps sound from the hallway. A thrill of anticipation runs through me. I would recognize the thud of my father's boots anywhere.

His shadow enters before he does, long and distorted on

the stone floor, shifting in the light of the candelabras overhead. And then, oh, then he is *here*, standing in front of me. *I'm home*, I think, as I take him in: his dark hair and high cheekbones, just like mine. *No*, I correct myself, *like mine* were. A pang of sorrow reverberates through me when I see how red his hazel eyes are, the bruised circles underneath. He must have been crying, despite the stoic, emotionless mask he wore at my funeral. I don't think I've ever seen my father cry. Not once.

I can't restrain myself. "Father!" I whisper in a choked sob, launching myself into his arms, crushing my face to his deep blue tunic, banging my cheek against its buttons. "I thought I would never see you again. I was so scared."

He stiffens, patting my head awkwardly, then pushing me backward till I am at arm's length. His face registers concern. "Are you unwell?" he asks. "Shall I have the servants bring you some ale? Some bread?"

I shake my head. "I *am* well, now that I'm home. I have so much to tell you, Father."

His eyes glisten. "I'm afraid I don't understand," he says slowly. "I'm not your father. I'm no one's father anymore." He takes a deep breath. "I buried my daughter today."

"No." I grab his hand with both of my own. He needs to understand. "That's what I need to tell you. Seraphina isn't dead."

He takes a step backward, his eyes darkening. "I saw her myself, when they pulled her from the river. My poor daughter was stabbed."

"Her body died, it's true," I say. "But her soul—it lives. And not just in Heaven, either. She walks the earth in another body."

He takes another step backward. I hate it, the distance he's putting between us, the look on his face that says he thinks I might be mad, like Cyrus's mother, a lost cause, a raving loon. "That's not possible, my dear. I know you mean well, but Lord Stuart shouldn't have sent you. You must leave."

"Father," I begin again, noting how his face grows more impassive each time I say it. "Listen to me. There are learned men, men of science, great scholars, who have developed a way to transfer a soul to another body." I decide not to name Johann and Cyrus, even though my father has called upon them many times for medicines and knows them well. Johann's threats still echo in my skull, and I don't want to make my family his target by doing exactly what he fears—exposing his incredible discovery.

"What do you want from me?" My father's voice rises in pitch, in intensity. "This is most cruel, to spread your lies over this house when we are in the throes of mourning."

"It's not a lie, Father—"

"I am *not* your father! Stop saying that word to me." His

ears are turning red, and I know from long experience that he's about to fly into a rage. I don't think I've ever felt more helpless.

"You *are* my father. It's me. I'm Seraphina." Oh, how I wish I could have led him to this point more gently, could have explained the science behind my revelation, could have argued my story more clearly. But I am desperate. It's my only move: the blunt truth.

"Get out of my house." He takes a step toward me, and somehow this is more disturbing than when he shrank away. "I don't know why Edmund Stuart would send you to me with these vicious falsehoods on your lips, and I don't care. Just get. Out."

I recoil from his hatred. It hurts me, just as badly as that woman's knife did when it pierced my spine the night I lost my human life. *No!* I shriek, in my mind. *He must believe me!*

"Remember the time you taught me to ride a horse?" I begin, the words all tumbled together. "And your stallion bucked? He threw me in the blackberry patch. My dress was ruined. I had cuts all over my face. Mother was so furious."

He pales. His rage drains away, slowly, terribly, becoming something else. Fear.

"Or the time you said you wished you had a son. I was ten. I could be a boy, I thought. It wouldn't be so bad. I could learn to hunt and become a knight. So I stole your dagger and hacked off all my hair. And again: Mother was furious. But I didn't care, I just wanted to be what you wanted me to be." My words become sobs. I reach for his hands again but he pulls his out of reach, takes another step backward.

"Remember," I continue, quavering, trembling, "when I was little? You said the only thing that would stop me from crying was when you let me tug on your beard. You said it hurt, but it was better than listening to me scream."

He falls to his knees and makes the sign of the cross. "Evil spirit," he hisses, "get thee away from me."

"I'm *not* evil, Father! I'm not. It's me. It's Seraphina. I can tell you more. I can prove—"

"Demon," he curses. "Witch. Devil."

"No," I wail. "No."

"I gave my daughter a proper burial. I said the prayers. Why did you send this fiend to me? Why?" He looks upward, as though expecting an answer from God himself.

"Where is my mother? Let me speak to her." I take a step toward him, and he scrambles backward, frantic, terrified.

"Foul spirit, you will not offend my wife." He begins to murmur to himself softly in Latin. He's praying, praying for me to disappear.

I approach him and place my hand on his shoulder. He's so solid, so strong, but he jerks away from me as though I were trying to murder him. "The demon made flesh." He curls his lips around the words, disgusted, but he draws himself up to his full height. "If you are flesh, I can kill you." He grabs my hair and pain stabs through my scalp.

"Please," I whisper. "Stop."

He doesn't respond, just pulls my hair, hard, yanking me with him as he leaves the room. Tears well in my eyes. My breath is caught in my throat like a trap. Something breaks in me.

"What's the matter, my lord?" Reginald exclaims. I recognize his voice through a veil of pain.

"Get this . . . *creature* out of my house. Now. And then get the priest. We need protection." My father gives me a shove, sends me sprawling on the cold floor at Reginald's feet.

And then his footsteps, the footsteps I would know anywhere, the familiar patter of his boots on stone—they grow faint as he runs away from me.

I feel something wet drip into my ear. Blood? Reginald hauls me to my feet and soon the guards are upon me, a fence of armored men and their clanking swords. Dimly, I see the doorway to our house pass over my head. I see the torches on the outside walls of the house. I see the gardens, orderly and perfect, as I am dragged past them and thrown through the open gate out into the road.

I land on my knees and look up just in time to see the gate close. I hear the crunch of wood on metal as the bar slides into place.

Banished.

My family thinks I'm dead.

And if Johann finds me, they will be right.

I end up by the river, the horrid, stinking river, from which my lifeless body was pulled. In the dark night, it is almost beautiful. But I will always hate the place where my old life ended and this new, strange one began.

I sit in a public garden, just feet from where listless water slaps against the stone wall at its bank. The tiny plot of land has begun to go wild, untended in the face of so many larger problems for the city. Oh, London. City of pestilence, city of thousands of deaths. *How many deaths are mine?* The beggar, the diseased girl in the garden, *me*. There are three lives that I've lost so far.

I bury my face in the early summer grass. Where can I go? Nowhere.

A horse's hooves pound on the road. My heart does not. It's given up.

"I've been searching for you, Seraphina," a voice says. I lift my head wearily. It's Cyrus, rushing to my side, his pale hair damp with sweat, his right hand bruised as though he's been in a fight. I think of the crack I heard earlier and wonder if it was Cyrus's hand against Johann's jaw.

But then his horse paws the ground, and all I can think of is the blackberry patch where my father's horse threw me when I was little. The way the sharpness of its thorns was so unexpected next to the sweetness of the juice that oozed from the overripe fruit. It ran into my mouth, tart and sugary, even while my flesh stung from multiple cuts and scrapes.

"You're alive," Cyrus breathes, almost reverently. It echoes in my ears the way a choir's song bounces off the curved stone ceilings in cathedrals.

"My father says his daughter is dead," I whisper to the river, not bothering to turn to look at him.

"He's wrong," Cyrus argues. "You are not dead." His voice is strong, male, and full of fire. *Destiny*, I remember him saying. *She makes me wonder.*

Is Cyrus my destiny? I have no home. I have no options.

Can it still be destiny if there is no other choice? Or is that the very definition of the word?

A small sob escapes from my lips.

"What did they do to you?" Cyrus murmurs. He pulls me into his arms, he touches my hair, my face with tenderness. He presses his fingers against my bleeding scalp. It stings.

I feel myself melt against him and force myself to shove his hand away. My eyes fly open. "Are you here to kill me?"

Pain flickers in Cyrus's face and his platinum hair glows in the moonlight. "No, Seraphina. I'm not going to hurt you." He presses a cloth to the wound on my head, where my father ripped out my hair. The pain stops, dissipating like smoke. "I won't let anyone hurt you as long as I live. That is my vow."

"My father says I am a demon," I tell him, closing my eyes. "My mother—" I can't even finish the sentence.

"I know."

"And Johann—"

"I stole his alchemy book. He'll be furious, but he won't come after us. Not yet." He looks guiltily down at his knuckles, which are bruised from when he struck his father.

"Please," I hear myself saying. "Take me away from here. From all this death."

"South," he answers. "We will go south."

"You would leave . . . everything? To be with me?"

I feel his hands stroking my hair. They move to my neck, to my arms. They bear me up and pull me close. For the second time in a fortnight, my body is found by the river. Only this time, it is Cyrus who finds me, who declares me alive instead of dead, who swears to protect me, as long as he lives.

"I would. Seraphina, you are the first person I've ever met who made me feel something that I can't explain. It's not logical." His voice surges, like the water below, then trails away.

"What do you feel?" I ask, my hair escaping its silk veil, drifting about my stolen face, my stolen life.

"Just give me some time to show you," he answers, dropping his gaze.

He laces his fingers through mine, and a sweet energy curls through my veins.

"We'll make a new life? We'll find a new home?" I ask, gazing into his ice-blue eyes.

"There's a whole world out there. Don't you want to see what it has in store for us?" His grin widens. A few paces away, his horse whinnies softly, like he's just as eager. "Don't you want to be together?"

He takes my hand once more, pressing his thumb into my palm, and I begin to understand what the word love means.

It's sweeter than blackberries. It justifies the existence of thorns. Cyrus could love me. He might already.

I lean closer to him, and he meets me halfway, his lips brushing against mine.

Maybe it was written in the stars, long before I was born. Or maybe I just decided it, creating destiny out of nothing. One way or another, my choice is made.

Cyrus leads me to the horse, whose hooves stamp on the unpaved earth. He leaps onto the horse's back easily, pulling me up after him. The horse starts to move and I tremble, remembering how easily I was tossed into the blackberry thorns. Cyrus wraps his arm around my waist.

"Don't worry," he says into my ear. His arm tightens. "I'm holding you. And I won't ever let you go."

How does forever begin? Perhaps just like this.